TARZAN®

THE GREYSTOKE LEGACY UNDER SIEGE

THE WILD ADVENTURES OF EDGAR RICE BURROUGHS® SERIES

TARZAN®
THE GREYSTOKE LEGACY UNDER SIEGE

RALPH N. LAUGHLIN

&

ANN E. JOHNSON

COVER BY TOM GIANNI

INTERIOR ILLUSTRATIONS BY MIKE GRELL

EDGAR RICE BURROUGHS, Inc.
Publishers
TARZANA   CALIFORNIA

Tarzan: The Greystoke Legacy Under Siege
First Edition

Trademarks including Tarzan (R) and Edgar Rice Burroughs (R) owned by Edgar Rice Burroughs, Inc. Front Cover by Tom Gianni and Interior illustrations by Mike Grell Back Cover Pencils by Thomas Yeates © 2017 Edgar Rice Burroughs, Inc.

Special thanks to John Gerlach, Jim Gerlach, Gary A. Buckingham, Bob Garcia, Jim Sullos, and Tyler Wilbanks for their valuable assistance in producing this novel

Number 4 in the Series

Library of Congress CIP (Catalog-in-Publication) Data
ISBN-13: 978-1-945462-08-5
- 9 8 7 6 5 4 3 2 -

TABLE OF CONTENTS

Acknowledgements   i

Foreword   ii

List of Main Characters   iv

Diary of Dian Fossey   vi

May 25,1971   vii

Chapter   *Page*

1. Call to Adventure   1

2. Same Time, Different Place   10

3. Return to Reality   14

4. Family Decisions   19

5. Shattered Peace   29

6. Out of the Cocoon   31

7. Escape to the Jungle   37

8. Where are the Bodies?   42

9. Jon Lost in the Jungle   46

10. Another Jungle   55

11. Rescued   64

12. Cursed   68

13. Captured by Guerillas   83

14. No News is Bad News   90

15. Village Gone Mad   95

16. Favors Called In   102

17. Journey Homeward   105

18. Escape to Safety   108

19. Steps Retraced   114

Chapter	Page
20. Arresting Moments	128
21. Korak Found	136
22. Inspecting Scene of the Crime	142
23. Identifying Friends and Foes	157
24. Grandson vs. Grandfather	163
25. Interrogation-Guerilla Style	169
26. Late Night Revelations	173
27. Escape to Confrontation	179
28. Gorillas vs. Guerillas	185
29. Korak Captured	191
30. Inside a Ceramic Cell	198
31. Jungle Full of Guerillas	207
32. Through the Back Door	214
33. Sisterhood	223
34. Up on Charges	228
35. Stand Off	233
36. On Moscow Streets	239
37. Day in Court	244
38. Blood Feud	250
39. From Russia with Haste	257
40. Diversionary Action	266
41. Compound Pow-Wow	273
42. Call to Action	279
43. Order Restored	288
44. Official Denials	292
45. Preservation Reservation	295
46. New Horizons	300
Authors' Notes	302

ACKNOWLEDGEMENTS

The authors thank the following people who aided us in the preparation of this book.

Anna Agell, LCSW and Eileen Boardman, LCSW for their knowledge of psychology essential to character creation; The Tuesday Night L Writers Group, Shirley Savage, Candace Guerrette, Rachel Kennedy, Ernie Hartman, and Laurie Notch for their support, feedback, and encouragement through several iterations of the manuscript; Eric C. Pederson, Shihan, Brunswick Martial Arts Academy, and 5th degree blackbelt in kempo karate for his insights into the mind of the martial artist and his expertise in karate and jiu-jitsu.

Michael Garner, Scott Holec and Todd Haley for sharing their detail insight of electronic data discovery and data forensics analysis; the Write-On Writers group – especially Bonnie Wheeler, Paul Karwowski, Vince McDermott, Dottie Moody, Patty Sparks, Gladys Szabo, Charlotte Hart, and Nancy Sohl for their continuous support; Jack Schump, James Yates-Laughlin, Allen Crain, Karen Bergren and Nicole Barritt for their insightful, constructive suggestions; Grant Connors for his military weaponry and wildlife behavioral knowledge; John Barritt- former Magistrate of The Crown's Court; and finally to Frank Connors for his unrelenting support and encouragement to bring this book to publication.

A special acknowledgement goes to Jim Sullos, President of Edgar Rice Burroughs, Inc., for his great insight and editing skills that have helped sharpen every aspect of the book.

Last but by no means least, credit must go to Ruth Shenna Foehring for saying "Yes" when propositioned about writing a Tarzan book. Had she said "No", the project would have never gone farther: Thank you Ruth for launching us on such a grand journey.

FOREWORD

As a grandson of Edgar Rice Burroughs, creator of *Tarzan of the Apes*, I take great personal interest in all projects related to the Tarzan Universe. My main consideration, where we have the ability to directly affect the content, is that each project reflects the core values, vision and the interplay of people, animals and the environment that he embedded in his writings.

We receive many Tarzan story submissions-books, movies, even plays. Each is evaluated through the lens of my grandfather's vision. When the manuscript of *The Greystoke Legacy* crossed my desk, I examined it as I would other such submissions. What I found was a story unlike any others. It introduces Jonathan Clayton, great grandson of Tarzan, as one of the main characters in a multi-faceted story placed in modern-day setting, with the active participation of all members of the Greystoke family.

When my grandfather wrote the first Tarzan stories, Africa was truly the "Dark Continent." Little was known about it, providing a ripe opportunity for his imagination to create lost cities, steamy jungles, strange creatures, alternate worlds, all combining to provide virtually endless storylines for Tarzan tales to provoke readers' imaginations

Modern Africa is no longer mysterious. Its landscape has been mapped, its interiors explored and its species identifed. Since my grandfather wrote, colonialism has vanished and nationalism has risen in its place. The Dark Continent has been illuminated.

Different times require different visions. Anything is possible in the unknown. As the unknown becomes known, possibilities shrink. For a story to meet this challenge a different vision is required. The story you are about to read provides that vision by combining fact and fiction in a most believable manner, integrating the personalities and actions of multiple generations of literary characters.

The Greystoke Legacy is ground breaking in that it is anchored in actual events and locations of the 1980's. This paradigm shift of story venues from fantasy to reality creates the opportunity to carry forward my grandfather's core beliefs, values and vision. He wrote of worlds where evil exists and people were willing to stand forth to oppose and conquer it...even at great risk to themselves and loved ones.

This seminal book opens the gates for the development of new and different Tarzan family adventures that I hope a new generation of readers will discover and enjoy. At the same time, I believe long-time followers of Tarzan will find this story, and subsequent stories, equally enjoyable and true to the Burroughs legacy.

I thank the writers of The Greystoke Legacy for their visionary approach and look forward to more Tarzan adventures based on actual and imagined circumstances. I'm sure Tarzan and his family will welcome the forthcoming new challenges as well.

John R. Burroughs

LIST OF MAIN CHARACTERS

John Clayton Tarzan , Lord Greystoke, Lord of the Jungle

Jane Porter Clayton Tarzan's wife

Jack Clayton Tarzan and Jane's son who also goes by Korak.

Meriem Korak's wife, Jon's grandmother.

Jackie Clayton Son of Korak, father of Jon

Irene Clayton Swiss wife of Jackie….mother of Jon

Jonathan (Jon) Clayton Great grandson of Tarzan.

Scott Horton Pilot for the Greystoke family.

Michael Garner British ambassador to Zaire.

Louise Smythe Long-time Secretary to Jackie Clayton

Nubiby Greystoke compound employee assigned to keep an eye on Jon as a child

Kuberi Son of Nubibly.

Mubuto A Waziri shaman

Ashanti Native girl who finds Jon and befriends him.

Madame DenishaVokolesky Grandmother of Vladimir Chertok

Vladimir Chertok Grandson of DenishaVokolesky and Nikolas Rokoff

Ian Farkwark In-house attorney to The Greystoke Trust (TGT)

Rupert Jameson Director of Information Systems TGT

Otto Finkster Director of Investments Div TGT

Leslie Langford Director of Human Resources TGT

Phillip Burpley Director of Currency Exchange TGT

Geoffrey Smithers Contact at The Exchequer

Hugh Noiseworthy An Associate Director at Britain's State Department

Terrik Leader of the band of guerillas that captures Meriem

Makpek A group leader in Terrik's band of guerillas.

General Zambossi Investigator of Dian Fossey's death

General Kanka Chertok's puppet general in Zaire

Todd Holley Official photographer for Dian Fossey

Gregor Gregorvich A Russian Major

Kerkuk One of three apes that accompanied Korak to Fossey's Camp.

Sir Thomas Bloweather Presiding judge of the Crown's Court

Sir Timothy Leggarder The Crown's prosecutor

Oscar Willoby Head of MI6, British equivalent to the CIA

"When you realize the value of life, you dwell less on what is past and concentrate more on the preservation of the future."

-Last entry in Dian Fossey's diary.

May 25, 1971

East Africa
The Greystoke Compound

Chapter 1: CALL TO ADVENTURE

JON CLAYTON looked back over his shoulder one more time. He had been waiting for this moment; been planning for it for some time. The embers of independence burned within him. He was seven, nearly eight, practically grown up. His physique was changing from undefined baby fat to lean and wiry muscles. He had grown three inches in the past year, reaching a height of four foot, nine inches. His mind strained to explore new opportunities, and there was no greater opportunity than to venture forth into his father's, grandfather's and great grandfather's jungle where they had discovered lost cities, lost civilizations, and hunted wild animals. They had their adventures. It was time for his.

He only needed the right moment of distraction to make his getaway. It came when Watticuo came running into the compound jabbering about something which Jon could not understand, but which excited the other natives. Nubiby, who was charged as Jon's watchful guardian, became so caught up in the excitement that he momentarily forgot his responsibilities. In the chaos, Jon seized his opportunity.

Jon looked back. No one was following him. He turned toward his destination, the primeval jungle, the jungle he had been forbidden to go near. He was prepared. He had his rope – borrowed from the tack room of the stable. He had his knife – a sharp butcher's knife procured from the kitchen when the cooks weren't watching, and he had his trusted companion, Samson – a Russian wolfhound that he had talked Nubiby into shaving to more or less look like a lion.

The vegetation grew thicker as Jon approached the jungle's edge. He had only been in the true jungle once before and that was with his father and Korak, much to the objection of his mother who had been very adamant about her dislike of life in Africa. He did not understand his mother's feelings. He loved the thought of the jungle and relished every opportunity he had to visit the Greystoke compound.

Jon and Samson followed the worn animal path into the dense jungle foliage. The light became dimmer as the canopy of the trees became denser. The cacophony of sounds intensified. He heard rustling in the tree tops as monkeys leapt from branch-to-branch with an outstretched arm, or by their tails. They began an incessant chatter, scolding him for having entered their domain. Their racket was suddenly obliterated by the earsplitting roar of a lion!

JANE CLAYTON SAT on the veranda of their African home, taking her normal mid-morning break from attending to the affairs of the Tarzan compound; an ever growing, time consuming job. What had started out as a small farm consisting of a few acres had over time grown into a gigantic agricultural entity that rivaled the size of the famous King Ranch in Texas. The initial few buildings that had been put up to keep a few animals and tools had grown into a complex of buildings housing a continuum of farm equipment, animals and storage facilities, not to mention an extensive water recovery and irrigation system that fed the many surrounding farms on the property. It even had its own fully equipped communications center, airfield and fully staffed hospital whose personnel was made up of local natives. As a result, there were over three thousand people who owned their own farms and actively contributed to the vitality of the compound; or as many referred to it as Greystoke Territory.

The central hub of the compound was the massive house that Tarzan had built for Jane. It had expanded and expanded again as the Clayton family grew; eventually including a house for the Clayton's son Jack, often called Korak, and his wife Meriem; followed by a dwelling for their son Jackie and his wife Irene. Korak and Meriem lived at the compound year-round; while Jackie and Irene visited from London as often as running the family Greystoke Trust would allow. Jane and Tarzan travelled extensively but always considered their African home to be their base, though they owned extensive property in Britain and the States.

Jane's reminiscing about all the changes that had happened over the years was shattered by several blasts from the Emergency Warning System of the compound; a system only be used when there was a crisis. She jumped out of her chair and ran to the main barn to see what had prompted the system's activation. Meriem quickly followed behind her.

Upon arrival, they found most of the staff of the compound milling around and talking faster than anyone could understand. Jane saw the back of Nubiby, the recognized leader of the staff, and called out to him. He heard her and turned. The look on his face radiated a combination of fear, concern and disaster, all at the same time. He pushed his way towards Jane and Meriem.

"Nubiby, what is the matter? What's happened?"

"It's terrible, my fault." was Nubiby's choked reply, hanging his head in shame.

"What do you mean it's your fault? Let me determine that. Start from the beginning."

Nubiby gathered his thoughts then commenced his story. "It started this morning just after we had started work. Watticuo came running in. Shouting, 'The man-eater's in the fields! The man-eater's in the fields!' Everyone became excited. We had heard an unsubstantiated rumor that there was a man-eating lion in the area, but didn't fully believe it. You know, because lions rarely stray this far from the plains.

"We questioned him, but he was adamant. He didn't see it, but he had heard its growling…like it was hungry. Everything was in turmoil. It took several minutes before some sanity was restored. It was then that I realized what had happened." He stopped as if he couldn't go on; as if whatever had happened was too horrific to tell. Jane urged him on. He removed his hands from his face, squared his shoulders and blurted out, "LITTLE JON IS MISSING. I'VE LOST LITTLE JON!"

Jane wanted to scream but instead reined in her panic and just said, "Go on."

"I know I'm supposed to be watching him all the time, but in the excitement about the man-eater I momentarily forgot about Jon. I started looking for him. I was sure he was around, playing like he was his great grandad. I checked the barns, the corrals, everywhere…but I haven't been able to find him. Old Mubuto said he thought he had seen Jon headed through the underbrush with his dog, Samson, towards the jungle…the same direction Watticuo had come from. But you know Mubuto; he's so old that his mind and his vision can't be relied upon. He just kept saying 'Ni wakati. Ni wakati. *It's time. It's time.*'

"I ignored his babbling and kept looking…but I've looked everywhere, and had several others helping me. We can't find him anywhere."

A frown came across Jane's face. "When, how long ago, did this happen?"

"Maybe an hour," then he looked at his watch and said, "Probably closer to two. I was sure we would find him."

Before Jane could respond, a battered Jeep pulled up into the yard. Two men got out. One was Korak; the other, Jon's father Jackie. They were returning from an early morning patrol of the fields and surrounding areas; specifically, they were inspecting the irrigation canals as the natives had reported seeing more than an usual amount of snakes.

"What is going on? We heard the siren," asked Korak.

Meriem answered. "Jon's missing….and has been for over an hour…Mubuto thinks he may have headed to the jungle…in the same direction that Watticuo said he heard a lion roaring." She was interrupted by the distant roar of a lion coming from the same direction it was believed Jon may have gone.

Korak had heard enough. There would be time for analysis later. He grabbed Jackie by the elbow, spun him around and they both jumped back into the Jeep and headed towards the jungle. For weapons, they only had the long spear that Korak used to probe for snakes in the irrigation ditches, while each carried their own hunting knife. An insufficient arsenal for most, but more than enough for the son and grandson of Tarzan.

JON FROZE IN HIS TRACKS. He looked down the trail. There was no lion in sight; but a second, even louder roar, proved there was a lion close by...very close by.

Samson growled from deep within his throat. Jon reached down to pat him, not sure whether such action was to calm Samson or for self-assurance. Samson stared down the path. They crept forward when a mere thirty feet away a massive beast stepped onto the path from the bushes. It was bigger than Jon had ever imagined, MUCH bigger. His mane was a spray of yellows and browns encircling one of the most frightening faces Jon could ever remember seeing. The yellow-green eyes flared with anger; his paws were the size of boxing gloves... boxing gloves with claws, his emaciated torso reflected the fact that he had not eaten in days. The lion cocked its head to the right and roared again, then slowly began walking towards Jon and Samson. It stopped only a few yards from them.

Jon began to think his jungle adventure might not have been the best idea. Perhaps he should have waited until he was a year or two older...and taller. When the lion roared yet again, Jon could see inside his mouth; a giant red tongue, large pointed teeth, and dripping drool. He thought how easily his head would fit inside it, and he began to shake. He wanted to run but he remembered his grandfather saying repeatedly "Never run from an animal. Runners look like prey, and prey is always

pursued". He didn't want to be prey. And besides, his feet would not move. Samson was barking now, advancing a few feet then retreating, back to Jon's side, never taking his eyes off the lion.

The lion crouched, pulling its muscular hindquarters beneath its body, readying to pounce. It had been several days since he feasted. His stomach was empty and called for fulfillment. Samson got too close and one large paw tossed the dog aside as if he was a piece of paper on a sidewalk picked up by a gust of wind. It was then that the lion charged Jon.

As his front paws lifted off the ground, a blur dashed past on Jon's left, blocking the lion's path to its intended prey. The blur carried a long spear. In one motion, he implanted the end of the spear into the ground, braced it with his right foot, and angled the point toward the chest of the onrushing lion.

As the point of the spear pierced the chest, another figure dropped from the tree above, landing squarely on the lion's back. An arm of steel wrapped around the beast's throat, while muscular legs locked into place inside the lion's back haunches. A gleam of steel flashed through the air and repeatedly plunged into the left side of the lion, eventually penetrating its heart.

The lion went limp… fell to the ground…dead. The two attackers jumped up, each placing a foot on top of the bleeding, lifeless corpse. Each looked at the other, with satisfaction, as if they had just won a cricket match. They turned from their kill to where Jon had been standing. He was gone… vanished.

BY THE TIME Jackie's wife, Irene, had responded to the ringing bell, Korak and Jackie were no more than a cloud of dust headed to the jungle. Nubiby was just completing relaying what had happened when she made her appearance from one of her many naps. It seemed naps were the only way she could cope with African life.

Meriem and Jane remained calm, explaining the situation to Irene who became a screaming maniac cursing Nubiby, the events and the very existence of what she called "the most God-forsaken place in the universe." She was sure that the terrible land had taken her only child, her only son, and she was not shy in naming Jackie as the root cause. Her son was dead – she was sure of it - and her husband, because of his demands of returning to Africa as much as possible, had killed him.

Jane could take it no longer, and was deeply embarrassed by Irene's actions and accusations. She moved in front of Irene and grabbed her firmly by the shoulders, then shook her. Irene gave out a blood curdling scream. That was when Jane slapped her across her face. She hated to do it in front of everyone, but she felt she had no other alternative.

The slap worked. Irene became silent, not moving, shoulders slumped in dejection. Without speaking, she turned away and stumbled, more than walked, back to her quarters.

BOTH MEN LOOKED AT EACH OTHER. Where had Jon gone? A small whimpering noise coming from behind one of the tall trees provided the answer. They ran over to him, but he shied away. He was too embarrassed. In his eyes, he had failed where his father, grandfather, and great grandfather had succeeded. He had let his family down.

They tried to console him but he wasn't having much of it. So, they decided that they would perform the initiation Rites of the First Kill (universal in almost every hunting culture) hoping that Jon would be emboldened and regain his lost confidence.

Jon wasn't too interested in getting close to Numa, but they took him over to the carcass anyhow. They opened its jowls and had Jon reach in and touch the teeth. He then picked up one of the massive front paws to feel the sharp claws. They had him pick the head up and scream at it to prove his victory over

Numa. As he did each act they smeared Numa's blood over him, telling him they were transferring the courage and strength of Numa to him.

Their attention was so focused on Jon that they forgot the first rule of jungle survival – "know your surroundings and what could be present at all times". It wasn't until they heard the rustling of a body flying toward them that their concentration was redirected. Both simultaneously turned to see Sabor, Numa's mate, hurtling through the air towards them. They had been caught off guard, and faced paying the ultimate price for their failure to remain alert.

They each drew their hunting knives and tried to prepare to face the onrushing menace. As the outstretched talons of Sabor were about to strike, she gave out a horrendous roar, arched her back and collapsed at their feet. The shaft of a long arrow vibrated from between her shoulders. Jon, Jackie and Korak looked beyond to see a tall bronzed body gracefully drop from a nearby tree and casually walk towards them; a length of rope, a nearly full quiver of arrows, and a simple long bow draped over his left shoulder.

Chapter 2: SAME TIME, DIFFERENT PLACE

ON ANOTHER CONTINENT, an old dowager who had once been beautiful, but now clothed in the embedded ugliness of bitter hatred, sat in her rocking chair and stared out the window of her twelfth-floor apartment at the carbon-stained snow below. She paid no attention to the cats surrounding her, not even the one draped over her shoulders. She was waiting, desperately waiting, to hear the news she had been yearning to hear for many years.

At one time she had been sought out by everyone that mattered to be part of their clique, their social group. She was of royalty, true royalty, the chosen among the chosen, most desirable among the most desirables. She was royalty and had married into royalty. It was her entitlement.

While she was in her seventies, her body's reflection was that of one much older. And so it should be. Life had not been kind to her, playing with her, repeatedly dangling greatness in front of her only to pull it away, leaving disgrace and humiliation in its place.

She had lived through times in which most of her friends perished in the tidal waves of chaos and insanity that had engulfed her country. Friends, relatives and others of a similar standing within society were taken out and slaughtered, their bodies unceremoniously buried in unmarked mass graves; their properties and riches ripped from them, taken for the alleged benefit of the State.

She was also a victim of her own distorted beliefs. She worshiped her first husband, Nicolas; her only true love. He had gone in pursuit of an untold fortune that would make them among the most powerful people of their country. He sent back word that he had found the treasure trove of a forgotten city: gold ingots, diamonds, rubies, emeralds. He bragged how he had swept the fortune from the grasp of a wild man. He promised he would soon return.

She had been ecstatic. She made grand plans to celebrate their new-found glory; but then, nothing. No returning husband. No treasure. It was as if he had evaporated from the face of the earth. She made inquiries but no one seemed to know or much less care. They were swept away by the national events of the day.

As regimes changed so did she. She changed her name each time she felt she and/or her children were threatened. She dreamed of that day when her children would be the instruments of winning back what had been lost…what was hers by right. The venom of vengeance that reeked from every pore of her being drove her ever forward and at the same time devoured and twisted her perception and soul. She lived bemoaning the past and simultaneously dreaming of a glorious future, never being able to reconcile with the present.

THE CLICKS OF THE MULTIPLE LOCKS on her door brought her back from her dark reminisces. She looked toward the door in anticipation. *THE NEWS. FINALLY, THE NEWS!* She was not disappointed. A handsome young man in his mid-twenties entered: Her grandson.

He stood five foot, nine inches tall and was dressed out in full military attire. The sheen from the insignia on his shoulders indicated that he had just been promoted to a lieutenant. Had it not been for his stooped shoulders, he would have been an additional two to three inches taller. His hair was full but there were clear signs of a hairline in rapid retreat. Wire rim glasses rested upon a narrow-pointed nose that was out of character for the oval face from which it extended. A leather messenger's pouch hung from his left shoulder.

Upon closing the door, he immediately crossed the room to his grandmother and knelt before her. A look of adoration covered his face as he looked into her eyes. She always made him feel special.

"I got it grand-mommy! I finally got it!" He said excitedly.

"Let me see." And with that the man reached into the pouch and pulled out a piece of parchment. The woman snatched it from his hand and pulled it close to her nearsighted eyes.

"This isn't it! This is your matriculation diploma. Where's…"

Before she could finish, he pulled out another sheet of paper. He dangled it in front of her. "I think this is what you're looking for."

She grabbed the second sheet even faster than the first one. Her preliminary scan reversed her mood. "Yes! Yes!" she shouted "This is what I wanted to see: Your GKES assignment. Yes. Yes!"

She lowered the paper and looked into his eyes as if she was trying to cast a hypnotic spell upon him. And, in truth, she was…and she did. His eyes locked onto hers, blocking out everything else. She spoke deliberately and precisely, "You have begun what needs to be done; the reinstatement of our family's name… its heritage… its fortune.

"Take this." She opened her bony hand, exposing a small silver medallion. "Keep this, always, as it will protect you against those who do not want or care if you succeed." The young man took the medallion and inspected it. It was about the size of a U.S. half dollar with a hammer and sickle engraved on one side, and a double headed eagle on the other. He placed it into the fold of his hand and dropped it into his pants pocket.

"You must proceed with caution, but do not dally. Our day of resurrection has been too long in coming."

She placed her aged hand on the grandson's cheek, "There are others who will be aiding you, people you know, and others you don't know, who are committed to our success. With their help, you will recapture what was wrongfully stolen from us."

The young man rose and looked down at his grandmother. "I'll do my best."

"NO!" she screamed, her eyes flashing with vengeance. If they could have thrown lightning bolts, the young man would have been knocked to the floor. "You will not '*TRY*', you will succeed. There is no other alternative. You are the family's Avenging Angel. Your father and aunt failed, but you will not. Nothing less than success is thinkable. Go! Begin the work for which you have been trained. It is your destiny!"

With that proclamation, the grandmother stretched out her arm, cupped his chin with her hand and gently pulled him down and kissed him on his forehead. "Now, be gone. I need my rest."

The grandson turned and left the apartment, saying under his breath, "As you wish grand-mommy…as you wish." The door locks clicked back into place as the old woman returned to her thoughts of the future and the envisioned return to glory. It was what she had dedicated her entire adult life to and now it would finally come to pass.

Chapter 3: RETURN TO REALITY

THE FIRST THING the assigned watchers saw was a cloud of dust on the horizon. Within moments the cloud became defined; it was Korak's jeep returning. Hobute, the appointed lead watcher, sounded the Emergency Alarm System once more to let everyone know that the party was returning. Jane, Meriem, and even Irene this time, came running.

As the jeep reached the outer edge of the compound it became clear that there was an additional occupant. The jeep entered the compound and braked to a stop. Korak climbed out the driver's side while Jackie, holding Jon, slid from the passenger's side. The backseat occupant placed one hand on the jeep's side wall and effortlessly cleared it, landing lightly on the ground. He reached back into the jeep and pulled out the carcass of a male lion. He turned and effortlessly tossed the body to a nearby native who nearly crumbled under the weight. "Here, Kabbe, take this to the kitchens."

Then without hesitation he reached back into the well of the jeep and pulled out yet another body. This one was the carcass of a female lion, which he tossed to another youth standing by. "Go with Kabbe." Then a head poked up and barked. It was Samson. His run-in with the lion, fortunately, had only resulted in minor wounds. Tarzan did not have to lift him out of the jeep; he jumped out on his own. He ran up the porch steps and lay down by the front door as if he had never left... and never intended to leave again.

Irene saw nothing of this. She was focused on the blood-covered body of her son in her husband's arms. Her shock of silence broke with a shriek of utter anguish and despair. "My son's dead! You and your damn jungle have killed him. He's dead! He's dead! And it's your fault! I will never forgive you - NEVER!"

By then Jackie was standing in front of the jeep facing a trio of angry ladies: Irene, accompanied by Meriem and Jane, who were holding Irene on either side, fearing she was about to attack Jackie. Everyone froze in place as Jackie lowered Jon to the ground where he stood...clearly not dead!

Irene could not believe her eyes. Joy and anger swirled in her mind. Her son was alive. But he obviously must be hurt. The volume of blood said it all. She took a hesitant step toward Jon saying, "Come to Mommy. Come to Mommy, my baby."

He and his mother had never had a strong relationship. Her Swiss background projected more aloofness than loving. As Irene reached out for him, Jon ducked under her arms and ran to Meriem. She stooped down and picked Jon up in her arms. "Come on Jon, I think you need a bath." Jon grinned back at her. "Okay."

Jackie moved to embrace Irene, but she pushed him away. For several moments, she stood there shaking her head not knowing what had happened, only knowing she hated Africa and all associated with it.

Jane, who had remained silent, spoke up, "Would you "boys" please let us know what you have been up to?"

Tarzan, who had moved next to Jane, said, "Let's all go in, sit down and we'll explain everything."

Jane walked over to Irene who was still standing in the same place she had been when Jon ran from her, placed her arm around her shoulder and said, "Let's go inside. The sooner we know what happened the better we'll all feel." Jane had lived long enough, and seen enough and heard enough, not to be upset by many, if any, events that might come her way.

"No. No. I don't want to do that. I have to lie down for a while." Jane conceded to Irene's wish and walked her to her room. After getting Irene settled down, Jane asked a couple of the household staff to watch over Irene, then she returned to the main bungalow to hear the details of events of the day.

EVERYONE TOOK THE TIME to clean themselves up before sitting down to explain the day's events. Tarzan sat in his oversized chair, which was not oversized for him. Jackie and Jane each sat on the overstuffed leather sofa, while Korak and Meriem occupied Jane's eloquent Queen Anne's style love seat. Jon was still nestled on Meriem's lap; all having their afternoon tea which the British are so fond to do.

With everyone settled in, Jackie related the events up to the point when Sabor attacked. It was at this point that Tarzan spoke up. "Yes, and you two were so focused on what you were doing with Jon that you completely forgot the first rule of the jungle – always know and be aware of your surroundings."

Korak spoke up. "That's not totally true. We did turn around when we sensed danger."

"Yes, you did, but if I hadn't been there Sabor would have been on you before either of you could have done anything."

Jackie looked at Korak, "He's right. When we turned around the only things we saw were her flared claws and gaping mouth flying towards us."

Tarzan spoke up. "I was returning from one of my daily trips (trips he took for his pleasure and enjoyment as he found jungle life to be more accommodating than life in the civilized sector) when I heard Numa's roars. I went to investigate, little knowing that I would find my off-spring about to become Sabor's lunch."

Tarzan looked directly at Korak and Jackie. "You both forgot that Numa and Sabor, can, on occasion, travel together

...and that it is almost always the female of a species who is the real hunter.

"Now, let's go find something to eat. I'm hungry after all this excitement."

LATER THAT EVENING when Jackie went to his bungalow to see if Irene's latest "nap" had calmed his wife's feelings, he encountered instead a second lioness...Irene, in a still furious mood. "Jackie, I've had it! Had it with you! Had it with your family! Had it with this jungle of yours!

"I've always hated it! I only agreed to visit here from time to time because of what the place means to you. But it means nothing to me. Nothing! Today has just confirmed my feelings. It's a vile place that at any moment something, be it an eight-legged arachnid or a lion, can jump out of nowhere and extinguish you in a moment. It nearly killed our son today, and I can't – I WON'T – live that way any longer."

Jackie moved closer to Irene, hoping that gently holding her would quell her feelings; but she would have nothing of it. She pushed him away.

"Jackie. The boy is scared to death. You can say what you want but he was totally, TOTALLY, traumatized today, and who knows what the long-term effects might be, thanks to your *beloved* jungle. NO! This is it!

"It's time that Jon has a proper education; a civilized education, one he can use in today's world, not in a backwater land that dwells in the last century. I'm taking him back to Switzerland and enrolling him in the best school I can find. You can either join us, or not. It's your choice. And don't try to stop me because my family carries as much influence in high circles as yours does. I can make sure you never see Jon again!"

Jackie, believing that time would extinguish her firestorm of anger, and out of his love for her, acquiesced to his wife's ultimatums. The next day, they made arrangements to cut short their most recent visit and return to the civilized world;

although deep down he did not consider it truly civilized because he knew it was ruled by the most dangerous and treacherous of God's creations, Man.

Chapter 4: *FAMILY DECISIONS*

E VEN DRIVING in from the Bern airport, Irene remained silent as she had for most of the trip home from Africa. Jackie had tried to engage her in conversation but she had repeatedly cut him off. He gave up, finally, and left her to brood. They would have it out later in private. He was concerned. He had heard words from her that shocked him. He hoped they were frustrations born of the trauma of Jon's encounter with the lion. He was afraid they were not.

Jon had been silent as well. Jackie decided not to force him to talk. Jon was only seven. He would get over it with the resilience of youth. It did not occur to Jackie that Jon had suffered a trauma to his psyche that would resonate for years. A few words from him might have alleviated the internal battle now going on in Jon's mind, a battle that pitted self-worth against the legend of his forefathers. Jackie, however, was unaware of the inner battle. He was certain the adults had resolved any confidence issues Jon might have with the Rites of the First Kill. And if fear of the lion had been the only problem, perhaps it would have worked.

But reverberating in Jon's seven-year old mind were the tales of his forefathers; of Tarzan and Korak who lived in the jungle and killed wild beasts as children. Even his grandmother, a girl, had done better than he had. Making it worse, in the few hours since the Rites, Jon had already forgotten the words of courage and strength, and now focused entirely on the blood and teeth and claws. In his teenage years, he would recall the Rite as "rubbing his nose in it" as some did with misbehaving puppies. He grew to believe that he was unworthy of the Greystoke name.

Jackie would eventually figure it out but not until the damage was done.

Arriving at their house in Bern, Jackie was surprised to see his in-laws present and waiting for them in the entrance. Irene's mother opened her arms to engulf Jon but he dodged and ran up the curving staircase to his room leaving the adults standing in the marble tiled foyer. The servants bustled around them bringing in luggage, discussing menus and guest arrangements with Irene.

Jackie had always had good relations with his in-laws. He thought that might be about to change. When the servants disappeared to their chores, the four adults faced each other in silence.

Julian, Irene's father, spoke first. "Perhaps we should retire to the drawing room?" He moved slightly toward the oak door on the right.

"Perhaps we should not. My wife and I have much to discuss and, frankly, this is not the time. It was a long trip. I am going to clean up. I am sure you have made yourselves at home." Jackie kept his tone in check and his stride up the steps unhurried, but he was seething. Irene had not told him she had called her parents, nor that they would be waiting for them on arrival. It felt very much like a sneak attack.

Later, Jackie came out of the shower to find Irene sitting in the Queen Anne's chair in their bedroom.

"You were rude, Jack. They only want to help. They want what's best for Jon."

"Rude? I thought I was quite reasonable considering I was the prey in the midst of a band of lions."

"A jungle metaphor? How appropriate. Our son was nearly mauled and killed by one of those beasts and you make light of it. "

"I do not make light of it. It was unfortunate. Nubiby has been vigilant and reliable for years. A seven-year-old boy who wants to escape will find a way…Especially our seven-year-old boy. He's quite resourceful. But it's over. Jon is safe."

"And he will remain safe. He will never, never go back to that place."

"That place? That place is my home. And he will go back. It is his home also. His grandparents, my parents, live there."

"It is not your home! This is your home. Here in Bern…This house, this civilized house in a civilized city in a civilized country. This is your home too…and Jon's. Here he will stay!"

"Irene," Jackie sat on the edge of the bed, towel around his waist, hair still dripping. "That is not reasonable. What of his grandparents there, and great grandparents? They have a right to see him, to teach him, to assist in his maturity to adulthood. You cannot deprive them of that, or Jon of their counsel. Africa is Jon's heritage as much as this house and Bern are."

"When he is an adult he can go wherever he wants."

"No. He will spend time at the compound with his grandparents. It is not an option."

"You are unreasonable. He was almost killed and you expect me to let him go back there. How can you even consider it? How can you live there? I don't understand it. I have never understood it. There is no civilization. They live like animals…with the animals. They are animals. I will not have my son associating with …" she hesitated.

"With what, Irene?"

She was silent.

"With the natives? With blacks? Is that what you mean?"

Irene raised her head and stood up. "Yes. That is exactly what I mean. Nubiby is obviously incompetent. A white man would not have lost him. You give them too much responsibility. They can't handle it. They are not equipped to handle it. It's not their fault. They aren't like us. They are savages. They aren't human. They look human but they aren't. I will not have Jon around them."

Jackie lowered his head and sighed inwardly. He sent his mind back to their whirlwind courtship almost a decade ago. He had thought himself a fortunate man – to win such a woman for himself. He began to wonder if he had truly won her. Perhaps she had won him. Never in the years he had wooed her, or the years since, had she expressed such beliefs. Or perhaps he had been too blinded by love to see it. Unlike Tarzan and Korak, Jackie did not live at the compound. The Trust was based in London.

Early in their marriage he and Irene had split their time between their London townhouse and their mansion on Lake Lucerne in Switzerland, rarely visiting the compound. Irene always seemed to have a reason not to go, usually an important function for one of her many charities. Jackie had been able to visit the compound only two or three times a year and then for just a day or two; and usually without Irene. He was actively growing the trust and that required his presence in London. Looking back, he realized how often he had gone to the compound without Irene. And, he suddenly realized, when she was at the compound, she was never at ease, never happy. An incident came to his mind. One of the Waziri women who worked at the main house assisting Jane and Meriem had tripped on a carpet edge and spilled a glass of iced tea on Irene. Irene had blasted her, calling her a clumsy fool. Jane had intervened and Irene had apologized saying she was shocked by the cold liquid and overreacted. All concerned had accepted that. Now Jackie wondered. Irene had not apologized immediately. In fact, looking back at it, she seemed sullen. He had chalked it up to surprise at the time. Now he was not so sure.

The subtle diversion of her eyes whenever he praised Nubiby came to his mind; and now that he thought about it, whenever he talked about a person of color. He suddenly recalled a conversation between them the first time they had visited the compound during their engagement. Many of the Waziri had gathered to greet the plane, including Nubiby's wife and children. Jackie had been standing behind her when the cabin door was opened and she saw the small crowd of Waziri gathered at the bottom of the stairs. A look of extreme distaste flashed across her face and she pursed her lips. He recalled asking if she was all right and her answer had been that certainly she was fine. She was just startled by the sudden change in temperature. It had been snowing in London when they departed and the temperature at the compound had been something over 90 degrees Fahrenheit. Jackie had believed her. Now he saw he had wanted to believe her.

Other slights and hastily covered nasty looks around non-white people scrambled through his mind. He had loved her completely and ignored them or found explanations to explain them. Fatigue, illness, surprise. Anything to avoid the truth. He should have seen it, should have expected it. She was a pampered debutante. In her upbringing, she was never exposed to other cultures and races. He began to feel a fool.

"Irene, why did you marry me? You knew my background, my grandparents, Tarzan and Jane. Surely you had to know we would spend time in Africa."

"Tarzan? That silly story? I cannot imagine that a grown man would still believe those tales. They can't possibly be true. A baby? Raised by apes? It's ridiculous. Apes have no ability to raise a human child. And that story about learning to read? It's utter foolishness. It takes years to learn to read with a good teacher; teaching yourself – that's just not possible."

Irene had not believed Tarzan's claims from the beginning. He was highly accomplished and at home in the jungle. That was obvious. But surely his upbringing had not been at the hands of apes. It was more likely to her mind that he had been rescued by the Waziri tribe and raised as one of their own. That would account for his love of their kind. The stories he

created were simply a product of his reluctance to admit that
he was raised by them. She understood that sentiment completely.

"Are you calling my family liars?"

"Yes, liars and cheats! They have used those stories to
build an empire and convince the weak-minded to buy into all
that conservation nonsense. I admired that once, thinking it
the genius of an astute and modern mind – to create such a
successful business based on fiction, but now I see it was not
genius. It was the product of a warped and diseased mind that
created a compound populated by the lower orders not fit to
be around our impressionable young son. I will not have him
in that place around savages and wild beasts.

Jackie stared at her. She stood before him, her face
flushed and her head raised. Her chin jutted out. How had he
missed these attitudes? How had she kept them hidden? Jackie
was seeing first hand one of Tarzan's reasons for avoiding civilized humanity whenever possible.

"Well, Irene, I see that you have been less than honest
with me for some time, since the beginning I think. Was the
Greystoke name prized so highly that you were willing to
prostitute your beliefs to attain it? And what does that make
you, in the end?"

"You are just like them: Savages!" she leaned back
subconsciously separating herself from the barbarian she had
married.

"And you are a conniving witch concerned only with
status and money. You have no morals, no compassion, nothing
worthy of the Greystoke family name. I am sorry you have it.
Jon will return to the compound. You may accompany him or
not. But you will not prevent it."

They stood face-to-face, Jackie's towel on the floor, his
fists clenching and unclenching, towering over a red-faced Irene,
her head tilted back, eyes boring into the gray equally resolute
eyes of her husband.

"Perhaps we should divorce. That way you can control who he sees when he is with you and I can do the same."

"A di…" Irene choked. A divorce was unacceptable among the good people at the pinnacle of the social elite. She would be ostracized, embarrassed. To admit she had married the wrong man, or, worse, that she couldn't keep him? "No, Jackie, wait…"

"Relax, Irene. I don't want a divorce. I don't want to put Jon through that. But…"

"Well, neither do I," Irene put a stop to whatever Jackie was going to say next. They simply would not put Jon through a divorce. She could not conceive of such a thing. He was seven. He would be devastated. He was too young to understand.

"But be assured. I will do it if you drive me to it."

Irene considered. Would he? A divorce would be disastrous, a custody fight even worse. But she was determined. Jon could not go back to that place that terrified her. It was unthinkable. He could be mauled by another lion. Worse, he could be influenced by those natives. She could not allow that. She must protect him. It was her duty as a mother. She tried another tact.

"Would you really do this to me. To us."

"I would. I have too. Jon is my son. He will know his heritage."

Irene sighed and sagged into the Queen Anne's chair. "I loved you Jackie. You were the most beautiful man I had ever seen. You had everything, money, English nobility. How could I not have fallen for you? You were my Prince Charming. Don't destroy me. Don't destroy us. "

"I think "Us" has been over for a long time. You are not who I thought you were, who you pretended to be. I do not want to destroy you. But I will not allow you to deprive Jon of his family. I will file for divorce if you force my hand."

Irene gave up all pretense then. "You can try. If you do, I will get custody. No court in the world would allow a child to live in that savage world." If he actually went through with a divorce, at least she would have custody of Jon, alleviating somewhat the criticism she was sure to experience from her fellow socialites.

"Don't bet on that. I have at least as many connections as you do and money will not be an object, for either of us. I will fight to keep him as you will fight to keep him. Perhaps you should consider him. And make peace – at least until he is grown. Unless you prefer to watch private lives unfold across world headlines. The paparazzi will be in our debt for a lifetime."

"What do you propose?"

Jackie considered that question. What did he propose? He did not think he could keep up a façade. He could not attend the normal social and charitable events with Irene and her family as he had been accustomed to do. They were frauds. So much time and money donated for lavish events, strictly for show, to a world that would adore and applaud them, and have no idea how much they were despised by their objects of adoration. Another reason for Tarzan's hatred of civilized humanity. In the jungle, a lion was a lion, not an antelope in disguise.

"I propose we decide tonight how we will proceed. How the two of us will interact with society. Where Jon will live, and go to school. It will be a custody agreement between us without the nastiness of a divorce. But this will be between us, Irene. Not your parents."

IRENE PROCEEDED DOWNSTAIRS, her mind awhirl, while Jackie dressed. What had she done? Jon would go back to that place. How could she bear it? How could she not? He was her son. Her only son. She would have to go to protect him, to see that those men did not instill in him a love of the jungle. To see that they did not make Jon like them. She shuddered at the thought. What had gone wrong? Their marriage had been so good. She had not lied when she told him she had loved him. She had. She did. It had been so easy then, at the beginning. Jackie had catered to her every wish. Why was he so against her now? She did not understand.

A single tear slid down her cheek. She brushed it off and did not see the small form hidden in the alcove just beyond the bedroom door. Jon waited for her to descend before returning to his own room, a much more confused child than he had been a mere thirty minutes before. He was certain it was his fault.

As Jackie dressed he recalled a discussion he had had with his mother and grandmother shortly before he entered college. They cautioned him to be wary of women who sought to marry the rich and powerful with no regard to love. They reminded him of the solid, loving, and committed relationships of his parents and grandparents, and urged him to be careful of those without their own resources. He thought he had. Irene had her own fortune and was already of the social elite when he met her. What possible reason could she have to marry him other than love? *She already had it all*, he thought. For some, apparently, having it all was not enough. She needed a trophy and he was it.

December 27, 1985

East Africa
The Greystoke compound

Chapter 5: SHATTERED PEACE

MERIEM CLAYTON STOOD on the veranda of the main house of the Greystoke compound, watching as the sun edged up over the eastern horizon, its red glow bringing a new day. Stretched out before her was the great African plain, still wearing its skirt of morning mist, creating a mystically haunting, surrealistic painting in hues of all shades of brown and green. The zebra, wildebeest, and antelope were just starting to rise from their nocturnal repose to begin their daily grazing. Only the sound of a distant bird penetrated the peaceful silence of the moment.

"This is the best time of the day...any day...just to enjoy the true beauty of Africa", she thought. There was a raw harmony between the earth, the air, and its occupants that is so easily lost in more civilized settings of glass buildings and paved roads.

Her vision couldn't take in the great expanse of the Greystoke compound. It was so different from when she had first come to it as Korak's bride. Then there were only Tarzan's and Jane's main house and a few make-shift farm buildings and thatched huts dotting the landscape. Today, the Greystoke compound was a thriving agricultural community. It was land deeded by the Colonial powers to the Greystokes after WWI for their help and assistance in winning "the war to end all wars." While it was not a country unto itself, no government dared to challenge the Greystokes' governance.

The Waziri huts were long gone, replaced with modern ranch-style houses for the nearly three thousand occupants who lived and worked on the land. They respected the Greystokes because they had brought prosperity and education to a land that had not known such before. The Greystokes shared the land with the native Africans, each helping the other to succeed.

"*If only Korak, Jane and Tarzan were here to enjoy the view*", she thought, "*then it would be perfect.*" But, they weren't. Korak would be back soon from his expedition to see Dian Fossey and see what could be done to save the dwindling number of mountain gorillas. He had called five days ago to say everything was progressing much better than either he or Dian had thought possible, and that he would be back in time for the annual "gathering of the family" on New Year's Day, or a day or two sooner.

It would be the first year beyond memory that Tarzan and Jane would not be joining them. Jane had talked Tarzan into taking a rare vacation to explore the mysteries of northern India and Nepal. (Truth be known, he acquiesced to Jane's request out of his love for her. When he was in his native jungle, from his viewpoint, every day was a vacation.)

The emergence of a billowing dust cloud on the right broke her reverie. She was momentarily puzzled. *Was Korak returning early without telling her?* It would be great to have quiet time with him without all the other family members.

The dust cloud grew bigger as it drew closer. She quickly saw that the cause of the man-made storm was emanating from many vehicles. It was too expansive to be coming from just one, or even two, vehicles.

Meriem was practically mesmerized by the cloud as it kept growing, spreading and advancing directly at the compound. A chill of impending danger ran up her spine to the nape of her neck. *Something bad was coming…but what?* She turned and started to go back in the house. As she reached for the door handle she heard a loud whistling noise, and before she could turn to see its source, the entire eastside wall of the bungalow exploded throwing stone, dirt, dust, glass and timber in every direction.

Chapter 6: OUT OF THE COCOON

"TEN MINUTES, JON. BUCKLE UP." Scott Horton's voice broke in upon Jon Clayton's musings in the passenger cabin of the Clayton family's private jet.

The ink was not yet dry on his bachelor's degree. He was leaving school and entering the adult working world. He was also parting ways with his family. They expected him to work with his father, Jackie, for The Greystoke Trust. His choice, however, was something else entirely, and he would have to tell them soon. This trip, in fact. The family was gathering for their annual New Year's Reunion. Only his great grandparents, Tarzan and Jane would not be there. He reviewed his reasons and logic again, dreading their reactions but thankful that only one grandmother would be there to turn disappointed eyes on him when he told them he was not joining the family business.

He had had a great life…a life of privilege and opportunity where anything he wanted had been his for the asking. That was the luck of being the sixth generation of the second richest family in the United Kingdom. His ancestors were of the privileged landed-gentry class. They were one of the few that saw the coming breakdown of the class system that World War I began. They embraced the change, entering the affairs of commerce, becoming one of the more prominent "Names" of Lloyds of London. The precious gems and gold that his great grandfather had extracted from the lost city of Opar added even more power and prestige to the family's position in Society.

In recent years, the family's fortune had accelerated exponentially through the astute investments of Jon's father,

31

Jackie Clayton. Five years ago, a car crash had taken the life of his wife, Irene, and left Jackie with damaged legs, a wheelchair and a teenage son. It was during his recuperation that Jackie began to focus more intently on the finances of the Trust. He made a series of aggressive investments that more than qua-drupled its assets in the intervening years.

Jon had reaped both the benefits of his great grandfa-ther's gold and his father's investments. He attended the best private schools in Europe, traveled extensively, and charmed high society in both London and Switzerland. His good looks and money attracted flocks of young ladies seeking glamour and wealth. He had learned from his parents' experience, however, and had so far resisted even the most tempting offers. He was not ready to settle down.

Nor was he ready for the conversations he would soon have with his father's family. Both sides of his family expected him to work in the Trust. His mother's family applauded his decision to major in economics and math. They would have been thrilled at anything he did that meant he wasn't living in Africa. His father's family was content to have him work in London with his father and hoped he would learn to love the jungle as they did. He would not tell them that was unlikely. His enthusiasm for the jungle had died with the lion when he was seven. He would not tell them that either.

He would tell them that he wanted to do something that was his alone and not connected to either family. He wanted to start his own martial arts school.

Jon had trained in martial arts from age seven and had loved it from the beginning. His father had introduced him to a dojo in Bern and later in London. Jon had excelled, earning a second degree black belt in karate and a first degree black belt in jujutsu. In college at MIT, he had continued his training and discovered an enthusiasm for teaching the youngest members of the dojo. He had found himself spending most of his spare time there, assisting and encouraging the younger students. During his second year in America he had met a like-minded

American working with a teen class on Saturday mornings. Doug was a junior high school math teacher who had encouraged many of his math students to take up martial arts.

The two became good friends, and spent many an hour over beer and pizza talking and planning a dojo of their own. Jon had the money and Doug the teaching experience. They had scouted a location in upstate New York and planned to open the next summer. This was the news he was dreading to tell his family.

Scott's voice again broke into Jon's thoughts. "Jon... come up here. Something's not right." The urgency in Scott's voice propelled Jon to the flight deck. Scott had been the Trust's head pilot for over ten years and was considered more friend than employee.

Jon entered the pilot's cabin and stood between the seats. Scott pointed to the left at dense black and gray clouds billowing up into the sky. Jon looked to the ground below. They came from the Greystoke compound.

"Take it down so we can get a better look."

Scott complied, dropping down to 1,000 feet as they neared the compound. There was little left to see. Every building had been leveled or was burning, including the main bungalow of the Greystokes. The airfield was pocked with craters. It would be suicide to land.

As they approached Jon could see scattered bodies and people running towards the jungle chased by men with guns. One man held what looked like a rocket launcher to his shoulder. It was pointed at their plane.

"What is ...?" The plane jerked and the right wing dropped sharply slamming, Jon across the copilot's seat into the glass of the side window, stunning him. At the same time the right engine burst into flames.

Scott reacted instantly. His right hand grabbed the throttles to cut power to the burning engine and give full power to the good left one. At the same time his left foot slammed into the left rudder keeping the nose from turning. His left hand on the yoke leveled the wings and lowered the nose to try to gain lift and speed. He succeeded in righting the aircraft but he knew it was in vain. In those swift seconds, they had lost five hundred feet. In normal conditions, he could fly with one engine on full power but he wasn't going to get full power in time. He had reduced power for their approach before the hit. Jet engines took time to regain full power. They were too low and too slow.

"Jon, we're going down!" In his peripheral vision, Scott could see that Jon had tumbled into the copilot's seat and was beginning to stir. He could not help. He scanned for a place to put down. They had only seconds. There wasn't much choice, the open fields of the compound or the jungle. They would be sitting ducks for the attackers in the fields but the trees would be certain death. He opted for the fields furthest from the site of the destruction. He banked slightly, losing more precious altitude.

"Jon, put your seat belt on. JON." Scott felt more than saw movement on his right and heard the click of a seatbelt.

They were just at tree level and Scott fought to keep the right wing up. Almost out of rudder, he lowered the nose for more lift and increased power on the left engine to compensate. The plan was to land parallel to the jungle and hope they could escape into it before any attackers arrived. It didn't work out that way. He ran out of rudder and the nose yawed to the right. The right wing dipped, touched the ground first and twisted the plane towards the jungle just yards away. Momentum carried them crashing into the trees at a canted angle.

Jon shook his head trying to clear the fog. He smelled leaking fuel and raised his head to see a tree sticking through the windshield. His eyes followed it back to Scott. The trunk pinned Scott to his seat much like an insect pinned to a piece of Styrofoam. Jon looked into Scott's blank and staring eyes.

SHOUTS AND GUNFIRE jerked him back to his own tenuous situation. He tried to crawl back to the main cabin to escape the plane but the twisted fuselage jammed the door. He pushed, shoved, and tore at the blockage but could not move it. There was no escape that way. Nor could he get to the survival gear Scott always carried. Retreating into the cockpit, he climbed onto the tree that impaled Scott. Wrapping his arm in his jacket he pushed and pulled enough of the glass away from around the tree so that he could squeeze out onto the nose cone. The shouts were louder, closer. He could smell smoke and glanced to the right. Flames were kicking up in the grass behind the bent right wing. He jumped down and struggled through the thick brush of the jungle.

The sounds of machine gun fire and the clamor of shouts and cries followed him, becoming ever louder. Every instant he expected the sting of a bullet, the slash of a machete, or the blast of an explosion that would fry him to a crisp.

When the plane did explode, it knocked him over. Landing on his right side, he felt the heat on his back but he was far enough away and behind enough foliage that he was uninjured.

He scrambled to his feet, heart pounding in his ears, and pushed through the foliage to get farther into the jungle. He did not look back as a second explosion shattered the atmosphere. A trail appeared and he ran down it away from the burning plane and the destroyed compound. He crossed another trail and ran down it, then another and another and another.

Chapter 7: ESCAPE TO THE JUNGLE

S O MANY TIMES, life and death are determined by a matter of split seconds. Had Meriem reached the inside of the bungalow three seconds earlier she would have been crushed by the collapsing walls, roof and flying debris. Instead, she was hurled off the veranda, landing on her stomach in one of the many surrounding flower beds.

She was dazed, but not knocked out. Her blouse and pants were ripped in various places where flying particles of stone, glass and other debris had pelted her. Blood ran down the side of her forehead from a four-inch gash across her left temple. Fortunately, like most head wounds, the abundance of blood didn't necessarily indicate severe damage. It took her a few seconds to regain her senses. She heard shouting and gunfire from all around. She started to get up, but immediately collapsed back to earth as what she saw turned her stomach and hardened her heart; friends and loved ones were being systematically run down and killed, either by being shot, knifed or bludgeoned to death by uniformed soldiers.

Old Bamhame, Jackie's nurse when he was first born, ran screaming across the compound, hollering for help from someone…anyone. No one came; they were too busy trying to protect themselves. Instead, a young attacker grabbed her by her dreadlocks. She thrashed about to no avail. In one rapid motion the soldier pulled her head back, raising her chin up high to expose her throat, then with his bush knife cut her from ear to ear. Blood spewed from the opened cavity. A gargling noise replaced Bamhame's screams, then only silence. The soldier

37

let go of the dreadlocks and let the body crumple to the ground and turned to see who his next victim would be.

Meriem's first instinct was to find Korak. He would be able to bring help. *Was he still at Dian's, or on his way back?* Almost immediately she knew that was impossible because the attackers came from the same direction as he would be coming. Their lines blocked her from reaching him. She had no other choice than to head West in hopes of finding some way to circle back around to reach Korak.

Her first moves were hesitant out of fear of being seen, caught, and most probably killed. Piles of debris, which were everywhere, became her shields from the attackers. It took nearly an hour until she finally reached the tall grass of the plains. It provided better camouflage allowing her to move faster even though she had to stay stooped over for concealment.

It took her nearly another seventy-five minutes to reach the edge of the jungle. She took one last look back and all she could see were the pillars of smoke ascending to the sky from their red-yellow flamed bases; and all she could hear was the silence of the completed massacre.

She turned and entered the jungle's edge, her only weapon being a long narrow piece of stone she had picked up from the garden. Ironically it was the same stone that had slashed her temple. It would do little good against an armed attacker, but it was better than nothing.

She climbed the nearest tree and gracefully worked her way to mid-terrace. As she sat in one of its crotches, she gathered her thoughts and tried to establish a sense of direction. Overhead the roar of jet engines reached her ears. She looked up to see a twin-engine plane pass over. She immediately recognized it as one of the Greystoke's private planes; she instinctively knew who the occupants were, her son Jackie and his son Jon. She watched as the plane dropped in altitude then made a wide banking motion circling back around. Out of a mother's instinct she said, "*Stay away! Get help!*"

Her thoughts were drowned out by the roar of a surface-to-air missile streaking skyward on a direct path to the airplane. She helplessly watched the impact, and the resulting jarring and jerking response of the plane. Its nose swung downward. She saw one of the two engines was gone, replaced by a fireball of flames.

The dense foliage made it impossible to see the final point of impact. She heard the breaking of trees and metal as the plane penetrated the jungle growth. The plane came to its final resting place. A momentary stillness, then a massive explosion followed by a brilliant ball of flames that rose above the tree line. Meriem put her head into her hands and cried unabashedly. *How could it be? How could it happen? Both Jackie and Jon dead… killed! Where is Korak? This must be a dream!* But it wasn't.

She lifted her hands from her tear-soaked face, extended her arms to the heavens, and gave out a blood curdling cry of grief and vengeance that only a bereaved mother and wife could make. It resounded across the tree tops, silencing all that heard it. She was once again the girl Korak had trained to the ways of the jungle after rescuing her from her Arab captors. The layers of civilization that had built up over time peeled away, bringing forth a formidable enemy for any that would cross her path.

AS SHE HEADED WEST, she heard the noises of men running through the jungle. She descended to the lower level of the trees for a closer inspection. There she saw nine men in military uniforms pressing their way through the jungle's undergrowth. They seemed to be chasing something, or someone. She knew that at some point they would have to retrace their steps as their back packs gave every sign that they were not prepared to spend overnight in the jungle. With that knowledge, she struck upon a plan.

She waited. It was nearly three hours until she once again heard the noise of the returning soldiers. This time they were walking not running, having exhausted their energies in the pursuit of their unknown prey. Their bedraggled formation, as well as their physical stature - slumped shoulders and sweat-soaked uniforms - made it clear they were returning empty handed, their prey having eluded them.

Meriem bided her time, waiting for the right moment. She counted the number of returnees. Number nine came in the form of a straggler who had fallen so far behind that he was out of sight of the others. As he lumbered on, Meriem tracked him from above, and then at the right moment, dropped onto the soldier's back.

The impact threw the soldier to the ground, knocking the wind out of him. Before he could recover, Meriem smashed her rock into the side of his head, squarely hitting the soft spot between the ear and the temple. His body jerked in spasm, then went limp. She felt for a pulse. There was none.

She quickly searched the body for anything she could use. The rifle was discarded into the underbrush, being too clumsy to carry in the trees. The knife was another matter. She detached the sheath and stuck it in her waist band. The backpack held some dry rations, a blanket… and three grenades. All could prove useful.

Meriem stripped the body, and dragged it to the center of the path so it would be clearly visible. Using the man's own knife, she ripped a large gash under the left rib cage and reached in and pulled out his heart. She pulled open the dead man's mouth and crammed in the bloody heart. It was a gruesome act but also strong "native medicine" that would terrify the other soldiers when they returned to find their missing comrade.

The voices of others calling out looking for their lost comrade came to her ears. They were close. She had to hurry. She gathered up her bounty and scaled the nearby tree. She remained motionlessly above as the others discovered their comrade's body. A choir of screams ensued. Two of the soldiers shot off wild bursts from their guns; less in hope of hitting anything, more in hope to scare away whatever jungle demon had slaughtered their comrade.

They debated whether to take the body back to their camp, or leave it. In the end, they chose to leave it. They would tell their superiors that he had wandered off and was probably killed by a beast of the jungle. It alleviated them having to explain the unexplainable circumstances in which they had found the body. Jungle demons should be respected.

Meriem waited fifteen minutes after the soldiers' departure before moving back up into the mid-terrace to begin her journey to contact Korak and find the necessary resources to avenge what had been perpetrated on the Clayton family. *Whoever said avenging angels couldn't be women, was wrong... dead wrong. He doesn't know me!*

Chapter 8: WHERE ARE THE BODIES?

THE RUSSIAN-BUILT Mil Mi-26 Helicopter, carrying Zairian Air Force markings, circled the area of devastation. Its two key occupants were pleased with what they saw, destruction on a massive scale. Nothing stood, other than a wall here, or there. The rest was rubble. It was devastation of a scale seen during the bombings of World War II.

Soldiers on the ground, upon hearing the approach, sought cover, armed their variety of automatic weapons and aimed them in the direction of the approaching helicopter. Their nerves were still on *"high alert."* Their commanding officer was the first to recognize the approaching aircraft. "Stand down. It's General Kanka. He's coming to inspect the good work you have done. Form up."

The soldiers scurried from their hiding places and formed two columns to receive their Commanding General. The chopper settled on a cleared area; the engine shutoff, the blades gradually coming to a stop. The side door of the helicopter slid open, from which twelve heavily armed soldiers emerged, The General's private security shield. They rapidly deployed to form a protective corridor for the general. The soldier closest to the door gave a nod towards the interior. Upon that signal, General Joseph Kanka stepped forth. He was a small man, barely five-foot tall, yet stocky in nature. Some people behind his back had compared him to a *"walking whiskey barrel."* He was as dark-skinned as a lump of coal. He wore thick oversized sunglasses and the furrows of skin on his forehead gave a continual scowl to his appearance. The ground troops came to full attention. The General saluted, and then said, "At ease."

Everyone was expecting the General to step forward to inspect the demolition and destruction of the Clayton compound. Instead the General looked back into the helicopter and gave a nod to someone inside. The General's silent assurance brought forth another person. He looked European, dressed in white, and wearing a panama straw hat. While he bore all the trappings of a diplomat, his body language spoke more like a hungry eel searching for his next meal.

He removed his sunglasses, revealing green eyes that continually darted from side-to-side, always searching for the first sign of danger...or opportunity. If eyes are the portals to one's soul, then his eyes illuminated the pathway to Hell.

The General didn't bother to announce his companion. Instead, he just motioned him forward and they walked through the makeshift honor guard. When they reached the end of the line, the commanding officer stepped forward, snapped to attention, and saluted. The General sent a sloppy salute in return and said, "Show us your accomplishments."

The commander did not waste a second. He pivoted on his heels and began walking through the compound, pointing out what used to be but no longer was: Stables now a smoldering hovel still carrying the stench of burnt horse flesh, tractors and trucks burnt almost beyond recognition, some parts completely melted down into hunks of twisted plastic and metal. The main house was shattered timbers, shards of glass and crushed concrete.

The diplomat spoke for the first time. "Where are the bodies? I want to see the bodies!" The words were English with a heavy Slavic accent.

"Yes! The BODIES! We need to see the bodies." It was the General reinforcing his companion's wish to see the bodies of the deceased. His tone and demeanor matched that of a person trying to seem more important than what he was – a messenger boy. The brief exchange told everyone present who was truly in charge.

The party rapidly moved over to an isolated area of the compound where the pungent stench of decomposing bodies invaded their nostrils. The stranger, as well as the General, withdrew handkerchiefs to hold over their noses and mouths with the hope of filtering out the foul fragrances. Bodies were randomly piled on top of each other.

The stranger turned to the General, "I only see black bodies. Where are the bodies of the Claytons? Why are they not here!?"

The General turned to the field commander and asked to specifically see the bodies of the Claytons. The field commander turned to his squad leaders who turned to their troops. A great collaboration pursued. An answer was reached. The troops whispered their answer to the squadron leaders, who did not appear happy with what they heard. The squadron leaders approached their commander with their findings. The answer was unacceptable. The commander turned to the General and said, "We have not found the Claytons. They must still be in the rubble."

The General's jaw jutted out and the furrows on his forehead grew even deeper. Before he could say a word the commander continued, "The men will set about clearing the main housing now. We will find you their bodies."

The General had the final words, "You'd better."

THE SEARCH WENT ON until dusk. More bodies were found, but none were the Claytons. The General was deeply embarrassed, flushed with anger. The stranger turned to the General and spoke a few words, "I told you to attack on New Year's Day, but no, you, because of a weather forecast, decided to attack earlier. Do you see now what happens when you don't follow my orders?" Without waiting for a response, the stranger turned away and walked back in disgust to the helicopter. He was livid. The entire operation had been for naught.

The General turned to his field commander. Before the underling could say a word, the General pulled out his pistol and shot the commander between the eyes. Then, he turned to his troops. "This is what happens when you fail me!" Pointing his index finger at one of the leaders, he shouted loudly, "You! You are now commander. Your single mission is to find and destroy the Claytons! There will be no failure! You will send me daily reports until you have succeeded. Is that understood?"

The General did not wait for a response. He turned and marched back to the waiting helicopter. His security ring followed, and within moments the helicopter leapt to the sky, leaving behind a bewildered group of soldiers who had no idea how they were to accomplish what they had been tasked to do.

As the helicopter disappeared over the horizon, soldiers began wandering off in a multiplicity of directions, heading to their home villages. They would take their chances in the jungle rather than dealing with a mad leader.

Chapter 9: *JON LOST IN THE JUNGLE*

JON RAN FROM THE PLANE. His heart pounded and heat scorched his back. A vision of the tree protruding from Scott's chest rose in his mind. He forced it down. Machine guns sputtered behind him and he ran faster

Thorns and nettles tore at his clothes and skin as he fought his way through tangled plants and vines that closed ranks behind him. The heat on his back cooled and the sound of the guns receded. Scott's surprised, lifeless face came into his mind. He forced the memory aside and ran on.

The vegetation thinned and he ran more easily. The guns were silent. He crouched down behind a tree, panting, listening, hoping his pursuers had given up the chase.

His mind swirled with the destruction, the crash, Scott's bloody hands gripping the branch that impaled him, and the harsh, jarring sounds of the guns. He shook his head and fell to his knees, then dropped his hands to the spongy moss of the forest floor, taking deep breaths. Dark spots rimmed his vision.

When his breathing slowed, he considered his plight. This was his first time in the jungle since he was seven. After the lion episode, he had returned to the compound twice a year as required by his father. But they were short visits, never lasting more than two weeks. In the early years, his mother had accompanied him and expressly forbid him to enter the jungle. He had been happy to comply. After she died, he had become adept at finding reasons not to go. Helping Nubiby, or one of his grandmothers, around the compound always seemed to work.

He had wanted that lion, dreamed of it, dreamed of making his family proud. But when face-to-face with the real "king of beasts," he was no match for it. If not for his father, grandfather and great grandfather, he would have been the lion's main course.

A flicker of yellow flashed across his peripheral vision and he jerked to the right. Nothing. No lion. He shook his head and realized he had come close to panicking. Great grandson of Tarzan, accomplished martial artist, two black belts, and he panics in the jungle. Gone was the acute awareness of his surroundings he had attained after years of training in the martial arts. Gone also was the calm acceptance of what is, replaced by fear and anxiety for what might come. He needed to regain his center and his focus; go with the jungle, not against it, using the opportunities it provided to advance, as he would any opponent.

Finally, when his heartbeat returned to normal, he stood and focused on his surroundings. The rainforest overwhelmed his senses. Hanging vines and lianas draped trees that soared two hundred feet in the air. The canopy blocked the sun creating the effect of a dimly lit hall with towering cathedral ceilings. He turned slowly taking in the emerald, lime and mint greens of the foliage, dotted here and there by the whites, purples and pinks of orchids. Passing birds flashed bright reds and yellows. Pale brown buttress roots rambled away from their trunks and tapered gradually into the ground. The scents of damp earth and rotting leaves intermingled with the smells of exotic flowers and unseen animals. His shirt and khaki pants clung to him like wet towels in the warm humid air.

The lion lurked silently in the trees' shadows, its yellow eyes locked on Jon.

Jon lurched backwards and tripped over a root. He landed on his back thinking the lion would, after all, have its lunch. He raised his head to see his death in golden fur springing through the air but it was gone. Vanished. He jumped to his feet and turned in a full circle. No lion. He scanned the foliage frantically. No lion. *Was it real?*

REAL OR IMAGINED, he needed to control his fear and get out of the jungle. He wanted and needed to return to the compound. But he had no weapons, and, much as he loved the tales of his fathers, and much as he wished it otherwise, he was not ready or able to swing from trees and rescue fair maidens. He would be lucky to rescue himself.

He tripped over another root and found himself flat out staring into two round eyes attached to a black hairy ball with legs; a spider, which from his vantage point on the ground, seemed bigger than his head. He choked and sprang to his feet, ready to run, but the spider ran first, skittering away into the thin undergrowth. He paused then and took stock. Knee-jerk reactions only heightened the danger. He squatted down with his back to a buttress root to think, brushing at the thorns, nettles, and debris that had collected in the rips and tears of his clothes. He yanked a thorn from under a fingernail and grimaced, pushing on the nail hard to staunch the blood flow. A breeze tickled his hair and a hand reflexively moved to scratch his neck. *Wait.* His hand paused in mid-air. *There is no breeze in the jungle.* The tickle suddenly morphed into something soft, prickly and heavy moving across the back of his neck. He jerked to his feet brushing it off with both hands. A bright orange and black mound the size of a football fell to the ground, righted itself and scurried away on a hundred legs. He spun around, running both hands back and forth through his hair, his stomach dropping.

He moved around the tree to a different root, searching the area above and below first before sinking down to think, swatting at insects. *Who were those guys? Where were his grand-parents? Did they escape?* His eyes registered a small downed tree trunk several feet from him, moving. *Now what? More hallucinations?* He stared. Not a tree. A snake. A BIG snake. His stomach churned but this time he took a deep breath, releasing it slowly, and moved cautiously but deliberately out of view of the snake. *Better.* Now he needed a plan. As a child – after the lion – he had not fantasized as other boys did of winning the super bowl or being a hero in some life-threatening situation. He already knew he would freeze. The martial arts had taught him to control his fear in mock fights and tournament situations. But this was not the dojo. He needed to control his fear and focus on survival, keep his mind busy, analyzing. *What do I have, what can I do, how can I make one thing better? Don't dwell on the jungle, the lion, the fear. Keep moving. Keep analyzing.*

He focused on his grandfathers. *What would they do? Probably call in the apes.* He slapped at a sting on his face and his hand came away with blood. The apes were not an option unless they found him.

Several Waziri villages had grown up between the compound and the river to the west. He had met the chiefs several times over the years during his visits to the compound. East, it would be. The Waziri would know him.

But which way was East? The canopy of the jungle blocked the sun. If he could find the sun, he could use his watch to find east. He considered climbing a tree but the trees he could see were straight and branchless. Triangular thorns the size of his hand marched up the tree next to him. There were no footholds other than thorns and no branches for at least the first hundred feet. Finding East with the sun was not an option.

HE DECIDED TO KEEP GOING in the direction he had been, hoping it was East. He had entered the jungle going East but his escape path surely was not a straight line. So, he guessed.

Daylight was dimming and he shivered at the thought of the approaching night. He knew enough from family stories not to stay on the ground. Night was feast time on the jungle floor. Sleeping in the branches of a tree was best but there were no low branches anywhere. He would have to settle for the roots.

He spied a tree with ten-foot high buttress roots, some horizontal, and growing close together. He collected a pile of sturdy plant stems, branches, and ferns, shaking them vigorously, then tied them with thin vines and hoped it was sturdy enough to hold him. He tossed his platform up and over two roots close together then scrambled up himself and sat down cross-legged to survey his accommodations.

Within minutes the light departed leaving him in pitch black and a gradually increasing cacophony of sounds. Whoops, laughs, trumpets, croaks, chirps and trills from low bass to high soprano punctuated the constant background static of crickets and cicadas. It was a chorus of creatures about which he knew absolutely nothing. Some were probably sizing him up for dinner. *They better hurry*, he thought, *if they want blood*. The mosquitoes were draining him fast. There was no respite and no part of his body that did not itch. He lay on his back looking up into blackness, the stars blocked by the high canopy above him. There was a whole world of animals up in those branches and he wished he could join them.

He considered his situation. There was a good possibility he would die here, taken out by a poisonous spider or snake perhaps, or one of the big cats. Or he could poison himself. He had no idea what was edible but he knew much was not. Water could be his demise, as well. Parasites lurked in standing water as did disease bacteria.

He propped himself up on his elbows and reflected on how utterly unprepared he was for this. He was the fourth generation of a family that thrived in jungle environments and the only male to shun that way of life. The lion had changed everything.

He fell asleep in the middle of these ruminations, waking several times through the night to the roars and cries of roaming beasts. Each time he forced down the adrenalin rush and remained still. Running in the jungle in the dark was not wise.

Dawn light woke him and he rolled over looking down at the jungle floor and contemplating his next move. An upright stick moved across his vision. No. Four feet of snake rose above the forest floor and moved rapidly, propelled by the wave-like movements of its lower body across the ground. A hollow pit opened in his stomach as the snake bore down on several bright green parrots perched atop a tree fern a few feet below Jon's eye level. Suddenly the snake struck a bird then fell back to the ground with the bird held firmly in its mouth and retreated into the undergrowth. Jon gasped. That bird had been four feet off the ground. The remaining parrots flew away and Jon considered never leaving his platform for the rest of his life.

He waited and watched for a long time, swatting absentmindedly. The snake did not return. Finally, he decided to find his way to the ground. His mouth was dry and he was hungry. The leaves were wet with rain that had filtered down in the night and he managed to lick a few drops but it wasn't enough. There were plentiful berries and fruit around but which ones? He wished he could find a way up into the canopy to observe the monkeys. If he watched them and ate what they ate he was probably safe.

A few minutes later he came across a trail and, determining the direction that seemed the closest to his concept of East he turned left and followed the trail for hours only to see it peter out and disappear. He sat down against a tree, wiping the sweat, mosquitoes and flies off his face and resisted the temptation to take off his sodden long-sleeved shirt. *This isn't working*, he thought. He turned around, retraced his steps and kept going.

Several trails led off from the path he traveled but he chose not to take them as the one he was on seemed larger. A few hours later he walked out onto an old dirt road, grown up with grasses and small plants but still recognizable as a road. *YES*, he thought. *Surely this will lead somewhere.* He went left but after an hour or so it also petered out disappearing into the trees of the rainforest.

Jon sat down on the road and considered, waving his hands automatically at insects buzzing around him. He did not want to spend another night in the jungle but it was getting close to sunset. There was more sky here but he could not see the sun. He could detect a shadow from the bigger trees and so figured East was to his left into the bush, not along the road that had developed from the trail he had followed. He hesitated to leave the road as it must have led somewhere once. He decided to stick with the road but needed a place to spend the night. The trees close to the road had lower branches, receiving more sunlight, so he climbed one and wedged himself in between two branches close to the trunk.

He woke up repeatedly, shifting from one painful position to another and spent much of the night awake listening to the random harmonies and quarrels of the jungle.

When dawn arrived, he continued down the road in the opposite direction from the day before, happy to see the sun most of the morning. He needed water soon and was surprised to see water shimmering in the distance across the road. He started to run, hoping it was not a mirage. A large body of water could mean a village.

Within a few steps sharp piercing pains in his shins and calves stopped him. He looked down to see he was standing amidst a column of black ants, many of them now crawling up his pants. He jumped off the column brushing at those he could see and smashing his hands at the tickle of others under his pants. A line of ants struck out from the column, quickly reaching him and adding their pinchers to the assault. He ran then, away from the column, still swatting but the ants had bitten through the khaki into his leg and would not be dislodged. His eyes followed the column to the shimmering body of water ahead: *Ants on water? No, not water at all. Driver ants. Army ants. The light was shimmering off millions of carnivorous ants.* He was dead if he stayed there. He turned and ran back the way he had come, wondering how fast a column of army ants could move.

Chapter 10: ANOTHER JUNGLE

THERE ARE MANY JUNGLES IN THIS WORLD; one of the most vicious is the financial jungle where man preys on fellow man, where money trumps morality, and where only the cunning and strong survive. It is in this world that Jackie Clayton, Tarzan's grandson, chose to hide after the car crash that killed his wife and condemned him to a wheelchair, his legs having been broken in multiple places by the force of the impact collapsing the dashboard into them.

Conquering the world of finance became an obsession. His astute investment strategies grew the gold bullion of Opar and the family's wealth into one of the largest global financial institutions, The Greystoke Trust. Its net worth was measured in the hundreds of billions of dollars.

In negotiations, he was hard, shrewd, and calculating. Those who negotiated a deal with him remarked "the mind of an enigma was easier to read." When it came to business, there were no feelings - only the numbers. If the numbers worked, fine; if they didn't work - no deal. Only the numbers mattered. His negotiations were always hard, even fierce, but never dishonest.

The Greystoke Trust controlled vast holdings throughout the world. It reached into every vital industry. Its means and methods were scrutinized by others who wanted to be as successful. The guiding axiom was to select only capital-based investments as they produced more rapid Return on Assets and Return on Investment than labor-based investments. The other axiom was *"Don't bet when you buy,"* i.e., know ALL sides of the potential investment, and know them better than any competitor.

Jackie, regardless of his negotiation tactics, realized the faith other financial and business institutions placed in The Greystoke Trust. He always insisted that his people maintain the highest moral and business standards in all their dealings – professional and personal. He understood The Trust's reputation was a keystone to The Trust's success.

The Trust was located at 17 Global Street. From the outside, it appeared to be an ordinary four-story brownstone just two streets off the main financial district of London. There were no exterior indicators of what went on inside. It seemed just another private row house residence.

The inside told a different story. It was not just one house but three. It also encompassed the interiors of 15 and 19 Global Street. The basement and the first two floors contained state-of-the-art computing and communications equipment where fifty-three of the smartest financial investment people in the world plied their trade on behalf of The Greystoke Trust. The third floor held the offices of the executives of The Trust, while the top floor, the fourth floor, was Jackie Clayton's personal penthouse.

DISTRESS TELEGRAPHED FROM JACKIE'S FACE. It was 8:19 AM London time. He had been at his eighteenth-century Thomas Chippendale mahogany partner's desk since 5:00 AM. His nightly leg cramps provoked early risings. That, however, was not the cause of his current mood.

Jackie's dismay stemmed from the documents that his long-time and trusted secretary Louise Smythe had just brought to him; the documents having been delivered by private courier from the office of the Exchequer of the Bank of England, the government entity responsible for overseeing financial transactions and stock trading.

She could tell by the look on his face that the news contained in the documents was not good. Her thoughts were confirmed when the first thing Jackie did was to look up from the documents and tell her to call the airport to let Jon know that he would not be going with him.

"Let him know I'll follow as soon as I can. Is the conference room open?"

"There's an all-day engineering meeting scheduled."

"Reschedule it. Notify Rupert, Ian, Otto, Leslie and Phillip to meet me there in thirty minutes. No ifs, ands or buts. I don't care what they're doing, or where they are. Get them there.

"Oh, and reschedule all of my appointments for today."

"What about your daily therapy? It's scheduled for four."

"Reschedule it for eight tonight. I should be free by then."

Louise knew from working for The Trust for twenty-five years, the last ten as Jackie's personal secretary, her presence was no longer needed. She returned to her desk to track down members of Jackie's inner circle: Ian Farkwark, The Trust's in-house attorney and a leading litigator, Rupert Jameson Director of Information Systems, Otto Finkster head of Investments, Leslie Langford Director of Human Resources, and Phillip Burpley who handled the Currency Exchange division.

As soon as Louise left Jackie wheeled his chair from behind the desk and started circling the floor, a habit he always did when contemplating highly serious matters. He looked down at the papers in his lap, then up to the ceiling as if looking for divine intervention. No intervention was forthcoming.

TWENTY MINUTES LATER Jackie wheeled into the conference room and moved to the head of the conference table. He was early, on purpose. He wanted to scrutinize each person as they entered the room. What did their faces reveal? *Confusion? Comprehension? Guilt? Innocence?* He would know. That was his expertise – reading people.

Ian was first to arrive. His fifty-four-inch girth mounted on a five foot, six inch frame waddled through the door. What he lacked in physical fitness he made up for with his incisive legal mind. There was none better.

"What's up that you had to pull me away from my morning scone and coffee?" Jackie just held up his right arm. Ian understood the signal: *Wait and all will soon be clear.* Ian crossed the room and plopped down into the one oversized armchair that was specifically his domain. It squeaked in protest.

Rupert came next, followed by Otto and Phillip. They received the same raised arm treatment. The room was silent. Then Leslie came in. He was always the last one, in his awkward, hesitant stumbling gait, typically carrying a disarrayed assembly of papers.

No sooner had he sat down than Jackie said, "Leslie, please close the door."

With everyone seated, Jackie balled up both hands, planted his knuckles on the conference table and rocked up to a standing position. His upper body strength was near Herculean. Two clicks announced the braces on either leg had snapped into position.

"Good morning gentlemen." All nodded their replies. Jackie intentionally paused to study each face. "At about forty-five minutes ago, I received a communication from the Exchequer stating that the Trust is being charged with a wide assortment of violations, including but not limited to insider trading, currency manipulation, and illegal diversion of funds." Everyone reflected a stunned ignorance.

"Needless to say, I do not believe any of this!" Exclaimed Jackie as he tossed the papers into the air. He waited for the last sheet of paper to land. "However, what I think, or anyone of you might think, the implication of guilt can be devastating to us individually and to The Trust.

"I have to respond within the next seventy-two hours. So, gentlemen, you have a lot to do in that short period of time.

We need to scrutinize each-and-every division to be sure we have not done anything wrong. We have excellent people working for us, but that doesn't mean that ambition may have turned one's head and allegiance against The Trust."

He turned to Ian. "Develop a plan that keeps this out of the tabloids and the general press. It's the kind of story they'd eat up…not to mention its negative."

He did not wait for Ian's response; he addressed each department head in turn.

"Otto, review our latest sales and acquisitions to be sure we dotted the "I's" and crossed the "T's".

"Rupert, check the formulations we're using…especially the newest ones for any "bugs" that were missed during Beta One.

"Phil, review the buys…and the sales. Scrutinize your people to be sure they're staying within guidelines.

"Leslie, go over the new hires for the last six months. Check and recheck their backgrounds. We need to make sure we are squeaky clean.

"Alright gentlemen, it's nearly quarter until ten. We will reconvene at four to see where we are…or are not. Come back with answers. That's it. Go."

The group rose in unison and headed to the doors. As the doors closed behind the last one, two clicks followed by a thud punctuated the atmosphere as Jackie released his braces and fell back into the wheelchair. All that he, and his family, had built was in danger of destruction. Only cold hard indisputable facts could extinguish the flash fire that these false accusations would ignite if the news reached the street.

AS JACKIE WHEELED BACK into his office, he swung his left arm in a circular motion, ending up pointing to the inner sanctum of his office. Louise knew the motion and its intent. She stopped what she was doing and followed him into his office.

"I need to talk to my dad and granddad… ASAP. Dad should be at the compound by now and granddad and Jane are…well you know where. You have their schedule. Put calls into both and interrupt me, regardless of what I'm doing, when you have one or the other on the line."

Normally Louise would head back to her desk to complete the given orders. Instead, she remained stationary in front of Jackie's desk, holding a newspaper.

Jackie looked up perplexed. "What? What is it?"

"You need to read this," extending the newspaper across the desk for Jackie to take.

It was a copy of the London Daily News with the headline:

DIAN FOSSEY KILLED BY UNKNOWN ASSAILANT

Kilgali, Rwanda (GPI) Dian Fossey, an American Primatologist who dedicated her life to the preservation of various species of African primates and their environment was found dead in her cabin at her campsite in Rwanda. Death was attributed to a severe blow to the head. A large, blood covered, machete was found close to the body.

The interior of the cabin had been ransacked as if someone was searching for a specific item. Large sums of money, as well as Travelers Checks, were left untouched.

Fossey was noted for her outspokenness and her on-going battles with the Rwandan Bureau of Tourism. Her attacks on the Bureau became more vociferous after poachers killed Digit, her most beloved gorilla. Fossey is believed to have on occasion tortured captured poachers and to have kidnapped children of suspected poachers.

She had formerly accused the Bureau of getting kickbacks from the poachers, in return for allowing them to roam free in protected areas.

Last month Fossey received a two-year visa. Prior to then she had been issued only two-month visas. Some sources

have speculated that the granting of the two-year visa
prompted people who opposed Fossey's work to take drastic
actions against her.

Jackie looked up at Louise, and shrugged his shoulders as if
to say, why is this important? Louise said, "Keep reading."

Initial Suspects Placed Under Arrest
Ruhengeri. Provincial Governor Protais Zigiranyr-
aro (Monsieur Zid) ordered the Karisoke Research Center
sealed and all of Fossey's staff placed under arrest. Key
suspects are Wayne McGuire, an American student at the
center, and Emmanuel Rwelekona, a former tracker who
Fossey had recently dismissed.

Son of Lord Greystoke Missing
Authorities are also looking for Jack Clayton as he was
known to be the last person to see Fossey alive. Clayton had
been visiting Fossey for the past two weeks, discussing
varying ways to save dwindling populations of African
apes, gorillas, and other primates. To that end, Clayton had
brought with him three West African Lowland Gorillas to
see whether the subspecies would mix with Fossey's Moun-
tain Gorillas.

A search of the camp's premises discovered the absence
of not only Clayton but also of the three apes that had ac-
companied him to Fossey's camp. Speculation was that he
had fled in the middle of the night, sometime after Fossey
was killed.

Campsite locals said Fossey had dinner with Clayton
and a representative of the Soviet Union's Foreign Eco-
nomic Relations Committee, one Vladimir Chertok. No
one knew the reason for the impromptu visit of the Russian

*diplomat, but there was strong speculation that it involved
the exploration for minerals on the grounds of the preserve;
something that Fossey had long fought against, but which
Monsieur Zid was strongly in favor. Staff members said
they saw lights on in Fossey's cabin after Chertok had left
the Center. Monsieur Chertok could not be reached
for comment.*

*Anyone knowing the whereabouts of Clayton should
contact the Rwandan authorities immediately.*

*Dian Fossey was 53. She was born January 16, 1932,
in San Francisco, California. She spent 18 years working
with and among the mountain gorillas. She will be buried
in the same cemetery that contains the remains of Digit
and other gorillas that have died at the hands of poachers.*

Jackie laid the paper down, and without raising his
head, said in a voice too calm for the situation "Call the compound. Get Meriem on the line. Then get Hugh Noiseworthy
at Whitehall."

FIVE, TEN, THEN fifteen minutes passed without any
feedback from Louise. Jackie grew impatient. *Where was everyone?* He punched the intercom button to Louise's desk. "What's
taking so long on those calls?"

"I'm not getting any response from the compound.
Only busy signals, as if there's trouble on the lines."

"Keep trying. What about granddad?"

"I've been working on getting through to the compound.
I'll call there now."

Three minutes later Jackie's intercom buzzed. He picked
up the receiver to hear Louise say, "I checked their flight, but
they never boarded, or checked in. So, I called The Grand

Ganges to see if they had extended their stay. I just got off the line with them. Lord and Lady Greystoke checked out two days ago…as scheduled. The concierge did say that they could be way-laid somewhere along the way because of avalanches in the area that have blocked some roads and rail lines. I asked them to call back if they hear anything as to their whereabouts."

"Keep trying the compound." Jackie slowly lowered the receiver back in place and then placed his head in his hands. *Where are they? Where are they? What else can go wrong?*

Chapter 11: RESCUED

JON RAN BACK DOWN THE ROAD until he thought he was safe. He glanced back, but saw no black columns of ants and those on his legs were well dug into his skin. Neither brushing nor scraping dislodged them and finally he grabbed each one individually to yank them off. It was a futile effort. The bodies separated easily but the heads and pinchers remained obstinately attached to his skin. He gave it up and took off down the trail. Wherever it led – it was away from the ants.

The branches of a tree on the edge of a small clearing provided sanctuary for another night. He dozed on and off, jarring awake as elephants trumpeted or cats snarled close by. Near dawn, he sank into a deeper sleep broken suddenly by a lion roaring from the base of his tree. It stood on its hind legs pawing at the bark as if to climb up to Jon. He scrambled further up the tree, missed his footing and fell toward the open jaws of the lion. His back hit the soft ground snapping his head onto a root, stunning him. He could not move and awaited the final ripping teeth of the lion. But the lion was gone. *A nightmare,* he thought when he could sit up.

Sleep evaded him after that and when dawn arrived he fell more than climbed out of the tree. His head was sore and his back ached. The insects, though, were in high spirits, but he had no energy to swat them. Damp leaves again provided minimal moisture.

Just keep moving, he thought. His mouth was sand, his tongue thick. Several fruits looked tempting. Soon, he would have to test his luck. He continued on down the trail more plodding than walking, stopping often to lean against anything upright, not caring about inhabitants, knowing distantly he might regret his inattention but his need to lean was stronger.

At nightfall, he had no energy to build a platform and found no clearing with low branches. Instead, he crawled between twisting buttress roots to the innermost spot beside the main trunk. He told himself he would pick a fruit in the morning, if he survived the night.

Well after dawn he opened his eyes. Four inquisitive parrots perched on the buttress root above him, heads tilted in unison. On another day, he would have marveled at their brilliant green plumage. Today he wondered how parrot would taste raw. He moved slowly both by design and necessity but the movement was too much for the birds. They flew away squawking before he had reached his knees to crawl toward them.

Black spots swam at the edge of his vision. Using the roots for support he dragged his leaden feet away from the tree. Perhaps he had waited too long. Every few steps he had to stop and catch his breath. He eyed the fruits close to him, finally deciding on one that looked similar to an orange. He pulled on it with both hands. Its exterior was thick. *Peel it?* His nails were useless on the tough peel. Finally, one thumb punched through into soft juicy flesh and his fingers scrambled to uncover the rest. Juice dripping down his arms, he raised it to his mouth just as a piercing shout startled him. The fruit dropped from his hands.

He leaned against a tree and looked down the path at a tall, beautiful young native woman dressed in dazzling green and yellow garb. She swung a deadly-looking spear back and forth between the fruit on the ground and his chest, all the while shouting a torrent of words at him like she was correcting a small child. He guessed he had not been wise in his choice of fruits.

He collapsed against the tree, legs stretched out in front of him, head hanging on his chest. He could never remember, later, exactly how she had convinced him to rise or to walk or for how long. He had memories of tugs and shoves, of her face in his face and soft coaxing words, followed by angry loud words. He just wanted to sleep.

JON BECAME AWARE OF THE BUZZING of incessant insects…and then unfamiliar words. He opened his eyes to razor sharp teeth honed to points, much like spear tips, inches from his face. He jerked away. The mouth smiled and moved back.

Jon tried to sit up, but a wave of dizziness and nausea washed over him and he gave it up. If these were cannibals he would not be putting up much of a fight. The girl with the teeth handed him a bowl of liquid that smelled like blackberries. He rose to one elbow long enough to drink it and then collapsed back to the mat, falling almost instantly asleep.

He next awoke to sounds of music and singing. It was dark but he could see firelight from the open doorway to his hut. He recalled the teeth and thought perhaps the festivities for him as the feast was commencing. But he wasn't tied up. Perhaps they thought him too weak to escape. He took his time sitting up this time. Damp leaves fell from him when he did. It occurred to him that he was no longer itching. The pain was also gone.

It took longer to reach a standing position and he was not going to win any races. He kept a hand on the low thatch roof and moved slowly to the doorway.

From the opening, he could see a large fire burning in the middle of a ring of huts similar to the one he was in. Tall black men clad only in hip wraps of feathers reaching to their knees, danced around the fire to a haunting rhythmic beat boomed out by tall kettle drums. Men, women and children surrounded the dancers, stomping their feet and chanting. They were clothed brightly like the girl in the jungle.

Jon debated. He could sneak away into the jungle but it was night, he was weak and could not climb. He would probably be dinner for something. On the other hand, if he stayed here he might be dinner for this village. He decided he preferred to die by man than animal. If he resisted maybe they would kill him fast. Slow roasting was no more appealing than snakes, big cats, or ants.

He stepped out of the hut.

Chapter 12: CURSED

THE VILLAGE HAD STOOD in this place in the jungle for a thousand years, unlike the others that had sprouted then disappeared, crushed by tribal wars or encroaching civilization. This village persevered, holding the jungle at bay. Its men hunted deer, boar, leopard, and man. Its women harvested fruits and cut back the ever-encroaching vegetation. This village was the last remnant of an empire its people had created and ruled.

The village warriors had always been superb practitioners of pain, masters at enhancing the path to death. Enemies turned their weapons on their families and then themselves to avoid capture and the horrors that would follow. The village warriors had never been defeated and the villagers took great pride in that to this day.

At the height of its power, the village's warriors vied among themselves to kill the enemy and then consume the kill. They believed that they absorbed the spirits of the defeated in this way. Within each warrior, the captured spirits fought among themselves enhancing the warrior, providing him with energy and adding to his prowess. When the warrior died, the spirits returned to the gods. If the gods were pleased, they would reward the warrior, perhaps with another life. So the villagers believed.

But this was legend and happened long ago. In the modern era, the once feared village tamed its appetites, or so it appeared. Its warriors no longer battled neighboring tribes. Its people farmed now and hunted less, trading produce for meat

68

with the pygmies who were now the masters of the deep forest. But the old ways were not forgotten. On certain nights at certain times of the year, the old tales were still told, the old rites still performed.

JON STEPPED into a darkness pierced with the fires from a hundred torches. No one noticed him or if they did, paid him any attention. He was still weak and leaned against the side of the hut, then sank down to the ground and leaned his back against it. The drums beat a hypnotic rhythm and the bare skin of the dancers glistened in the firelight. Others clapped and swayed to the beat. He was captivated and kept time drumming his fingers on his legs.

The smell of cooking meat and spices filled his mouth with saliva. The girl with the teeth materialized beside him holding rolled leaves wrapped around something that smelled like sweet potatoes and bananas. The Waziri made this or something like it at the compound. He took it from her and ate with enthusiasm. She smiled and her fang-like teeth reminded him he was probably in the hands of cannibals. Perhaps this was internal marinade? When she walked away he noticed she was shorter than the dancers. *A Pygmy?*

He awoke the next morning not remembering how he had moved back to the pallet in the hut. A bowl of liquid and another leaf roll lay next to him. He consumed both then fell back asleep. He slept for most of the next two days, waking periodically for food and drink.

Finally, on the third day he felt more like himself. He walked out of the hut into bright sunshine and the smells of cooking spices. Children ran and played between the huts, shouting and yelling at each other, chasing a ragged ball. Brightly clothed women tended fires. Several ground a type of grain in shallow containers. Others flattened dough on the sides of rocks lining a fire.

He saw only children, women and old men. All ignored him. He thought about approaching one of them but could not think how to communicate. *And what would I say? Take me to your leader?* He laughed inwardly and watched for a few minutes, then decided to wander. Maybe someone would communicate with him.

The village occupied a clearing in the jungle, an area carved out of vines and tree trunks. Twenty or so small thatched-roof mud huts arranged in concentric lazy ovals surrounded two stone-lined pits, each big enough to fit a small elephant. Several of the huts had stone bases and each had its own small stone-lined cooking fire in front tended by one or more women. One large open rectangular building across the oval from him rested on an ancient stone foundation.

No one spoke to him or seemed to notice he was there. He tried to catch an eye here or there, but they all refused to look at him, except the pygmies. They would catch his eye but then look away. Beside one of the larger huts he saw two large copper pots big enough to fit several men. They appeared well used.

One hut was peppered with skulls and skins. He recognized crocodile and leopard skulls among numerous smaller animals unfamiliar to him. Leopard, deer and boar pelts hung between the skulls. Large animal bones dangled over the door. His stomach turned over. They were rib bones and surprisingly human.

He moved in for a better look when suddenly a tall well-muscled man, pelts dangling from his waist and bones draped across his chest, burst through the door, shouting and wielding a spear. Frizzled black hair dusted in white powder stood out in all directions. Intricate designs of raised whorls and scrolls scarred every inch of his cheeks. He stopped abruptly, planted his feet on either side of Jon's and thrust his face within inches of Jon's nose. Startled, Jon stepped back. The man followed, pounding his spear on the ground and shouting louder, spittle flying into Jon's face. Jon flinched, wiped it away and stepped back again, this time several steps. The man jumped after him, landing almost on Jon's feet, screaming now, his face contorted and his eyes bulging as if they would pop. Jon held up his hands to apologize for whatever trespass he had committed. The man facing him did not budge.

Jon fell back again and the wild man followed smashing his toes into Jon's and leaning forward, forcing Jon to lean or move back faster. The wild man heightened his tirade, eyes bulging and scars rising as if they too wished to enhance the harangue.

From somewhere behind him, Jon heard a shout and the wild man suddenly stopped, peering at the newcomer with disgust. Jon backed away. The newcomer approached the wild man and the two began to argue. The spear became an object of punctuation, pounding on the ground or thrusting into the face of the newcomer. Finally, they both stopped and stared at each other. Then the wild man leaned in and hissed five distinct words, pausing between each one. Then he pounded his spear, spun around, and disappeared into his hut.

The remaining African turned and looked at Jon, scanning him from head to toe. He broke the silence and said "Come wi' me", in a perfect Scots brogue.

Jon's eyes widened.

"No expectin' that now were ye," the man smiled. "Come. I am chief here. We will talk. And eat."

The chief led him to the open pavilion, passing numerous protruding stones, some of which surrounded rectangular patches of barren ground that gave the hint of an archaeological site.

"This was once the residence of the king who ruled over many villages of our tribe. Only one village remains now and there is no king…just a chief." He swung his arms wide to include the whole village.

Jon was relieved. Here was someone who spoke English and had knowledge of the West. His fears of cannibalism seemed childish.

"Who was that man?"

"He is our shaman, healer, spiritual leader. You in the West call him witch doctor. He does not like white men."

They sat on woven mats at one end of the pavilion. Three women served them and withdrew to sit at the far end.

The chief talked throughout the meal, giving him a short history of the tribe and explaining his Scot's brogue. Two branches of the chief's family broke out of the village several generations ago. They moved to the city and established themselves in business. Some sold goods to local miners. Some opened restaurants. Over the years they became successful, expanding into other businesses.

They often took in and supported male members of other branches, sending many overseas to acquire western educations. These individuals were expected to return and further the family holdings. The chief had been one such lucky young man. He had been sent to Edinburgh to study business.

Disaster struck in his third year. Guerrillas destroyed the small African town, killing most of his family and wiping out the fortune that supported him. He had been forced to return to Africa to his home village. His father had died at the hands of guerrillas several years ago and he had been chosen to replace him.

"And that is my story. Now tell me why you are wandering around lost in my jungle."

Jon hesitated. He did not know where he was or who was responsible for the destruction of the compound. He had no idea who he could trust. Perhaps this chief had links to those from whom Jon was running. On the other hand, he and his village had saved Jon's life and the chief seemed to have no cause to support the guerrillas. Jon told his story.

"I know of the Claytons," the chief said when Jon had finished. He did not expound. "Their compound is a few days from here."

"Where exactly?" Jon asked.

The chief picked up a stick and drew a map in the dirt, showing him the river, the compound and the village. "It is not to scale of course. You are very far north." Anticipating the next question the chief continued. "I do not know who is behind the attack. There are many guerilla groups protesting this or that. They attack sometimes for no reason. Some just like killing, I think."

"How long would it take to reach the compound from here?"

"Two days if you travel fast," he said, "and if you know where you are going."

"Ah. That's the problem."

"Are you certain you want to go back? Perhaps it would be easier to travel down river to a city where you could contact the authorities, and your family."

Jon considered that. He was unsettled in his mind as to what he should do. Going back with no weapons or resources seemed foolish, but he desperately wanted to know if there were survivors. Did his grandparents still live? Did they need help? Going on to contact the authorities and his Dad was tempting, though, and seemed the most logical course. His father might not yet know. Jon had no way of knowing if the attack had been reported anywhere. The chief didn't know.

"Can you spare a boat?" He asked the chief.

"I think we can spare a canoe. If you leave at first light tomorrow, you should be in Kompese by night. The authorities there might or might not be able to help you."

Jon asked about the girl who had saved him.

"Ashanti," the chief sighed and motioned to the end of the pavilion. "She is the one in green." He motioned to her and she walked toward them. "She has a mind of her own. This is not a trait admirable in an African woman."

"Really?"

"African women are expected to be docile and obey their husbands, unlike your women in the West. She was sent to us by her father, a cousin in the city who was unable to tame her wild ways. My father thought his warriors could tame her, so he offered to take her and marry her off. But none of the warriors wanted her except Tendaji. The others did not want to exert the effort it would take to beat her into submission. I told my father it was a mistake because Tendaji would botch it and he should send her back. He refused. To do that, he would have had to admit defeat at the hands of a woman. He gave her to Tendaji and told him to act like a man. Then my father died and left the problem to me."

The slender girl glided across the pavilion and stopped before the chief. She was almost as tall as Jon. At the chief's hand motion, she melted into the space between them. Jon was mesmerized, entranced by the intricate whorls and curves tattooed into her face.

"Tendaji means 'makes things happen' in Swahili. The ancestors joked with his parents, I think. He more often 'let things happen,' especially with Ashanti, and it is creating problems with his other wives and the women of the village. They are jealous of her. He favors her and lets her do as she wishes, such as hunting, like the men. No other woman is permitted to hunt or wants to hunt, I think. If he beat her the other wives would at least see that she is like them. But he refuses to beat her. Tendaji is an idiot. He is besotted with her and does not see the danger."

"Danger in hunting?"

"No. Not in hunting. You will see later. But for now, it is good for you that she hunts, eh?" The chief slapped him on the knee. "I will introduce you."

"Tell her I am grateful to her for saving my life."

The chief translated. She answered in the same language.

"She says she would do the same for any child."

"Child?" Jon looked sharply at her.

"As I said, she speaks her mind. But she is correct. Any child in the village would have done better in the jungle than you did."

Jon sighed. Ashanti spoke again.

"She asks if all white men are as ignorant."

Jon raised his eyebrows. "Give my condolences to Tendaji."

The chief laughed and slapped his knee again. He sent Ashanti away.

"Come. Let me show you my village."

Jon was happy to go. He had a plan now. He would leave in the morning and canoe to Kompese where he could contact his father. He had time to kill and was intrigued by the chief and his villagers.

"You are lucky. Had any of the men found you they might have killed you on sight. The country is in a state of political unrest. It is a free-for-all, like the American Wild West. There are so many groups fighting and killing for this or that. Some fight to change the government. Others want a religious state. Foreigners search for diamonds or minerals and are willing to kill for them; poachers look for any animal part they can sell and kill any who oppose them; militant groups with no stated purpose just seem to like shooting people. The military is no match, and is probably infiltrated by those groups. It is impotent. Too many uninvolved bystanders are killed, including members of this tribe. The warriors are suspicious of any and all outsiders. Strangers are not welcome of any skin tone."

Jon was surprised. He had not kept up with the events in Africa. His father had talked about some of these issues but Jon rarely internalized any of it. He never loved this part of the world. He had not intended to become involved in compound activities or widely in any of this country's affairs. His father and grandparents had such matters well in hand.

"I think I may have met some of those military types myself."

The chief smiled. "So, tell me. Are you CIA?"

"Central Intelligence Agency? Are you serious?"

"I am. They are everywhere in Africa, as is the Russian KGB. Not a few Cubans as well. How do I know you aren't CIA?"

"I don't know. What makes you think I am?"

"CIA travel alone or in small groups. Easy to get separated. Get lost. We don't see too many tourists in this area. Any white man is suspicious."

"I'm not. Wouldn't the CIA train their operatives in jungle survival?"

"You would be surprised."

As they passed the big pots he had seen, Jon asked about them. The chief waved a hand. They were nothing, just pots to boil the big animals such as leopard and deer, and the occasional elephant.

They stopped at every hut, it seemed to Jon. The chief would speak and Jon would nod and say "Hello" in English. Now, the women looked him up and down. Several approached him and wanted to squeeze this or that part of him. One woman came from behind and pinched his butt. He jerked away and stared at her. The chief rattled off something in Swahili and quickly moved them on. He dismissed their actions to Jon. They were not used to seeing white men and wanted to feel the flesh and bone to assure themselves he was not a spirit.

At the next hut, several of the smaller women conversed with two village women. Jon asked if they were pygmies.

"Yes. Part of our pygmy tribe."

"Your tribe?"

"Yes. They live in the forest but come to us when we need them."

"When you need them?" Jon had heard his father speak of pygmies used as slaves.

The chief paused and looked away, then, "They are more proficient in hunting the forest than we are. They hunt for us and trade for food from our fields."

They had reached Jon's hut and the chief left him in front.

"I would not venture into the jungle, but feel free to wander the village. Our shaman is conducting a special ceremony at dusk, and then tonight is a feast to celebrate one of our ancestors. You are welcome to join us."

Jon settled cross-legged on the ground outside his hut to watch the villagers about their daily activities. He felt some measure of calm for the first time since the crash. Tomorrow he hoped to begin to find answers about the fate of his family. For today, his life was no longer in immediate danger and he could do nothing else. He allowed his mind to absorb and appreciate the energy of the village.

Several women struggled to move a big copper pot next to a central fire pit. Others stacked wood beside it. He wondered what big animal the pygmies had brought for the feast.

SHORTLY BEFORE DARK villagers set the big copper pot on the embers of the central fire and added wood to build it up. People began to gather. Two pygmies came from the forest dangling a large boar from two poles they carried on their shoulders.

Jon recognized Ashanti. She held a scrawny chicken and approached a man Jon assumed was Tendaji. They conversed briefly. Ashanti kept her head down and Tendaji leaned towards her and said something to her. She flinched, then moved slowly to stand behind him. Another woman, also holding a chicken, glared at her and moved away.

The witch doctor emerged from his hut clad in a loin-cloth with a leopard pelt draped over his shoulders and the leopard's head snarling silently from atop his head. His face and body were streaked with white paint and he carried a six-foot staff carved with grotesque human faces contorted in expressions of anguish, terror, and despair. A human skull grinned from the top.

The witch doctor strode briskly to the center of the assembled villagers, causing several to scamper out of his way. He pounded his staff on the ground and scanned the gathering. The entire village was now in attendance. Jon rose but stayed where he was leaning against the hut.

He could understand little of what was going on. The witch doctor harangued the crowd, frequently pounding his staff or raising it to the heavens. The spellbound villagers stared in rapt attention. Jon thought the witch doctor the equal of any fire and brimstone speaker in the West.

"He is denouncing witchcraft. He says it is evil and must be stomped out," the chief said coming to stand beside Jon.

"Witchcraft?" Jon asked.

The witch doctor lowered his arms then and Ashanti approached him, looking only at the ground and holding tightly to her chicken. She knelt beside him facing towards the crowd but never raising her head.

"What is she doing?" The chief did not answer. One woman after another approached the witch doctor and spoke. Most were angry and pointed repeatedly at Ashanti. Jon turned to look at the chief, raising his eyebrows. Finally, the chief spoke.

"The women speaking are accusing Ashanti of witch-craft. The one who just spoke said Ashanti has come to her in dreams saying her sons will never grow to adulthood, that Ashanti will see to it they meet a bad end."

"Are you serious?"

The chief shrugged. "It is a common enough complaint. This one speaking now says Ashanti used witchcraft to give her son the illness that killed him last month. It was probably malaria but none will believe that."

Jon stared at him.

"You are not in England white man."

"This is not 1400."

The chief shrugged. "It is Africa."

"You are the chief, are you not? "

The chief laughed. "You betray your ignorance, white man. The woman moving to speak now is a co-wife. Last week, her son and another child were killed by crocodiles in the river. She claims Ashanti bewitched them and sent them into the river as all children of the village know to avoid the river. And it will go on. Three or four more I think."

Jon could not believe it. Who still believed in witches? "And then, what? Will you burn her at the stake?"

The chief laughed again. "Not exactly. After all who wish to speak are done, the shaman will ask the ancestors if she is guilty or innocent. This one speaking now is interesting. She says Ashanti must be a powerful witch and we would do well to be rid of her."

Jon watched as the woman pointed at Ashanti and then spat at her. Then she turned toward Jon and the chief. She extended her arm and finger toward Jon and spoke angrily, then spat in his direction.

The chief chuckled. "She doesn't like you."

"What did she say?"

"She claims you are an evil white man and Ashanti, who obviously summoned you here, must be very powerful to summon someone from another race. She wants Ashanti to die."

"Oh, come on. This is ridiculous. You aren't going to let this happen, are you?"

"It's not up to me. It's up to the shaman now. And the chicken."

"Chicken?"

"Watch."

The witch doctor took Ashanti's chicken. Tendaji approached him and said something.

"What is he saying? Is he defending her?"

"No. He is telling the shaman which way the chicken will fall to say if she is guilty or innocent. He said, 'beak in the dirt'."

Jon stared at him, open mouthed.

The chief sighed and said "He's calling heads or tails. If the chicken dies on its front, she is innocent. If it dies on its back, she is guilty."

"I don't believe this."

"Believe it, white man. Tendaji cannot defend her. If he does, they will all think she has bewitched him. Then he will be on trial. Tendaji is an idiot. He brought this on himself. She is his youngest wife. And he favored her. The co-wives are jealous and are seeing to it that she is removed."

"So, they will have her killed because he likes her better?"

"No. They will have her killed because she is a witch. They believe this, heart and soul. Unless the chicken dies on its beak. Then she will be free."

"I don't understand."

"Bad things happen. There must be a cause. Sometimes it is difficult to accept what is. Witchcraft supplies reason and eases pain." He tapped his head. "Pain here."

The witch doctor had cut the chicken's throat and was chanting over it as it bled out, twitching in his hand. Finally, he threw it. The chicken landed on its back, twitched a few times but stayed on its back.

"Why a chicken?"

"It is a way for the ancestors to speak through the shaman to the people. To make their wishes known, to answer questions. The shaman asks if Ashanti is a witch. The ancestors answer by causing the chicken to die on the side that is appropriate."

Jon shook his head in disbelief. "That isn't what it looked like to me. He threw the chicken after it was mostly dead. The shaman decided which way it went."

The chief shrugged again. "He is responding to the ancestors. And the people."

"The people?"

The chief did not respond. Another woman approached the witch doctor with a chicken. It was the woman Jon had seen earlier with Tendaji.

"Is she accused also?"

"No. She is the first accuser. The shaman will ask the ancestors if she was truthful."

The witch doctor waited for Tendaji to call the side, then performed his chant. He slit the throat of the chicken and threw it immediately. The chicken struggled in the dirt, flopping on its beak, then its back, writhing out its final agony.

Jon looked at the chief. "He didn't control this one."

"The outcome is irrelevant."

The chicken finally died on its back.

"She lied," the chief said. "But it doesn't matter. The ancestors condemned the witch."

"Don't you mean the witch doctor condemned her?"

The chief shrugged and pointed back to the witch doctor who was pounding his staff on the ground. He raised his free hand to point at Jon and spoke in a loud and commanding voice. Jon turned to the chief for translation, but the chief was gone.

Suddenly hands grabbed him, picked him up and carried him toward the witch doctor. He kicked out with his feet and arms but could not break free. In seconds it seemed, he was in the center of a circle of warriors with spears and elongated shields that towered above their heads. Villagers crowded behind the warriors. Some held children on their shoulders for a better view of the spectacle to come.

Opposite Jon was the witch doctor, now devoid of leopard skin and staff. He held a machete in his raised right hand and pointed directly at Jon.

Chapter 13: CAPTURED BY GUERILLAS

MERIEM SPENT THE FIRST DAY OF HER escape preparing for her trek across the rain forest to get help. Her size belied the strength and agility that her body possessed. She always loved being in the jungle because that was where she had met Korak. And even after they were married, they would go back into the jungle for two, three or more days at a time. Those were some of the happiest days of their lives.

This time it was different. She was on her own. At least she knew that Korak was safe at Dian Fossey's camp. He would hear the news soon enough and return immediately, and upon finding her gone he would set out in search of her. To aide his efforts she used the knife to mark trees along the way with three radiating lines, giving the appearance of a star burst. Korak would know it was her mark and not just a random slash on a tree's trunk.

Meriem, having earlier thrown away the rifle as it was too heavy and too difficult to carry, needed a better weapon for protection. She needed a spear that she could carry across her back and use to kill small animals for food, and drive off any larger animals that might cross her path.

Her first thought for the spear was to find a straight branch and attach the knife to one end. Contemplating that she might need the knife for other purposes, so she set out in search of an appropriate rock. She circled the area at the mid-terrace level until she saw a small outcropping of rocks. She dropped to the ground and within a few minutes found a suitable elongated stone that would work. She used another stone to sharpen the sides of the first, and to create a notch on either side of the stone so as to hold it better in place on the staff.

Back in the trees she found the perfect branch, strong, straight and of the correct diameter to fit her hand when she grasped it. Using the knife, she cut the branch from the tree then cut a six-inch groove down the center of the branch, inserted the stone into the groove and proceeded to secure it in place with shoe laces from the dead soldier.

She felt she also needed a rope of some length for access to the upper terraces where low hanging branches were not available, to possibly snare food, and as an aide in traversing hostile terrain that she might encounter. The most suitable material from which to make the rope was the uniform of the dead soldier. First, she tore the trousers into long strips, then the shirt. She braided two of the cloth strips with lengths of dogbane harvested from a nearby jungle clearing. Intertwined they made a taut, strong rope. When completed she had a rope approaching twenty-five feet in length…long enough to serve her needs, yet light enough to carry without hindering her actions.

When she completed her various chores, it was late, too late to start her journey. Instead she set about trying to find food. She had not eaten all day and hunger was starting to dominate her thoughts.

She knew the best place to find food was near water, and using her heightened sense of smell that she had developed while living in the jungle, headed down a small game trail in the direction of what her nose said was a water source. Within a mile of walking she found the source, a small tributary of the Congo River. If she couldn't get meat, she could at least get fish to abate her hunger. The water was clear enough to almost see to the bottom. She took up a kneeling position on the bank with the spear poised, ready to strike the first fish that swam within her range of attack. Within ten minutes she had impaled her supper.

THE NEXT DAY MERIEM set out to find help. She moved through the jungle with a heavy heart. Her son and grandson dead, literally shot out of the sky. As the depth of the loss deepened, so did the resolve grow to vindicate her loss.

As she moved through the jungle she split her time between traveling through the trees and proceeding along the jungle floor. The alternation of travel helped to ease the strain on her muscles. Muscles had to have time to rest and refresh. It had been more than a little while ago that she had last done such sustained strenuous exercise. Thus, while her progress was steady, it was also slower than what she would have liked. She had to move slowly for another reason.

In the early days, she had to be aware of the animals of the jungle, separating them into those she had no problem in avoiding, those she could fight and those that meant food for her body.

It was a different predator that now stalked the jungle that she feared; Guerillas...bands of heavily armed men, women and children who had taken to the jungle to fight against the ruling governments, to replace those governments with equally corrupt governments of their own.

Many of these groups were aided, funded and armed by the Cubans, Chinese, U.S. Intelligence agencies, and the Russians, all vying to gain control of the rich assortment of minerals that lay hidden below the jungle floor. The same countries funding the guerillas were at the same time wooing the official governments of the same states. The resulting turmoil served their desire to create an atmosphere of chaos that best suited their manipulation of the local governments for global ambitions.

ON THE THIRD DAY as she was nearing the foothills of a mountain range a loud booming noise came to her ears. She paused momentarily but then proceeded on her chosen path, not wishing to get too close to the source of the boom as it meant humans, and humans, in the midst of the jungle, meant danger.

Five minutes later another boom sounded, then after a short pause, yet another. She could tell from experience that the regularity and strength of the explosions ruled out military ordnance being fired.

Her curiosity got the best of her. She changed her course and headed towards the source of the explosions, first through the mid terrace, and then on the jungle floor as the growth thinned. She cautiously stalked forward for a better look. What she saw was a small clearing, probably made by elephants, in which there were several men. She moved to the edge of the circle of underbrush that outlined the cleared area to get a better view. She waited, and watched. Three of the men were working with an array of what appeared to be scientific equipment. Eight others, armed with AK-47s, formed a perimeter around the three.

As she stooped to watch, the three stepped back twenty feet from their equipment. This action was followed by one of the men pushing a hand-held control that set off a small explosive charge where they had been. The men moved to the equipment and began feverishly writing down data that the dials of the equipment were displaying. Meriem immediately knew what they were doing, taking seismic readings to detect oil and valuable minerals that might be buried under the surface.

She sensed movement behind her. She had been so intent on watching what was going on in the clearing that she had lowered her guard. Before she could even standup, let alone turn around, a hand clamped over her mouth and a knife point dug into her side. A voice whispered in her ear, "Don't move… and don't make a noise. If you do, you die!"

She tried to turn to see who the attacker was, but her action was met with complete resistance. This time the voice hissed in her ear. "I said, 'Don't move.'" She instinctively knew that there was little she could immediately do, so she adhered to her unknown assailant's orders, waiting for a more appropriate time to act.

The men in the clearing began packing up their equipment, their area testing completed. Within five minutes all eleven men moved off into the jungle in a direction that was away from Meriem's position.

Without realizing it, the man who was firmly holding Meriem slightly relaxed his grip on her. It was the opportunity for which she had been waiting. She stomped on the man's foot, lashing her body to the left, digging her left elbow into his rib cage, and biting his hand that was clamped on her mouth…all simultaneously. His grip loosened. She spun back to her right, completely breaking loose.

She started to run. She got seven steps before invisible hands plucked her off her feet. Her legs churned in midair. Then, something slammed into the small of her back, a direct hit to her kidneys. The pain shot through as if she had been electrocuted. As she buckled to her knees a sack was thrown over her head…a rope pulled tight. Everything went black.

A voice said something, but she was in too much pain to comprehend. She was lifted to her feet and pulled forward, her feet churning in the dirt as she struggled to get a footing. The voice sounded again, "Kutembea! Kutembea!" *Walk! Walk!* The language was Swahili, a tongue Meriem knew quite well. But she faked ignorance in hopes that her captors would think she did not understand and therefore would talk more freely among each other as they headed off to an unknown location.

IT WAS NEARLY a two-hour march to her captors' campsite, made more difficult as the hood was never removed. Hands, pushing and shoving, navigated her over the jungle terrain.

Finally, their small group slowed. She could tell that they were coming to a campsite because the quality of the air changed. The refreshing air of the jungle was replaced by the stench of rotting meat on discarded carcasses, the unpleasant odors radiating from clothes that had gone too long between washings, and pungent fumes of human waste. She had to call upon her utmost inner control to keep from gagging.

Meriem was jerked to a halt. The voice that had whispered in her ear, and then shouted at her to "walk," spoke out in Swahili, "Look what I have found. She will be my new woman!"

Another villager spoke up, "Is she so ugly that you have to keep a hood over her head?" Several voices burst out in laughter. In answer to that ridicule, the hood was yanked from Meriem's head. She lowered her head and squinted her eyes because of the sharp contrast between the sunlight and the darkness that her eyes had resided in for two hours. It was not the most appealing pose she could have struck. More laughter.

"Kutosha!" *Enough*! It was a new voice; a stronger more forceful voice than before. "You may have brought this woman here, but I am your leader and I will decide whose woman she will be! Is that understood?"

Meriem looked to see from where the voice came. She saw a tall, muscular built man nearly six feet tall; an African, in his early to mid-thirties. His full head of brown/black hair was cropped short and had tinges of gray interspersed throughout it. He wore camouflage patterned pants and partially laced up combat boots. He was shirtless. It was clear by the way the others responded that he was their leader. His word ruled.

He moved up to her, grabbed her chin and pulled her mouth open. Meriem was so startled that she didn't resist. "Sound teeth." Then he pulled her hair. She screamed but he just said, "Good." He then began slapping her body, testing her firmness: her arms, her buttocks, her thighs. She tried to pull away. She tried to kick back. All he did was laugh and say, "She has spirit."

He then looked at Meriem's initial captor and said, "Thank you. You have brought me a very fine specimen. She will be mine. You can have Myopee, my old one. Take this one to my tent. Bind her arms and her feet. I believe there'll be a little training to be done."

"You have robbed me of my find. That is not fair. She should be...." a monstrous sized fist slammed into the side of his face, sending him literally flying through the air. He landed hard and rolled over three times. He came to a rest next to a make shift lean-to. Miraculously he remained conscious, though a bit groggy.

The leader stepped forth and leaned over the prostate figure on the ground, "Makpek, do we have an understanding?" Makpek shook his head in the affirmative. Then the leader looked around the camp at the rest of its occupants and said, "Does everyone understand?" The chant was united. "Ndiyo! Ndiyo! Ndiyo!" *Yes! Yes! Yes!*

Makpek slowly rose, walked over to Meriem and the two men that were still holding her and said, "You heard Terrik. Take the woman to his tent...and be sure she is bound, hand and foot. Go." Without hesitation, the two men pulled and dragged Meriem to Terrik's tent and an unimaginable fate.

Chapter 14: *NO NEWS IS BAD NEWS*

THE FOUR O'CLOCK MEETING didn't take long. No clues had turned up nor any divergences of behavior from Trust operational procedures. Operational programs clean. New hires clean. Trading practices clean.

The only good news was that Ian had gotten a commitment from Geoffrey Smithers at The Exchecquer to do some political maneuvering to slow down, delay and temporarily impede the investigations from going forward. He would not, or could not, reveal the party or parties that had brought the charges. Such action would only provide a three to five-day window before the charges crawled out of hiding into the public light. On the positive side, it was two or three more days than they had before.

"Obviously, we need to dig deeper. Look at the relationships. Work them. See if you can find out who is making such allegations. If we know who, then we can get to the why and defend ourselves.

"We'll reconvene at eleven tomorrow. Get some results."

The silence announced the end of the meeting. All left, each contemplating what to do next. Each knew they had to come back with results the next day, *but what?*

IT WAS NEARLY 3:00 AM in London, but Jackie was still in his office. His therapy session had been the only interruption. He was conducting his own investigation, investigating his division heads. No one was immune from the search for resolution.

Other than once going to her apartment to change clothes and freshen up, Louise had been a constant figure in the office, responding to whatever Jackie needed. The early editions of *The Financial Times* and *The Guardian* had been delivered to her desk. As she started to get out of her chair to take the papers into Jackie, she gasped at *The Guardian*'s headline. Forgetting formalities, she dashed into Jackie's office, ran up to the desk and just stood there holding the newspaper out to Jackie with absolute terror blaring from her face. Jackie looked up, puzzled by Louise's actions that were so out of character for her.

"What?" he said. She just poked the paper at him. Then he saw what had her so upset.

The lead headline shouted, "**AFRICAN MASSACRE**." The supporting text said several plantations in central Africa had been attacked by guerilla troops, slaughtering anyone in their path. It listed the names of several of the plantations that were destroyed, the Greystoke estate was third on the list.

Jackie just stared at the print, then threw the newspaper down on the desk. "This can't be! There's a mistake! Turn on the TV. Let's see what the BBC is saying."

Within moments a picture came up on the screen, showing an aerial view of billowing clouds of smoke rising up from smoldering, charred rubble below. The voice-over of the reporter provided the latest information.

"The scenes you are seeing are from film shot by a local bush pilot as he was returning to his home. We do not have verification of the validity of the footage, however, the Zairian government has verified that such an attack by rebel guerillas has been made and that the government, until it can ascertain the situation, is not letting anyone into the devastated areas.

"They are concerned that whoever did this might still be in the area. When asked about who specifically could have done this the government spokesman was quick to say, 'In our opinion, we firmly believe that these terrible acts against the people were carried out by the Zairian Freedom Fighters, the rebel group that would replace our current government with their anarchy.'"

The video shifted to show what appeared to be a burnt-out area adjoining the jungle. The broadcaster continued his narrative. "Unconfirmed reports have said that a plane, possibly a Learjet, had been shot down during the attack. We won't know if this is true until we're allowed into the area. This destruction, we are told, is representative of the other plantations in the area that were decimated: total devastation, total destruction of equipment, of buildings and of people. This is Frazser Hamilton reporting for the BBC, now, back to the studio for the local weather report."

Jackie recognized landmarks. *That's the compound! That must have been Jon's plane! Oh, my God, this can't be!*

His head dropped to his chest, his shoulders rolled forward as his hands came to his face. He cried; only momentarily, but he cried. It was the first-time Louise had ever seen him show such emotion. It threw her completely off guard but she quickly regained enough of a degree of composure to ask, "What can I do?"

His voice started as a whisper but slowly rose, speaking to himself, oblivious to Louise's presence. "Too many coincidences...too many things...too close...too lined up. We're at war...but with whom? If they have killed my family I will kill theirs ten times over!"

Then he looked at Louise with a look she had never seen before, one bordering on that of a savage beast cornered, fighting for its life. The Greystoke bloodline had come to the surface! *Let the battle commence!*

"Get me Noiseworthy. By God he can get off his..."

Louise interrupted, "But it is three thirty. He'll be asleep... somewhere." She had to add that because Noiseworthy was notorious for his sleeping around and about. He had made several indiscrete advances towards her, which she had repulsed. She didn't like the man, but he did hold a position of great importance.

"I don't care where he's sleeping…or with whom. Get him. Just get him!"

Chapter 15: VILLAGE GONE MAD

J ON WAS SHOCKED. He had to fight, unarmed, a machete-wielding witch doctor? His heart crashed to his feet.

The last two days came together. His encounter with the witch doctor and the Chief's request that he wait a day and a night for the canoe took on new meaning, as did the invitation to the ceremony and feast. He should have seen it coming. The chief had said as much but Jon was so shocked at the witchcraft accusations against Ashanti that he had not considered the repercussions to himself. Not that he could have done much. He was alone and weaponless, at the mercy of the elements and now the witch doctor.

He considered his options. Bound by the circle of warriors, he could not run. Weaponless, he was at a disadvantage against a machete and the warriors in the circle. His opponent was big and strong, and would not go down easily. On the positive side, Jon was quick on his feet and the large circle gave him maneuvering room. He was skilled in the martial arts. That and a bit of strategy gave him a chance, small though it was. He thanked his father silently for signing him up at that first dojo, years ago.

He shook his arms to loosen up. Strength returned to his muscles. He would not freeze and, if he lost, he would not be an easy kill. He had trained for this.

Torchlight glinted off the steel of the machete the witch doctor pointed at Jon. Once the most celebrated warrior in the tribe, he had chosen to fight the white man. The chief had

95

advised him otherwise, suggesting the witch doctor had not fought seriously for years, implying he was too old.   One of the villages' young elite warriors would gladly dispatch Jon for him. But the witch doctor was a proud and arrogant man. He missed the accolades accorded him as the tribe's most accomplished warrior. This victim was young and weak. He had been saved from the jungle by a woman. He would be an easy kill.

Jon began to move around the circle away from his opponent, preparing his mind for battle. Through years of martial arts training he had achieved *zanshin*, a state of heightened awareness and focus that few ever achieved. It had become his normal state of mind, until he entered the jungle. The trauma of re-living his childhood failure with the lion had blocked it. When he needed it most, it was gone.

He calmed himself inwardly, releasing his thoughts and emotions to flow away like a slow-moving river. He thought and focused only on the void. This was *mushin*, the state of mind-no mind, a mind without fear, anger, or anxiety; a completely reactive mind. And a mind ready for battle.

Ashanti, crouching between two warriors, watched the fear and tension leave his body like ice melting under a blazing sun, returning to its natural state.   To the untrained eye Jon appeared lax, uncaring, defeated. The untrained eye was wrong.

The warriors stood behind their six-foot tall shields. Some pounded the earth with their spears, sending the sound vibrating through bone. Others waved machetes above their heads, slashing at invisible foes. The villagers outside the circle stomped, clapped and sang, swaying in unison, waiting for their shaman to cleanse the village of the evil that had come amongst them.

The shaman swung his machete in slow arcs, his grin widening as he moved around the circle, closing in on Jon. *This puny white man is no match.* He tossed the machete from hand to hand. Perhaps he could remove the head in one swing. He laughed out loud.

The witch doctor advanced, swinging the machete in front of him, grinning widely. He thrust at Jon, who dodged but not quite quickly enough and the machete ripped a sleeve. The witch doctor thrust again, several times, more rapidly, each time gaining a small tear but missing flesh. Jon dodged and retreated. The witch doctor toyed with him, playing to the crowd who oohed and awed when the machete connected.

Jon was close to the edge of the circle and the warriors. The witch doctor swung again and the blade sliced across Jon's chest leaving a trail of red. The villagers chanted and clapped louder. The spears pounded faster and the machetes swung higher. The end was near.

Jon backed up against the shields, hands raised and cowering, blood oozing from his chest and dripping onto his khaki pants. A smirk twitched the lips of the witch doctor. He stood before what appeared to him to be a cringing and terrified white man. He raised the machete high above his head, arrogantly confident of his imminent victory. As the machete began its downward arc, Jon dove into the dirt to his left and rolled hard back into the surprised warriors, scattering feet and bodies around him. He grabbed the bottom of a spear and jerked it sharply away from its startled owner. The witch doctor recovered from his downward swing and turned to find Jon on his feet, holding a spear. The warriors and villagers gasped into stunned silence.

The witch doctor's lips merged into a hard line. This was a minor setback, a lucky white man, nothing more. He would take his time now. The white man had made him look the fool. For that, he would die a slow and painful death.

The spears resumed their obsessive rhythm. Jon embraced it, heart pulsing to the beat, adrenalin surging through his veins, lifting him up. He no longer needed the plan, no longer needed to convince the shaman that he was weak. The spear changed everything. Jon had mastered the *bo*, or staff, years ago. The spear was a perfect *bo* and it gave him the advantage. He now had a longer reach. He smiled to himself. Bring it on.

He saw no tangible way out. The witch doctor would kill him or he would kill the witch doctor, in which case the warriors would then kill him. Either way he was dead. His only choice was how to meet his death and he resolved to honor his grandfathers. The witch doctor would die first.

Jon glided sideways toward the center of the circle, keeping the spear always pointing at his foe. The witch doctor followed, swinging the machete hypnotically, back and forth, left to right.

The witch doctor shook his head. An accomplished warrior, he recognized the danger of the staff but could not believe this weak white man, who could not survive alone in the jungle, was a match for himself. A solid hit with his blade would split the spear. He smiled. It would just be a more interesting kill.

Jon held the spear with both hands under his left arm like a *bo* or staff and waited. He had the advantage of a longer reach. The shaman circled to Jon's right, away from the spear. Jon followed, the spear-point always aimed at his foe. They began a slow dance, each waiting for an opening.

The witch doctor lost patience first, moving right, then quickly back to his left and lunging towards Jon, expecting an opening and an easy slice to the neck. But Jon had not moved to follow the feint and easily parried, connecting sharply with the wrist holding the machete. The shaman swung his blade in a circle over his head and down to the other side, but Jon snapped the back of his spear as a *bo* up to meet it again striking the wrist of his opponent. There followed a brisk tango of swings and parries with the shaman attempting to strike flesh or split the spear and Jon blocking the wrist, arm or the flat of the blade. Neither man appeared able to penetrate the other's guard.

The shaman showed signs of tiring, his responses a tick slower, imperceptible to most. Jon, trained through years of sparring, perceived the change. He put all his power into the next block, again targeting his opponents' hands. The shaman winced and Jon grabbed the opportunity striking the shaman's knees outside, first one then the other, rotating his spear with lightning speed before his opponent could catch up. The shaman lunged toward Jon's chest. Jon dodged right and struck the side of the witch doctors' head then rotated the back of his spear up under the wrist holding the machete. The shaman almost lost his grip but recovered and stepped back quickly just barely avoiding the upward thrust of the spear towards his groin.

This was not going as planned. He backed away. Jon followed and attacked, charging inside the machete's radius, blocking, parrying and forcing the shaman to the defensive. His opponent moved continually backward until he was up against the shields of his warriors. He was swinging the machete well parrying Jon's strikes but Jon was fast and the shaman was now breathing heavily. And he had nowhere to go except sideways along the shield wall.

Jon followed pressing his advantage whipping his spear in a blaze of speed to the shaman's head, abdomen and knees, ending with the back of his spear thrust hard into the shaman's stomach. The shaman fell sideways into a shield and was pushed upright. The machete rose and Jon moved to parry when his right foot tripped, over what he was never certain: perhaps the foot of a warrior. He would never know. Trip he did however, giving the shaman a minute opening which he took, slicing into the spear that Jon inadvertently raised to counter his fall and regain balance. He backed away, no longer having the advantage of reach, with a piece of spear in each hand. The shaman followed swinging the machete with his left hand.

Jon now returned to his original plan, emanating fear and weakness, hunching his shoulders, averting and widening his eyes, cringing at each strike of the machete, and waiting for his opportunity.

The witch doctor advanced, not smirking now, intent only on finishing the kill. He moved toward Jon, swinging his machete fiercely and with both hands.

Jon parried each attack, taking a few cuts. He had his own opportunities to inflict a few nicks but resisted, staying with the plan.

He moved around the circle, tripping several times then righting himself before the witch doctor could close. With each misstep, a collective gasp arose from the villagers, expecting that now, finally, their shaman would inflict the deathblow.

The circle began to contract. The warriors moved in, reducing Jon's maneuvering room. *Time to end it.* He paused and bent over, hands on knees, breathing hard. The witch doctor moved closer, a smirk returning to his lips. Jon feigned surprise and moved backwards until he felt a shield at his back. Suddenly he was shoved violently forward and stumbled, almost falling at the feet of the witch doctor. He scrambled to his feet, holding up his hands and cringing, still clutching the remains of the spear.

The witch doctor threw his head back and laughed. It was his last. Suddenly, the ball of Jon's foot connected with his chest and knocked him violently backward. He staggered, swirling his arms, hands futilely grasping air for support, struggling to stay upright. Again, Jon kicked him in his chest and then in quick succession, three times more. The witch doctor continued to stumble back unable to regain his footing. Jon gave him no quarter; snapping front, side and roundhouse kicks to his abdomen, chest and face. But the witch doctor refused to fall, and he soon would be up against the circle and could regain his balance against the shields.

Jon needed to end this. He lashed out with a sidekick high on the chest then pivoted and whipped around in a full circle landing a vicious kick to the shaman's head. Bone snapped and the witch doctor went down. The machete bounced in the dust. Jon straddled the body and thrust the spear down into the chest, piercing the heart. The witch doctor's last sight was of Jon grinning above him.

Jon ripped out the spear as the adrenalin surged to a crescendo. He had prevailed. He lived. Exhilaration filled him. He thought he would soon be dead but there was one last rite he would not be denied. He put a foot on the witch doctor's chest, raised his face to the sky and shouted out the victory call of the bull ape to all of the jungle, as Tarzan, his great grandfather had, done before him.

As the call died away, so too did the adrenalin. Jon looked down at the body beneath his foot and was stunned. His arms dropped as he took in the blood pooling at his feet, the surprised look and the glazed eyes of his dead foe. What had he done? This was not a karate match. There would be no mutual bow of respect; this man was dead. Regardless of the man's intentions, Jon had killed, taken a life, an act that could not be undone. His great grandfather would have had no remorse, but Jon had called himself a civilized, enlightened man. Bile rose in his throat and he turned to the side and threw up.

He felt a tug on his arm. Something pressed into his right hand. He grasped it and looked down. Machete. Someone yelled in his ear. He did not understand. *What was she saying?* Ashanti grabbed his arm, tugged harder, and pulled him with her as she ran. He did not resist. As they ran, the sudden silence reverberated through his mind. No birds called. No monkeys chattered and no angry warriors attacked. And then they were in the jungle.

Chapter 16: *FAVORS CALLED IN*

ONE, TWO, THREE AND THEN FOUR DAYS passed without any breakthroughs on any front. The Trust team was still digging to find out the source of the alleged misconduct that could destroy The Trust and the Greystoke family.

At the Exchequer, Smithers was encountering resistance in holding back and diverting the young hawks that were pushing for the prosecution of the charges against The Trust.

Noiseworthy had little more information. He had been running into political roadblocks and inefficiencies in getting any additional information about what had happened at the Greystoke compound. He had never met such resistance. He was frustrated to no end.

No word on Tarzan's and Jane's whereabouts had surfaced. Korak was still among the missing.

Louise knew Jackie had the patience of Job. She had seen it many times during negotiations, but also knew it could only be stretched so far. She was waiting for the moment when the buildup of emotions would become a volcanic eruption. The moment arrived.

"Why the bloody Hell..." his words drifted off into space. "If other people can't get answers, we damn well can. I'm through waiting.

"Louise, call John Barritt at Com-Cor. By God, we hold enough stock in his company to get some action."

"It's eleven-thirty..."

"Yes, but it's just five-thirty in Houston. He should still be there. If he's not, tell them to track him down."

Louise stepped outside Jackie's office to her desk. Four minutes later Jackie's intercom buzzed. "Mr. Barritt is on line three."

"Thanks Louise." He picked up his receiver. "Hello John. How are things?"

"I should be asking you that question Jackie. We've only heard bits and pieces, but what we have heard doesn't sound good. What's happening?"

"That's what I'm trying to figure out. I'm not getting anything out of the politicos here. All hell has broken loose and my visibility is zero…zilch!"

He filled Barritt in on what little he knew. Then, as if to change the subject Jackie asked, "How's that high-mobility imaging system you've been working on? The reason we invested in Com-Cor?"

"We've just started field testing. So far, so good."

"Excellent! I'm going to give it a REAL field trial. I need it in Africa, NOW!"

"But…"

Barritt didn't get to complete his sentence as Jackie dashed on. "No buts, ifs or ands. I need eyes on the ground and THAT system is my best chance. If I weren't confined to this damn wheelchair, I'd already be there. I need boots on the ground! Wheels don't cut it! How soon can you pull your team together?"

"Jackie. It isn't that simple. We'll need to assemble a crew that's willing to go. Schedule the transportation. Get visas. And, what about protection? They'll be going in essence into a war zone. My guys aren't trained soldiers…they're trained electronics guys."

"Don't sweat the small stuff. Just get your end pulled together…the crew and the equipment. That's all. As soon as we hang up I'm calling Red. You know Red; Red Slocum, head of Red Water Securities. He'll pull together a team of a dozen former US Navy SEALs and have them equipped and landed at Hobby within five hours. Have your tech team ready to go. I'll get the visa clearances here...and everything else."

Barritt acquiesced. He knew it was useless to argue with Jackie at this point. He would be making the same outrageous demands if the shoe was on his foot. In addition, he didn't want to take the chance of losing The Greystoke Trust funding. "Okay. They'll be ready. Let me know what else you need."

"That's it. Thanks John. I knew I could count on you." With that he hung up and called Louise to get Red Slocum.

FIFTEEN MINUTES LATER everything was in motion. Jackie had spoken to Red Slocum, providing him with as much detail as he had. In fact, Red had anticipated the call, having known and worked with Jackie for more than twelve years, he had already begun the scramble to get a team in place. He didn't have to worry about a plane; he kept a Boeing 737, fully equipped, ready for just such rush emergencies because in his business he understood that time was of the essence and nearly all clients only called when they were already in trouble. He didn't worry about the expense. He knew that Jackie was always good for it. Unlike so many other clients, The Trust always paid the day it received his invoice.

The fatigue that Jackie had been fending off finally broke through his defenses. It rolled over him like a twenty-four-foot wave. He gave into it, knowing that things were moving. *"The politicos might be mired down in the swamps of bureaucracy, but I don't have to be."* He turned from his desk, wheeled out his office doors to the elevator that would take him to the penthouse for a few hours of recuperation. Rest and clearness of mind are strong allies which can many times mean the difference between success and failure in times of high conflict.

Chapter 17: JOURNEY HOMEWARD

THE TWO FIGURES MOVED ACROSS the open savannah of the great African plains. One walked more on all fours while the other walked upright. This was unfamiliar territory for them. The wide-open spaces containing vistas as far as one could see were frightening. Their home was in the lush green canopy of the jungle where one could only see a few feet, not miles; where one's enemies were always well hidden, not highly visible.

They moved in single file, trading the lead from time to time, as if a cycling team trying to conserve their mutual energies for the undeterminable distance that must be traveled before reaching their sanctuary.

The first day of their journey they made the mistake of traveling during the day. The heat of the sun beat down upon them and they soon realized that they needed to find shelter or suffer the consequences from the sun's burning effects. They determined that going by night would be best. It would be cooler, at least cooler than the heat of the day.

Night travel had its own risks. Numa the lion, Sheeta the leopard, Buto the rhinoceros, and Horta the wild boar were all more active at night. Their fragile safety lay in their acute hearing of potentially hostile advances, and their ferocious shouting when danger did approach; sounds that the would-be assailants had rarely heard.

Finding water turned out to be the greatest challenge. When they did they had to be acutely aware of the presence of Gimla the crocodile. What gave all the appearances of a stagnant floating log could in an instant turn into a death threat from Gimla's tail and its gaping fang-filled mouth. Gimla was always close by…and always dangerous.

Ultimately their safety rested in the fact that while they were strangers in a strange land, they were just as strange to the local inhabitants as those inhabitants were to them.

They eventually set upon a schedule of traveling in the early morning, resting during the heat of the day, then more traveling into the early evening, and finally finding nightly refuge in one of the few trees of the savannah.

On the eighth day, tired, weary and a bit on the dehydrated side they spotted the edge of the jungle. Even in their deteriorated state they found the energies to jump and shout about, very much like a man that had just found a treasure trove of gold, silver, diamonds, emeralds and rubies. It was in this impulsive jubilation that they almost lost their lives.

In their excitement, they had let down their guard. An old lion, dispatched by a younger and stronger lion from the pride that he once ruled, heard their shouts. He did not understand what they meant; only that he had not eaten in several days and that the noise represented an opportunity to feast on fresh meat, a chance to dispatch his gnawing hunger. The old Numa moved through the waist-high brush until he was within ten feet of his intended prey. It was a most strange sight indeed; two creatures, one hairy, the other virtually hairless, shouting and jumping about.

Which one to attack first? Which one would be easiest to catch? Probably the hairless one. These were the thoughts of the old Numa as he drew his hindquarters beneath him for his final leap and charge. Numa brought his concentration to full power and launched himself toward the hairless one.

Even in celebration, the body reacts to the danger. First by raising the hair on the back of one's neck, then by pile driving adrenalin into one's muscles. As the lion was in midair, the travelers turned to face the perceived danger, armed only with a single sturdy branch the hairless one had picked up along the way.

The hairy one sprang to full height, leaped into the direct path of the lion, and began to beat its chest, while baring its ferocious fangs. At the same time, the hairless one charged the on-rushing lion. He ducked under the lion's outstretched paws, grabbed its mane and swung up onto its back. Locking his legs on the inside of the lion's hindquarters he swung the branch over the cat's head slipping it up under the chin. With his position secure, he began pulling back on the branch, cutting off the lion's air supply.

The lion was driven into the ground, then bucked, shook and rolled trying to dislodge the hairless thing from its back. The adversaries rolled over and over on each other, but the grip of the hairless one only drew tighter.

Meanwhile the hairy one watched and waited. The battle paused and that was the moment he needed. He rushed in, grabbed the lion's head in a vise grip of his mighty hands, and using the full force of his body, twisted. A crunching, grinding noise announced the snapping of the lion's neck. The body quivered, then went limp. The lion would roar no more.

Each victor looked at the other. Two mature males ready to charge the other, answering the call of long embedded genes and chromosomes. The fire in their eyes from the rampaging testosterone and adrenaline said it all. Two giants of herculean strength ready to tear the other apart in blood lust, as their ancestors had surely done.

Then, the bond of friendship broke through; dampening the fire of heritage. Muscles relaxed and then a sound seldom heard across the great wide expansive plains of Africa resounded, the victory cry of the great apes, not from one but from both in a terrifying unison.

Chapter 18: ESCAPE TO SAFETY

ASHANTI KEPT JON'S HAND tightly grasped in hers until they were well away from the village. Then she stopped and dropped his hand leaving him adrift in the suffocating darkness. He froze, heeding the rustle and ripping of vegetation that assaulted his ears, hoping Ashanti was the cause of it. He started when she touched him, slipping something around his waist. His hand found hers and he realized she had knotted a thin vine around him. A tug told him she pulled the other end to her own waist. Jon felt like he was two years old though he recognized the wisdom of the tether. Their hands were free and they would not lose each other in the dark. Even so, he was glad his friends and family would not see it.

Ghostly blue-green light startled the blackness of the jungle night. Mushrooms sprawled across the ground or marched seemingly into thin air, stepping up invisible tree trunks. Insects winked in and out. Stunning as it was, the bioluminescence was of no help to them. Jon tripped over roots more than a few times. He noticed with chagrin that Ashanti did not.

He had no sense of time. It could have been hours or minutes when Ashanti stopped. The smothering dark retreated slightly and he raised his eyes to see sky and stars. They were in a clearing. She took Jon's hand and held it against a tree, then against a limb of the tree. He understood. They spent the night in the tree, Ashanti on one limb, Jon on another.

He did not think he would sleep but found himself jerking awake at one sound or another of the jungle. A snake slithering down the tree was his biggest fear. He figured any big cat would have pounced already. Just before dawn, the witch doctor appeared beside him on the limb, shaking his spear and jeering. Suddenly he turned the spear and stabbed Jon in the heart, blood spurting over the witch doctor's laughing face. Jon started, awake in a cold sweat, almost falling out of the tree. He felt his chest. No spear. It had seemed so real. Ashanti was already on the ground. She poked him again with her bow and said something he took to mean "hurry up."

They moved rapidly in the daylight following game trails. Jon expected a spear in his back at any moment and frequently looked behind him until he realized the futility of it in the closeness of the jungle. He would not see them coming.

He wondered where she was taking them. The events in the village swirled in his mind and he kicked himself more than once for trusting the chief so quickly, lulled by the sound of his own native language. He marveled at his defeat of the witch doctor, and at Ashanti's presence of mind at the end. She had been in as much danger as he but had thought to grab her bow and arrows, and then him, while picking up the witch doctor's machete and thrusting it into his hand. Without her, he would surely be dead.

In the early afternoon, she finally stopped, knelt down and rooted among the plants with her knife, then dug out a bulbous root. She placed it on the ground and smashed it with the hilt of her knife. She handed a glob of the paste to Jon and motioned that he should smear it on his skin, as she was doing. Almost immediately, the insects besieging him diminished as did the itching. He looked at her, surprised, and said "Thank you." She nodded and they continued.

They made good speed. Jon refused to think of what could be watching, following, preparing to pounce, bite, or enwrap. He put all his concentration on staying close to Ashanti, trusting she knew what she was doing and where she was going. She was a witch. What could possibly go wrong?

In the late afternoon Ashanti stopped suddenly, making strong shushing gestures as Jon started to speak. She moved them off the trail to crouch down between buttress roots and put her hand over her mouth. They waited. Shortly the sounds of something big, stomping down the trail, reached him. As it got closer he crouched lower and lower attempting to become one with the tree. The sounds receded and Ashanti rose. Jon followed.

They stopped periodically to eat, Ashanti choosing the menu. They ate vegetarian, not taking the time to make a kill. She searched through the vines and lianas as if they were clothes on a rack, finally choosing a liana. She cut it letting the bottom drop away and lifting the top to her mouth. Jon was astounded to see water trickle from the liana into her mouth. She cut another one for Jon and laughed at the face he made from the bitter taste.

A short time later Ashanti stopped suddenly and Jon plowed into her back, knocking her forward. She caught her balance and pointed straight ahead. Jon followed the line of her arm and saw a panther standing a few yards in front of them. *Sheeta*, he thought. It bared its fangs but made no move. Jon stared at its yellow eyes watching them. Its muscular legs could spring in their direction in a heartbeat. Jon felt Ashanti move beside him, slipping her bow off her shoulder. The large cat growled a second time then disappeared into the undergrowth. Jon breathed a sigh of relief. As they passed the spot where the panther disappeared, she pointed and said the word for panther in her language. Jon repeated it and gave her the English word, which she repeated. The rest of the day they exchanged words constantly.

Just before nightfall, Ashanti built a platform of branches covered with a shelter of banana leaves. A few inches off the ground and enclosed, it would protect them from insects and most animals. Inside, as they settled down for the night, she said something he thought was an attempt at English. It sounded like "nif." He tilted his head. She stared at him and repeated the word in Swahili.

"Ah," he said. "Knife. Not nif." He drew out the long 'I' sound which Ashanti was not used to. He repeated the word in Swahili, "*Kisu*". She tilted her head and said it correctly. They laughed and quickly went through the words of the day, adding the parts of the body or most of them, until it got too intimate for Jon and he switched to a charade spinoff, acting out various verbs such as eating, walking, and cutting.

That night the witch doctor appeared again in his dreams. Jon sat in a large pot of boiling blood-red water with half a spear sticking out of his chest. The witch doctor shrieked and screamed in his face while he stirred the pot with his machete. Jon jerked awake with Ashanti's hand on his arm. His clothes were soaked in sweat. She removed her hand and sat cross-legged beside him speaking softly in Swahili. Her voice was mesmerizing and his breathing slowed. They remained side by side until dawn arrived.

Jon attempted to ask Ashanti where they were going. He drew pictures in the dirt of the village, the river, and the Greystoke compound as the chief had shown him. The chief had used the word "*Eneo*". He hoped that was right. She watched him draw in the dirt, then pointed at the compound and down the trail in the direction they had been going. He hoped she understood. There was little he could do about it at this point if she did not. He was not Tarzan and could not find his way alone through the jungle. Yet...

Jon was now less engaged with survival and began to consider his situation and the future. What would he find at the compound? If no one was there, what would he do? Where would he go? He could not return to the village. He would have to find civilization and return to London. And what would he do with Ashanti? What would happen to her, as she could not go back to the village? After a while, he decided he would have to take things one at a time and deal with each event as it occurred.

Still, what if they were all dead: Meriem, Korak, Tarzan, Jane? He regretted the years he had avoided them. He regretted not redeeming himself in their eyes.

In the afternoon of the fourth day, Ashanti suddenly stopped and said, "Quiet. Men come. Hush."

Within seconds, natives emerged from the jungle surrounding them. Some carried spears. Others held machetes or drawn bows and arrows. All had elongated oval shields. Jon recognized them as warriors from the village he and Ashanti had left four days ago. These men had tracked them through the jungle for four days and they did not look happy about it. They stood perhaps five feet apart. Jon did not think they could make a run for it and survive, although he was tempted to try.

The circle began to close, the shields getting closer until the warriors were shoulder to shoulder. The circle was less than fifteen feet in diameter. One of the warriors detached from the circle and approached them. Jon moved instinctively to put Ashanti behind him. She kicked him and let loose a string of Swahili. The native approaching stopped and raised his spear, pointing it straight at Jon's chest.

Jon hoped this was to be single combat again. He could dodge a spear or deflect one from close range. He knew Ashanti was also light on her feet. He took a step towards the warrior who immediately stepped back, out of range of Jon's feet.

Someone laughed.

"Not this time, *mzungu*" Jon recognizing the Swahili for "white man." He could hear the chief but could not find him in the circle.

"You are beaten. Put down your machete," the chief said, adding something in Swahili.

Jon got little of it but he did understand "down." Immediately Ashanti answered with one of the less than polite phrases she had taught him. He looked at her in amazement. Her bow was fully drawn and pointed at the warrior whose spear was pointed at Jon. The archers of the warriors drew theirs, all aiming at Ashanti. *Checkmate.*

The warriors began to chant and the circle slowly closed in. Jon could not see how it was happening as they were already shoulder to shoulder. Then he saw it. Warriors were dropping out, one at a time, and forming a second surrounding circle, allowing the first to shrink.

They didn't have much time. Soon they would be captives and Jon did not relish being boiled alive as Ashanti had described in words and pictures to him on their trek. Jon looked at her. She did not take her eyes off her target, but nodded. She also wanted to end it now, go out fighting.

Jon turned towards the direction of the chief's voice and spotted him. He would rush the circle at the chief's location while Ashanti took out the warrior in the center and probably not many more. He tensed his hand around his machete, prepared to raise it and give one last bull ape call to the jungle of his grandfathers as he charged.

Just at that moment, a machine gun scattered its contents into the canopy above them and shocked the warriors into silence. Black men appeared dressed western style in jeans and t-shirts holding AK-47s pointed at the warriors. The warriors closest to the guns began to melt away to the sides, opening the circle. A machine gun chopped up leaves and dirt at their feet and they stopped.

Jon almost laughed. It was not exactly the frying pan to the fire, since the fire, in this case AK-47s, was a preferable means to die than what was planned for them by the chief. It was too bad though. If he had to die, he really wanted to take the chief with him.

Chapter 19: STEPS RETRACED

JON LOWERED HIS MACHETE. Ashanti lowered her bow and moved closer to Jon.

He didn't see any options. The guns would mow them down before they could run behind a tree or anywhere for that matter, assuming they could get past the warriors.

The chief yelled to someone in the newly arrived group. Jon picked out a few words but most of it was lost on him. Ashanti listened intently, moving her gaze back and forth between them. Guns were pointed and spears were raised. No one was backing down.

Jon spotted the other speaker but he was too far away to see clearly. He assumed they were some of the guerrillas the chief had spoken about and would not be likely to leave anyone alive, although he might get lucky and be held for ransom. Ashanti would not, though. He wondered if these were the guys who had attacked the compound. Those attackers had possessed sophisticated weapons. They had brought down a Learjet. They must have had good connections with someone outside Africa. So...Live or Die. It was a tossup so far. And it seemed to be out of his hands. He did not see any move he could make that would have even a remote chance of survival. So, he waited.

Suddenly Ashanti grabbed his arm and shouted "Down" in his ear as gunfire erupted. They both hit the ground and the warriors scattered. The gunfire stopped abruptly and Jon heard the rustling and smashing of vegetation as the warriors disappeared into the jungle. A voice called loudly from the retreating warriors, "It's not over, white man."

Jon did not respond. He felt Ashanti rising beside him and grabbed her arm to keep her down. She shook him off and rose to her feet. He followed her up, questioning the wisdom of it all the way. She knew more of the guerillas, if they were guerillas, than he did and they had let the warriors escape. He would have to trust her.

Fifteen men who were partially hidden among the ferns, trees and vines, lowered their weapons. One of them yelled and sprinted towards them. Jon raised his machete but Ashanti pushed his arm down. He turned a questioning look toward her. She pointed at the running man and grinned at him. Jon turned back and recognition hit him just as Nubiby's arms enveloped him and squeezed. Relief spread through his body as Nubiby pushed him to arm's length and proclaimed his joy at finding Jon alive to the other Waziri gathering around them.

"We saw you go into the jungle after the plane crash. Where have you been? We thought you were dead or taken hostage. We searched and found your tracks, followed them a little way, then lost them. I was afraid you could not survive in the jungle."

"I thought the same thing. I was lucky. I remembered a few things from the family stories and happily Ashanti found me." He turned to Ashanti.

Nubiby and Ashanti spoke together in Swahili and the group surrounding them soon broke out in laughter. Jon raised his eyes at Nubiby.

"She says you have strong white magic. You killed a witch doctor. Is that true? Did you kill a witch doctor?"

"I got lucky."

"But she says you are as a babe in the forest." Jon grimaced but Nubiby slapped him on the back.

"No matter. You learn fast. Come. Mubuto will be happy to see you."

"What about my grandparents? And the Waziri? Who else survived? Who were those guys?"

"Korak, Tarzan, and Jane were not there. Korak was with Dian Fossey in the west. He is late in returning. Tarzan and Jane were traveling in Burma and Thailand. They also should have arrived by now. Only Meriem was here at the time of the attack. We think she escaped into the jungle and have been searching for her as well."

Jon was relieved. At least they were safe. And his Dad was safe in London. Only Meriem had been in danger.

"And we think your grandmother killed one of them."

"YES!" Jon punched his fist in the air as Nubiby continued.

"She left marks which we followed but they stopped or else we could not find them. In any case, she is still out there somewhere…unless she set out to find Korak. Fifty of the Waziri died. But many escaped and are returning slowly, a few every day. The attackers did not intend to leave survivors. We do not know who they were. Mubuto thinks he knows but he won't say. Perhaps he will tell you. You should return to the compound and talk to him."

"How far is the compound?"

"Half of a day's walk that way," Nubiby pointed in the direction Jon had been going before the village warriors caught up to them. "Several of us will go back with you. The others will continue searching for your grandmother. We have other groups out in different directions. If she is alive we will find her."

"If she were alive, wouldn't she have returned by now? Just to see what happened?"

"Yes, I believe she would. That is why we are searching. We think, if she lives, she is in trouble, either injured or perhaps captured by guerrillas or a tribe such as the one you found. She could live in the jungle alone for years. But she may be sought by many and I do not think she will be as successful against witch doctors as you. You must tell me how you did that. I know of this guy – he was no weakling. That is rare among witch doctors. But this one was once a warrior. A very good warrior. And she says you had no weapon, that you kicked him to death?"

"It was nothing. A few karate kicks connected."

"Ah, karate…I have heard of it. You are no longer the small child afraid of Numa."

Jon grimaced. He did not want to talk about the lion. This was one of the reasons he had avoided the compound for years. They always remembered the lion. The men of the family had had to rescue him. And they always remembered that too.

Nubiby sent most of the Waziri off to search in new directions, eliminating the path of the retreating village warriors. Nubiby, Ashanti, and the remaining five Waziri returned to the compound, reaching it later that afternoon.

JON WAS SHOCKED AT THE DEVASTATION. No buildings remained standing. Craters covered the ground, while piles of charred wood dotted the landscape marking the former locations of barns and houses. The main house was a pile of rubble. Groups of Waziri worked amid the destruction, clearing debris and building mud huts. Several heaps of unusable materials burned adding to the war zone effect. Other huge piles waited to be burned or were salvage, Nubiby told him.

They approached a circle of mud and thatch huts. Nubiby said, "Nothing is left of our houses. We have built old style huts temporarily. We hope to rebuild as before."

"Hope? Surely we will rebuild all of it."

Nubiby considered Jon thoughtfully. "We do not know who is left. Until today we thought you were dead. We have heard nothing from Korak, Tarzan, or your dad. They are probably fine. But it is strange that a week has passed and nothing has been heard from any of them."

Jon did not reply. Yes, of course. Rebuilding was the least of his problems at the moment.

Nubiby pointed to a hut. "This is Mubuto's hut." From around the side of another hut a large wolfhound bounded towards them.

"Samson!" Jon yelled. He was surprised and thrilled that he was still alive. He had to be at least 16. When he heard Jon's call, he picked up speed and bolted into him, knocking him down and then sitting firmly on his chest, licking his face. Samson had not seen Jon in a long time.

Ashanti laughed loudly, as did most of the Waziri in range.

"OK! OK! OK! I missed you too. I did. I swear. Let me up." He rolled him over to the side and got up. Samson would not let him go, his nose constantly nudging his hand, arm, or leg. Jon laughed and scratched his head.

From overhead, the whoop-whoop-whoop of helicopter blades caught their attention. Three helicopters approached from the east.

Jon turned to Nubiby. "Expecting company?"

"No. Run." Jon and Ashanti sprinted for the nearest cover. The Waziri working on salvage scrambled for guns and disappeared into the brush. Nubiby ducked into a hut and emerged with two machine guns and ammo. He raced after Jon, catching him in a copse of trees short of the jungle.

"Not here. The jungle," he yelled at Jon and pointed towards the denser vegetation a football field beyond.

"You go on. Take Ashanti. I'll catch up." He wanted to know who these guys were. Were the attackers sophisticated enough to have helicopters? And if they did, why had they waited until now, a week later, to show up in them?

Nubiby opened his mouth to argue, then closed it and sent the Waziri into the jungle. He and Ashanti stayed, as did Samson who refused to be parted from Jon.

Nubiby handed Ashanti the second gun and showed her how to shoot it. The recoil startled her. She stamped her foot and threw it at him, then grabbed an arrow for her bow. Nubiby stared at her open-mouthed. Jon laughed.

The helicopters had not landed. One hovered close to the main house and disgorged twenty men on ropes to the ground. Manned machine guns in the open doors backed them up. The men wore camouflage and their faces were wrapped in black ski masks. Jon could not tell their race. Immediately upon reaching the ground they formed a large expanding circle. The remaining two helicopters took up positions at opposite ends of the main compound and repeated the actions of the first.

Nubiby tugged on Jon's arm. This time he didn't argue. They ran to the jungle and joined up with the other Waziri. Jon asked about the wounded: Surely there had been wounded in the original attack. Were they in danger?

"There were few wounded. After the blasts, the gunmen killed all who could not run away. The only wounded who escaped were those who could walk or run, or were carried. There is nobody left to be in danger."

Jon sighed. It got worse and worse. "Okay. We must find out who they are. They might be friendly."

"They did not look friendly to me."

"I know. I know. But it's been how long since the attack? A week? Surely someone else would have come to check things out."

"Or not. Many believe it is best to stay away. Pretend ignorance. One's life is extended in this manner."

"My dad would have sent someone by now."

"That is true. Would he send warriors...with no markings on the aircraft?"

Jon sighed again, "Warriors, yes…in an aircraft without markings, no. Why would he? Okay. You are probably right. Doesn't matter though, I still want to know who they are."

Mubuto approached them, walking slowly with the aid of a wooden cane curved like a snake. His hair was gray, almost white. His skin wrinkled like a prune over his thin body. When he got close, he shook the cane at Jon and said, "The gods have saved you, young man. Soon, the jungle will take you back."

"Take me back? What do you mean?"

"Your mother was wrong to take you from the jungle. It will have you back." Mubuto hugged him and then walked away. Jon raised his eyes at Nubiby who shrugged. Jon called after the retreating Mubuto, "Wait. Do you know who caused all this?

"Do you know who *these* guys are?"

Mubuto waved his cane in the air and kept walking.

Jon threw up his hands. Death and destruction of the compound, warriors who wanted to kill him, commandos wanting who knows what, a witch he thought might be partial to him, and now the jungle wanted a piece of him, or maybe all of him. *Was that a prophecy?* Mubuto either didn't know anything about the attacks or wasn't willing to share. First things first: Make a plan, then follow it.

He conferred with Nubiby and Ashanti. There had been limited contact with the outlying Waziri villages. The compound communications system was destroyed in the attack. Drum messages were kept to a minimum as no one understood the source of the attacks. The few Waziri from outside the compound that Nubiby had heard from were angry and looking for those responsible.

Five Waziri would remain with them in the vicinity of the compound. The others would proceed to the nearest Waziri village that had not been attacked. It was a day's fast march away. There, they would wait one day and attempt to contact Jackie in London if the village radios worked. They were notorious for not working. If no word came from those remaining at the compound or no radios were available, they would leave in pairs in different directions to reach a city where they could make contact with London and Jackie.

Nubiby was not happy with the plan. He did not believe the commandos now in the compound were friendly and he wanted Jon to leave the area. Jon refused.

Despite living in the compound and western weapons, the Waziri had maintained their native warrior skills. They were superb spearmen and bowmen, and adept at bird call messaging across short distances. Nubiby kept five of the best and sent the others off.

NIGHT WAS ALMOST UPON THEM. They scattered around the main force getting as close as possible without detection. Their mission was to identify the intruders and send signals back to Jon and Nubiby. If not, they would meet at dawn and decide their next move.

They could not get close enough. Nubiby's binoculars were little help in the dim light. The jungle was too far away and the brush thinned out close to the compound. Jon returned to the copse of trees they had taken refuge in earlier. He watched as commandos erected tents and dug holes for support poles sporting lights at their tops. The area would be well lit, he thought. Perhaps that would help him identify the intruders. So far, he had caught not a glimpse of skin or insignia. He thought he might have to sneak into a tent to learn anything and did not relish that task.

In the end, it didn't matter. Shortly after dark, commandos from the compound fanned out with night vision goggles and without warning quickly surrounded each of them. Jon, Ashanti, and the Waziri, with hands on heads, were herded together in front of the main tent.

Jon still could not tell who they were or even their race. Each of their captors was covered head to foot in dark green mottled camouflage. Ski masks covered their faces. Not an inch of skin showed. Dark glasses replaced the night vision goggles. Few words were spoken and those few were in Swahili.

They stood in front of a tent the size of a basketball court. A maze of smaller tents surrounded it. The lights gave the illusion of daytime.

One commando approached Jon and motioned with his gun toward the main tent. When Jon did not move, a second commando pushed him firmly but politely from behind. Jon gave up resisting and entered the tent. Several men in camouflage, and with ski masks removed, hovered over a table covered with maps, speaking English with American accents. They were white. A gray-haired man straightened, removed his black-rimmed glasses and scrutinized Jon. He had the physique and bearing of a marine, Jon thought.

The man moved a map and picked up a photograph, putting his glasses back on long enough to consult the picture. He looked up at Jon.

"Jon Clayton. Your father will be very happy to see you. Sorry about the welcome."

"Who are you?" Jon did not confirm his identity. Maybe his dad sent these guys and maybe he didn't. This could be a hostage set-up. There were no markings on the equipment. He thought *What legitimate group would do that?*

"Red Slocum. I am a friend of your father." He reached out his hand across the table. Jon ignored it.

"You're American?" Jon wanted confirmation this guy knew his dad. But just how he was going to do that, he was not sure.

The man did not immediately answer. He turned to one of the others and asked, "How long until the satellite feed is set up for the camera."

"Five minutes," the reply came from behind a row of computers.

The grey-haired man turned back to Jon. "I understand your reticence, son, but I assure you, I am here at the request of your father. We are setting up a satellite link to him now and you will be able to talk to him. Unfortunately, the video only goes one way. You will be able to hear him but not see him."

Jon remained silent, thinking. He was leery of everybody. He had no idea yet who blew up the compound, only that they had sophisticated weapons, as did the men in whose custody he now was. He suspected they were not the bombers, and were friendly, possibly sent by his dad. But his assumptions had been wrong before. He was not ready to confirm an identity that would be instantly attractive to the ransom minded. He did not really believe the American government would be involved in such actions, but these men did not bear the markings of U.S. Forces. They had no markings at all. He kept coming back to that. *Even if these guys weren't who they said they were, what was he, Jon, going to be able to do about it? Nothing,* he thought. He was caught again.

Red considered. This was Jon Clayton. The photo confirmed it and even without that, he would have recognized him as a Clayton. He looked like his father did at that age.

"Let's go outside, under the lights and you can talk to your father." The man walked around the table to the tent flap and raised it, waiting for Jon.

Jon felt he had little choice. He was led to a portable video camera and followed the coaxial cables with his eyes to the satellite dish and transmitter box a few yards away. Red stood in front of the camera and waited. Jon stood to the side. The audio feed was two way but the video feed was only to London.

A technician behind the camera said, "Feed coming up in 3-2-1-now."

Red looked into the camera. "Jackie, are you there?"

Jon started and looked at him. Jackie? Could it be?

"Red. Did you find Jon?"

Jon pushed Red aside and stood in front of the camera. "Dad, thank God."

"Jon. Thank God you're alive! I thought you were killed in the crash. Are you okay? Is Meriem there with you?" In London, Jackie exhaled deeply.

"I'm fine, but Grandma isn't here, but we don't know where she went. Nubiby sent Waziri out to search but they haven't found anything yet. Dad…what happened here? Who did this?"

"I don't know. That's why I sent Red. Tell me what you saw."

"Nubiby could tell you more. Scott and I didn't see it all – just the smoke and then we crashed. They shot us down."

"Is Scott okay? Where is Nubiby now? Let me talk to him or to anyone who saw the attackers."

Jon looked at Red. "He's one of the guys you captured."

Red turned and spoke to someone and Jon went back to his dad. "Nubiby's coming. Scott's dead. He died in the crash. Dad…"

There was a brief silence. "I am sorry about Scott. He was one of the best. Jon, too many things are happening at once. The family seems to be under siege. Criminal charges are being brought against The Trust and…."

"For what?"

"There's more. Tarzan and Jane have not been heard from in seven days. We can't reach them. And Korak has been accused of the murder of Dian Fossey. Rwandan officials are looking for him. No one knows where he is."

"Dian Fossey is dead?"

"Yes, murdered by all accounts."

"But Dad, Korak would not kill her. They were friends."

"I agree, son, but he was there the night she was killed and now he can't be found. Innocent or not, it looks suspicious;

which is why I am going to ask Red to fly you home. Now. Tonight. I don't know what's going on. I need you here."

"To do what? Play with numbers? Run errands? Answer the phones? You have plenty of people to do that. I need to go after Grandma."

"Nubiby and the Waziri can do that. You need to be here."

"No I don't. I need to help find Grandma."

"No! Absolutely, not! You're coming home now. She could be anywhere after a week, halfway to Fossey's camp, in the hands of guerrillas, or dead. She knows how to live in the jungle. Let the Waziri search. I need you here."

As he said it, Jackie realized just how true that was. He needed his son safe in London. They could very well be the only two Claytons left.

"Dad, she's your mother, my grandmother. I can't …."

"Yes. You can and you will. You are my son. She would agree with me. Come back here now. You have little enough experience in the jungle."

Jon dropped his head. That damned lion. Then he raised his head back to the camera. "You might be surprised. Dad, I have to do this."

"Jon, be reasonable. Think! This could be an attack on the family. You may very well be a target. Anyone with you would be in danger as well."

Jon smiled. "Then, I'll have to go alone, as grandfather and great grandfather did."

Jackie's hands turned white clenching the arms of his chair. "No! I forbid it." He stopped, realizing he was yelling. In a lowered voice he said, "Let me talk to Red. You are coming home."

Red moved toward the camera but Jon stopped him with a hand on his chest. This was not going to happen this time. He looked into the camera wishing he could see his father's face. He was going after Meriem and this might be their last conversation.

He took a deep breath and said. "Dad, I am going. Red cannot stop me. I am past the age of majority. I am sorry you do not understand. I love you dad, but if you want me stopped you will have to come down here and do it yourself."

As soon as the words passed his lips he regretted it. His dad in a wheel chair could not physically stop him. It was simply revenge for the lion allusion. He was damned tired of that reference. Yes, he had little experience in the jungle but that was changing. He had Ashanti and he had Nubiby; and he had killed the damned witch doctor. That had to count for something.

Jon turned away to leave but then stopped and turned back. He interrupted his father who was yelling something to the effect of "Jon, you get back here right now!"

"Dad," he paused waiting for his father to realize he had returned to the camera and to stop yelling. "Dad, thank you for insisting I take martial arts training. It saved my life. Love you." He walked away, leaving the camera for Red.

In London, Jackie unclenched his hands from the arms of the chair and blood resumed flowing to his knuckles. He sagged in the chair.

Nubiby with a commando escort approached the camera. Jon stopped them to speak to him.

"It's Dad," he said, pointing back to the camera. "He wants to talk to you. I am going after Meriem. I would welcome your assistance. But I am going regardless."

Nubiby looked at him astounded. "Of course, I will help you. Why would you think otherwise? I am your friend and protector."

"You haven't talked to my dad yet."

Nubiby nodded his head. "Yes. Of course, he does not want you to go. You knew little of the jungle until now. But the Waziri will be with you. And I would imagine Ashanti as well." His eyes twinkled at that.

Jon told him what his dad had said about the family being a target. Nubiby was not fazed, "That is nothing new. The Greystokes have always been targets." Nubiby waved his hand at the rubble. "He just doesn't want you to go. He is your father. Now that the compound is in safe hands, we will go in search of your grandmother."

Chapter 20: *ARRESTING MOMENTS*

THE ELEVEN AM MEETING PROVED productive. It was Rupert who brought the good news to The Greystoke Trust's inner circle.

"In reviewing the ops codes at the binary level, we found several irregularities. We compared them to the dates of blips Otto found in the investment records and found that they matched."

"And your conclusion…"

"It appears that the irregularities are intrusions into the system from outside, i.e., we're getting hacked. It appears that whoever is doing it is waiting for us to log a trade. And as soon as they see one on the system, they take that information to initiate their own transactions to either neutralize our trade or to even take our anticipated gain from the trade away from us. The overall effect gives every appearance of insider trading. I'd rather call it Pirating."

"Have you put a fix in to block the hackers?" It was Jackie again. Without waiting for an answer, he continued on. "How do we track the hackers? And stop them."

Rupert was ready. "First, we have not blocked the port through which they've been coming in because by doing that it would make it virtually impossible to locate the hacking source. Instead, we're creating our own hacking program that will in effect backtrack the intruding programs to their source. With any luck, the next time our system is penetrated we'll be able to physically find the intruder's location."

It was Otto who spoke next. "With your permission, we want to execute a fake trade as bait for the pirates. Then even if Rupert's program isn't totally successful, we can check the market to see who is trying to take advantage of our trade by using the information. That will give us two ways to run the intruders to ground."

Jackie's turn, "That sounds good. Ian, are there any legal ramifications to this?"

Ian momentarily pondered the question before answering, like most lawyers who believe that by doing so lends more weight to their opinions. "Doing a 'fake trade' could be seen by other parties, such as the Exchequer, as a fraudulent act. It's my opinion that you should first create a document outlining the prospective trade and the purpose of its use and that it is not intended to be carried out.

"Second, as soon as you know that the mouse has taken the bait, cancel the trade. If it goes sour on them, they aren't about to report it, nor where and how they got the information to make such a trade."

"Rupert. Otto. Follow Ian's guidelines. Also, run it by me for final sign off only because if everything hits the fan I want to take the blame.

"Any other input?"

"Yes." It was Rupert again. The other thing that we discovered is that the hacking seems to be happening on transmissions coming through one terminal. There are three people who regularly use that terminal: Frank James, Juan Sanchez and Bill Fields. We're checking logs to see if we can time the hacks with who's on the terminal at that time."

Jackie turned to Leslie. "Have you done any deep dives into the HR records of those three?"

"Yes. I've got their records right here", he said tapping a pile of manila folders. Actually, right now, they're in the HR conference room, waiting for a presentation on benefits. Didn't want to tip our hand but wanted them available for you at a moment's notice."

"Excellent. Let's see if we can't short-circuit the whole thing now. Go get the first one."

OVER THE NEXT FORTY-FIVE minutes each one, James, Sanchez and Fields, was personally vetted by Jackie and the other members of the management team. Each was confronted. Each confessed. Each claimed they needed the extra money to live in London. Then when each thought he would be fired in disgrace, he was told that he would not be. Instead, each was told "You should be discharged, then turned over to the Exchequer for prosecution. Those regulatory jackals are always looking for new flesh to devour. You will keep your position provided you make restitution of the monies stolen and you agree to undergo a special training program that will help you manage your personal as well as business accounts. You will be under tight scrutiny and any slip ups and you will be shown the door....and introduced to people at The Exchequer."

Jackie turned to Leslie. "We need to update our comp procedures. It's a disgrace - on us - for employees to feel they can't live on what we pay them. Give me your recommendations in the next three days. Understood?" Leslie nodded his understanding.

"Concerning Smithers, I'll tell him we found the source of the problem, that it was internal, and we have taken appropriate steps to eliminate a recurrence. He should have no problem in getting the charges dissolved. Anything else?"

No one else spoke up. A feeling of success, and relief, floated through the room.

As Jackie adjourned the meeting, there was a commotion outside followed by the conference room doors flying open and a total stranger strutting into the room. He carried a fedora in one hand and several sheets of paper in the other. A battered rain coat was draped over his left forearm. His suit didn't quite fit, it definitely came off the rack; while his scuffed shoes were well past receiving any shoe polish, or any form of improvement. Two other similarly dressed men followed behind him.

Rupert and Otto stood up to bar the stranger's progress into the room. He ignored them, took two more steps into the room then looked around, zeroing in on the end of the table. "Are you Jack Porter Clayton, Chief Executive Officer for The Greystoke Trust?"

"Yes, and who might you be?"

"I'm Chief Inspector Greenwood, Allyn Greenwood, and I hereby place you, Jack Porter Clayton, under arrest. You have the right to remain silent."

The whole room went still. Everyone seemed in a stupor. It was Ian who broke the silence. "My dear sir, I think there has been some mistake. I've already talked to Geoff Smithers at The Exchequer. There was no mention of any arresting of anyone. You must be mistaken."

"I don't know a "Smithers" at The Exchequer. Besides, this is not an Exchequer matter." Again, heads turned trying to seek some semblance of sanity out of what was spinning out of control.

"If not The Exchequer," Ian said," then what the hell is this intrusion about?"

"And who might you be?"

"I'm Mr. Clayton's barrister, Ian Farkwark. And, he's not going anywhere until you clarify why you're here." He shifted his great bulk forward as if creating a human roadblock to the inspector and his men. "Well?"

Greenwood held out the pile of papers he had been holding. "These papers are all the necessary explanations."

Ian looked through the papers, then turned back to Greenwood. "Would you please allow me a moment with my client?" Greenwood, feeling now he had the upper-hand, nodded his consent, turned to his two companions and all three stepped back out of the conference room closing the doors behind them.

Ian turned to everyone else still in the room. "I think this matter is best discussed with Jackie in private so, I suggest you go about the tasks you've been assigned while we handle this matter." Everyone picked up their materials and exited. Once the room was cleared, Ian turned to Jackie.

"Jackie, if anything in these documents is true we have a very, very serious matter on our hands. This stuff makes The Exchequer's situation look like a walk in the park."

Jackie exploded. "For God's sake, Ian, cut to the core! What are we being accused of that warrants my arrest?"

"From my brief scan, you are being arrested for crimes against the Crown."

"What?"

"More specifically, you, through The Trust, are accused of funneling funds to several terrorist groups including the IRA."

"That's tommyrot! Why would I ever do that? You know I'm not disloyal to the Crown! I don't play politics! It's idiotic to think differently!"

"I'm sure that the charges are tommyrot, but according to these documents, funds going into known IRA accounts have been traced back to us. The Crown claims that they have direct testimony from a highly reliable and reputable source as to the validity of the charges. Couple this with The Exchequer's matter and it would seem The Greystoke Trust has become a sieve for illegal transactions."

Jackie took a deep breath, paused to collect his thoughts and said, "Alright. Alright. You're the legal genius. What do we do now? Can you keep me out of prison?"

"For once your state of immobility might be a blessing. I'll call Noiseworthy and see what can be done. In the meantime, it's probably best that we go along with Inspector Greenwood. If you have to make a stay, it shouldn't be a long one."

Jackie took another deep breath. "Alright, but first I need a moment with Louise. Someone has to stay on top of things while I'm incapacitated. Will the bastard at least allow me that?"

"Let's find out." Ian looked through the glass wall of the conference room and motioned for Greenwood to come in. "Thank you for allowing my client the privacy he requested. He understands the severity of the charges and has pledged to work with whoever is necessary to get matters resolved.

"He has agreed to come with you, with my accompaniment. He has requested an extra few minutes to put things in order prior to the departure. I'm in hopes that you will find that small request to be acceptable."

Greenwood, the man of many words once again nodded his agreement and then said, "Ten minutes. That's it. And you're lucky I'm so sensitive." His smirk belied his words.

Jackie wheeled over to the phone in the room, punched three numbers and said, "Louise. Please come to the conference room." Louise was in the room and the door closed within thirty-seven seconds. She had tried to stop the three-man invasion, but they just walked through her as if she wasn't there. She knew she would be summoned.

"Sit down Louise, there are a few things we need to discuss." Jackie waited for her to sit down. "There's been a major screw up involving The Trust. I won't go into details but to say that the charges are very serious and I'm being arrested." Without noticing Louise's look of incredulity, Jackie continued. "While I'm gone, which should not be long if Ian's judgment is correct, I need you to keep things on an even keel here. I trust you to do what is necessary to keep operations running." His steel grey eyes looked into her eyes, "Can you do that for me?"

"Certainly, I will keep everything running until you get back."

"Good. You're in charge. Make me proud."

"Oh, I will. I will."

Jackie turned to Ian and said, "Let's get this over with." He then began wheeling himself to the door and Inspector Greenwood waiting beyond. Ian fell in behind and the entire parade of people marched to the elevators, down to the waiting cars and onto the jail cell awaiting Jackie's occupancy.

WHILE JACKIE WAS BEING PROCESSED, Ian called Noiseworthy at Whitehall. It didn't go well. When the processing had been complete, Ian met with Jackie in his cell. "I've talked with Noiseworthy and he is not happy about events. He's sure you're innocent.… but, others are pressing the matters and there is nothing he can do to get you out of here. Bail is not granted in such cases, and Whitehall is not willing to let you out on your own recognizance. The only good news I can provide is that they want to press the case as quickly as possible. As such we've agreed that the initial Commitment Procedure Hearing should be held within ten days. Until then, unfortunately, you will have to remain here."

It was not what Jackie wanted to hear. "You said I'd be in and out in no time. Now you're saying I'm a permanent resident here in Hotel Bailey. You're not doing your job." Jackie's anger and frustration hung heavy in the air.

"Jackie, I know you're distraught, but I am doing my job. Because of accessibility to such massive amounts of funds, combined with you owning property all over the world they fear you'll try to flee. I've tried to convince them that is not the case. My pleadings fell on deaf ears, closed minds."

Jackie, frustrated, shouted back, "Claytons don't run from problems…they face them."

Ian continued. "The whole key to this matter is their eyewitness who's brought the case to them. There are documents supposedly signed by you that initiated the cash transfers. I asked who this key witness is. I demanded to have access to him. But, they wouldn't hear of it. We have to wait until the Commitment Procedure Hearing. That's why they won't let you out. They think the case is ironclad against you. Is there anything you want to tell me?"

Jackie was furious and the scowl on his face said everything. Ian bowed his head in submission and frustration, closing his eyes in an attempt to keep from seeing what bleak future lay ahead for Jackie and the Claytons.

Chapter 21: KORAK FOUND

J ON AND ASHANTI SLEPT HIGH in the canopy. They had spent two days searching the jungle in vain for signs of Meriem. In the morning, they would travel to a Waziri village on the river, there to meet with the other groups searching from the compound at the same time.

The distant beat of drums awoke them. The full moon above the horizon and the drumbeats triggered a memory in Jon.

"Is that the Dum-Dum of the apes?" he asked.

"Yes," she said, amazed that he would know of it. "They will go on awhile. Go back to sleep."

"No," he said, reaching for his rope to scale down the tree. "C'mon. I want to see one."

Ashanti was stunned. *Surely, he was not serious.* As his head disappeared below the canopy, she realized he was. She scrambled to catch up, arguing with him as they descended.

"This is crazy. They will kill us."

"They won't see us. We'll stay concealed in the trees."

"Apes go in trees, you know."

"They go into a frenzy at these things, like sharks do when they smell blood. They won't even know we are there."

"They will smell us."

"It won't matter. They'll be too intent on the ceremony."

A wild and terrifying shriek of a bull ape pierced the chatter of the night jungle and sent shivers up Jon's spine. He knew that call, Tarzan's call. He had practiced it endlessly as a small child, much to the chagrin of all those in range of his voice. Another bull roared his challenge and was answered by another, then another and another.

They had reached the jungle floor. Jon turned to Ashanti, "We need to hurry. Come on. The ceremony has started."

"How do you know that? No humans ever go there. Nor should we."

"Tarzan and Korak described Dum-Dum ceremonies to me as a child. Let's go. Hurry."

Jon wanted to see a Dum-Dum ceremony. It had been one of the most fascinating stories Tarzan and Korak had told him as a child. He had fond memories of them acting out the parts of the apes, dancing around the drum and mock fighting each other for the kingship. Of course they had hammed it up for a seven-year old, but to this day, it made him smile.

Ashanti and Jon made their way through the dark jungle, Ashanti lighting their way with both flashlights while Jon wielded the machete. The full moon shed little light at ground level.

Ashanti was not happy. She knew of the Dum-Dum ceremony. All jungle people did. And they all had the good sense to be somewhere else when the apes went crazy. But here she was, following this white man, into the den of the beasts. What was she thinking? She sighed and swept a flashlight in an arc behind her, searching for the reflecting eyes of cats or other beasts that might think them an easy meal. She knew exactly what she was thinking. She just wished he was think-ing it also, but did not fool herself into believing that he did.

The drums grew louder. They were close. She could feel the vibration. Jon took a flashlight from her and they both scanned the trees around them. Some had lower branches. They climbed up until they could see the moonlight reflecting off the clearing through the foliage. They knew where to go now and climbed down to find a tree with a better vantage point. They went mostly by feel, not wanting to betray their presence with flashlights. The sounds of frenzied apes accompanied by drums covered the sounds of their approach.

Quickly they found a tree edging the clearing and climbed up, stretching out on branches to view the ceremony below. The apes danced wildly around the big earthen drum in the center of the amphitheater. Jon could clearly see the female apes beating a rhythm on the drum with bones. He was sure Tarzan and Korak had talked of sticks but these old females were pounding out their haunting beats with what Jon thought were the femurs of a large animal.

He watched the bulls with fascination. One of them stood out from the others as the only hairless one. He stared. The arms were short, not reaching the ground. This was no ape. This was a human and it had to be Tarzan or Korak. No other human would be accepted into a Dum-Dum. Jon stared, waiting for the dancing to give him a better view. Finally, the human looked up at the rising moon for a brief second and revealed his identity. It was *Korak*. He lowered his arm to the branch just below him and nudged Ashanti, whispering to her.

"That's Korak, my grandfather. Do you see him?"

"Your grandfather? Are you sure?"

"Of course, I'm sure. He's my grandfather…"

She stared at him in disbelief.

"I'm going down there." He rose to a sitting position.

"What?" she hissed. "Are you crazy? They will kill you."

"No, they won't. Korak won't let them. He's my grandfather."

"You are one stupid white man. At least wait for the dancing to end."

Jon consented to that and they sat together in the tree watching as the dancing continued. Fifteen apes danced wildly, bounding, prancing and strutting their pride around the clearing, snarling and growling, saliva dripping from bared fangs. They leapt high in the air, beating their chests and roaring their challenge to any foolish enough to accept.

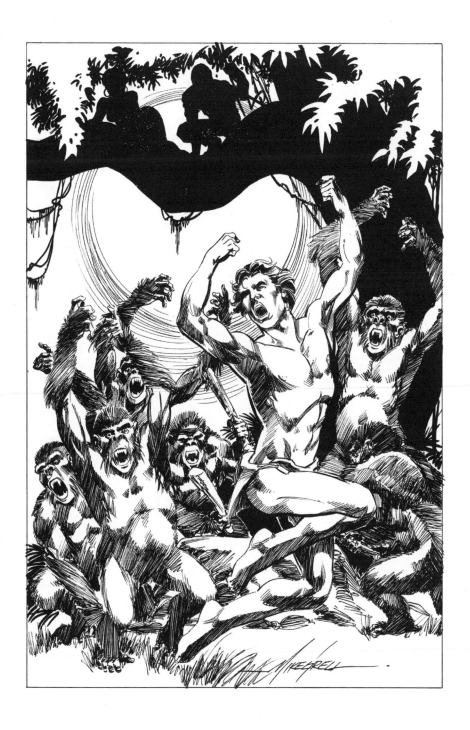

139

The old females beat their bones on the drums harder and faster. The apes matched their intensity leaping higher, screaming louder, and beating their breasts with such ferocity that Jon thought surely ribs would be broken. They had missed the first part of the ceremony, the ritual hunt and slaying of an already dead foe or sometimes an old king who had been challenged and lost. He could see the mangled body of what once must have been an ape lying in front of the drum and wondered if this was a king making. If so, one of the apes now dancing would be claiming the kingship.

The drums suddenly ceased and the dancers stood waiting while the three old females rose swiftly and scurried to the back of the clearing joining the other females and the young. Korak approached the mutilated corpse and ripped off his share of the feast. As he retreated to the side of the amphitheater, the other bulls descended on the corpse, ripping and shredding the remains, snarling and shoving each other as they vied for the most delectable parts.

When he saw Korak take the first piece, Jon knew the identity of the new king. *But why? Why would Korak go back to the apes? Could it be true that Korak had killed Dian Fossey and now was hiding out among the apes?* He did not believe it. Korak and Dian were fast friends. They saw eye-to-eye on conserving the anthropoid populations and what should be done with poachers. Korak did not think Dian was wise in some of her interactions with the natives, but they were definitely of one mind on conservation. Jon knew all of this from Meriem's extensive letters on the subject. She had maintained a constant correspondence with him since he was seven.

Jon's attention was drawn back to the clearing. The females and young were arguing over what was left of the corpse. The Dum-Dum was ending and the feasting commenced with the apes now quiet and scattered around the clearing or in low branches of the trees. Jon observed a female with a young ape riding her back, approaching the tree in which he and Ashanti were hiding. It was too late to move. The ape grasped a branch and started to bound up into the tree when she caught the scents of Jon and Ashanti. She shrieked an alarm, jumped to the ground and scampered to the far side of the clearing. The bulls sprang to their feet, jumping up and down, snarling, and waiting for their king to respond. Strangers were not tolerated in the amphitheater.

Korak moved towards Jon and Ashanti's tree.

"Grandfather," Jon called expecting recognition. Instead, he received a cocked head in response.

"Grandfather. Korak. It's me, Jon. Your grandson." The only response was a cocked head in the other direction.

"I'm going down there," he said quietly to Ashanti. "Whatever happens, don't kill him."

"And if he kills you?"

"He won't."

"Mambo mzungu," *Crazy white man*, she said.

Jon smiled slightly. "Swear to me you won't kill him."

"Okay," she said, adding under her breath, "Kijinga mzungu," *Stupid white man*.

"Probably so," he said and jumped to the ground in front of Korak. The bulls clustered behind Korak, hooting, howling, and baring fangs. Several charged, stopping at Korak's back, then retreating, only to charge again. They impatiently waited for their king to dispatch the interloper.

Chapter 22: INSPECTING THE SCENE OF THE CRIME

THE SECRETARY to Michael Garner, the British Ambassador to Zaire, immediately recognized the voice on the other end of the phone and said, "The ambassador is on another call...with the Prime Minister...but don't hang up!" He was uncharacteristically nervous and excited at the same time, "I am putting you on hold... just momentarily...the ambassador will be right with you."

The secretary burst through the doors to the ambassador's office shouting, "He's on the line. Line three." The ambassador cut the prime minister off in mid-sentence. "He's calling in now. I'll call you back."

The ambassador punched line three and launched a rapid-fire of questions at the caller. "Where have you been? Where are you? What in blue blazes is going on? Do you have any idea what's been happening?"

The caller remained calm. "It's nice to be missed, Mike. Let me take your questions in order. First, Jane and I have been holed up in an isolated chalet in the foothills of Nepal. An avalanche cut us off for three days. We just arrived in Kathmandu. That's when we heard the news. I need information. That's why I'm calling."

The ambassador launched a new verbal offensive. "You sure do need my help. By the time everything is sorted out you may need an act of Parliament to survive. How soon can you get here? I need you here ...to make some sense out of this insanity."

"Mike," frustration crept into Tarzan's voice, "That's why I'm calling you! How soon can YOU get us flights...commercial or otherwise?"

"Stay put. Give me the number where I can reach you. I'll be back to you in 15 minutes, even if I have to scramble half of the RAF."

The number was given; the promise kept. Within two hours an RAF Shadow R15 had landed at Tribhuvan International Airport, taken on two passengers and their luggage and was again airborne enroute to Jomo Kenyatta International Airport, Nairobi, Kenya.

SIX HOURS LATER the Shadow 15 touched down at Kenyatta International and taxied to a remote end of the runway where three black limousines were parked. As the aircraft's doors opened, so did the doors to the limousines emptying their human contents onto the tarmac.

After a momentary pause an additional figure emerged from the middle limousine, Ambassador Garner. He was nearly six feet tall, and held his athletic looking body in a firm, erect carriage, almost military. His face exuded confidence. His full head of brown dyed hair belied his true age. He buttoned, unbuttoned and then re-buttoned the middle button of his suit coat. He next realigned his tie, for the fourth time. Settled in, he began walking towards the plane to meet the two passengers who at that moment were descending the staircase that had been rolled-up to the plane's hatchway. The parties met at the bottom of the stairs.

"It's an honor, Lord and Lady Greystoke, it's been..."

Tarzan's impatience interrupted. "Cut the diplomacy, Mike. Give us the straight facts."

The ambassador turned to his entourage, motioning them to step back out of hearing range. All complied as none wanted to be part of the discussion that was about to take place.

"Alright John, here's where things stand. Jack is wanted for questioning about Fossey's murder by the Rwandan government, but he's nowhere to be found. Neither is his wife.

"Serious charges have been brought against Jackie and The Greystoke Trust, up to and including possible acts of treason." Jane gasped and shook her head in disbelief. Tarzan gave no indication of his feelings.

"Your plantation has been destroyed, along with several others in that general area. The remains of a crashed and burned fuselage have been found. Inside were the charred remains of the pilot. Upon impact, a tree branch punched through the cockpit window and impaled him to his seat. He never had a chance. The few legible markings indicate the plane was registered with your Trust."

Jane shouted out, "Jon and Jackie were supposed to be on that plane!" Tarzan put his arm around Jane, but remained stoic.

"According to Jackie's office, Jon was on the plane and Jackie stayed in London. Only one body was found…that of the pilot. Where your great grandson is, is anyone's guess.

"To be blunt, besides Jackie, you are the first Claytons that we have been able to find.

"The Prime Minister has issued an arrest warrant for Jackie; and I'm supposed to be taking you into custody, right here, right now." Tarzan's back instinctively straightened. He was not about to be arrested.

The ambassador noticed the change in Tarzan's composure and continued, "John, we go back too far and have known each other too long, so I'm putting my trust in you. I'm not arresting you. What do you want to do?"

John Clayton remained silent for a moment then spoke. "Mike, your trust is not unwarranted. Restraining me would be no good for anyone. Your synopsis confirms what I have surmised. Here's my plan. Here's what I need.

"First, I need Jane safely escorted to our compound. She can address the matters on the ground. Second, I need to get to Fossey's camp to see it for myself. Jack's not a killer. He's being framed and by seeing the site I may be able to find new clues that haven't come to light yet. Can you make those two things happen?"

"What do you intend to do about the charges? They're what have the PM going crazy over. The Greystoke Trust is a pillar of integrity. Its investments control the fate of many companies around the world. If that pillar collapses there could very well be a tidal wave of fear sweeping through the stock markets around the world. That can't happen. The PM's looking for stability."

"Tell Prime Minister Thatcher, she has my word that I will personally stand responsible if any of the charges are true. On the flight, Jane and I talked about all this and we truly believe that these individual events are tied together by an invisible thread. I need to find that thread, and when I do, everything will unravel revealing our innocence and the person or persons behind these events."

The ambassador's face couldn't hide the argument going on inside him. "Okay. I'll make the arrangements…under one circumstance, you check in every twenty-four hours and keep me informed of what you find. If one minute past twenty-four hours goes by without hearing from you, I will have no other alternative than to detain all the Claytons that we can find."

"Fair enough."

THE CAR HAD BEEN FOLLOWING a single-lane dirt road which without warning changed into a mere footpath. The driver braked to a sharp stop, then turned to his passenger with a combined look of indecision and confusion. The passenger ended the driver's consternation. "Wait here. I'll walk the rest of the way. I should be back in two to three hours."

And with that, the tall man stepped out of the car and headed up the footpath.

Ah, the smell of the jungle. The rotting vegetation, the flowering fauna, mixed with scents of various residences of the jungle was exhilarating to the passenger. It was the fragrance of his real home.

He chaffed under the restraining clothes that he was wearing. They were the dressings of civilization. He would have much preferred wearing his loincloth, carrying his trusted rope, bow and quiver of arrows, along with his father's knife hanging at his side. But, he knew this mission required the airs of civility... to act as a British Lord of high respectability.

As he was ascending the final steps up to the entrance to Dian Fossey's camp an armed guard stepped out from the bushes lining the trail. "Halt! You cannot enter. This is a crime scene. Go away!" A normal person would have been startled by the sudden appearance of the Rwandan soldier, but the visitor's acute senses had alerted him to the soldier's presence one hundred yards prior to coming upon him.

The visitor held his position, reached into his safari coat pocket and withdrew a piece of paper which he handed to the soldier. The solder read it, looked up at the person before him, then looked back and read the paper again. It was a letter of introduction, granting Lord Greystoke, John Clayton, access to the camp's premises and the right to conduct any investigation that he saw fit to do. It was signed by His Excellency, President Juvenal Habyarimana of Rwanda.

"You are Lord Greystoke? You are Tarzan of the Apes?" Astonishment wallpapered the soldier's face. He had heard of such a person, but like so many others thought Tarzan was a fictional character created by some writer in some faraway land who knew nothing of jungle life. Instead, Tarzan was real... standing right in front of him. The soldier tried to gather his composure and said, "Come with me. I will take you to General

Zambossi. He's in charge." The two walked into the camp area, the soldier constantly looking from the letter to Tarzan.

As they were walking into the compound, a figure strutted toward them. It was General Zambossi, who was a "squat" man, wide of girth and just over five feet tall. His wild hair looked like the snapshot of a large fireworks explosion. Some said he kept his hair that way to help overcome his height challenge. He tried to overcome his sensitivity of his size with an inflated belligerence toward anyone he met for the first time. In his own mind, he thought it gave him the upper hand in any conversation. He made the mistake of trying to do so with Tarzan.

The soldier handed the General the letter who looked it over and then said, "How do I know you are the person claimed to be in this letter? This letter is nothing! It has no meaning. What real proof do you have of who you claim to be?"

With that, the General began to tear the letter in half. But before he could do so, a massive, yet gentle hand reached out and encircled the general's hands. "I am who the letter says I am." As the words were spoken, Tarzan's gray eyes burned into the general's carrying the message that if you want to truly challenge my identity, do so at your own risk.

The General got the message but was hesitant to admit defeat. "What is it that you want to see? We have gone over everything. It is clear. Your son was here with Ms. Fossey. She was killed. Your son is gone without explanation. The facts speak for themselves. You would do better by telling us where your son is hiding."

Tarzan held his anger...but not entirely. He bent his entire six foot, five inch frame over the stump of the man before him, bringing his face within inches of the General's, and said, "I will see for myself. Myopic eyes can miss the full picture."

The implication was clear. The General had met his match. He pulled in his arrogance and extended an invitation to look around as much as Tarzan cared to do. Then, he turned on his heels and marched off toward the barracks from which he had come. The embarrassment of the confrontation had been enough; but to have it done in front of one of his underlings was too much. He would seek his pound of flesh later...in another way.

TARZAN APPROACHED FOSSEY'S living quarters. Rather than entering, he first circled the building, noting the location of entrances and the placement of any foliage that could be used for hiding. On the southwest corner of the building's back side he noted a gaping hole in the wire mesh intended to keep any animals from getting under the building.

He knelt down and examined the ground. The first things he noticed were small pieces of grayish brown hair that had snagged on the wire mesh. Individual strands seem to point from inside to outside; while others pointed in the opposite direction. He pulled off a portion, rolled it between his thumb and forefinger. Then he sniffed it. He knew the scent, and he started to begin to imagine what had happened.

He rose and walked around to the front where he climbed the three steps to the front porch. The door, while scarred from use over time, showed no sign of forced entry. He opened the door and stepped into the living room. To his left, he could see the kitchen/dining area, a step down from the living room level. Both rooms were in total disarray. Tables turned, shards of glass, chairs broken. Dian Fossey's desk had been rifled, paper strewn all over the place.

Photos were scattered everywhere...Hundreds of them. Fossey was obsessive in recording the activities of her ongoing research. She wanted to have pictures to answer any potential donor's questions. Tarzan bent down and scooped up a handful. There were several of Dian with Digit who she had raised from his birth. There were other pictures with her faithful staff of park rangers. He turned a few over and noticed that some had been stamped: "Photo by Todd Holley." It made sense that

Fossey would employ a professional photographer so that she could be in as many shots as possible. An idea started to form in Tarzan's mind. He placed the photos on the desk and continued his search.

He stepped into the kitchen. Dirty dishes were still in the stagnant sink water. Every piece of furniture not nailed down had been thrown about. A waded-up piece of paper in one corner of the room caught his eye. He went over, picked it up, and unfolded it. He read it, then folded it and put it in his inner coat pocket.

Next, he went into the bedroom, which was behind the living room. Everything was tossed there as well; whether by the occupants or the investigators was unclear. What was clear was the white chalk outline of where Dian Fossey's body had lain. Brown splotches of her dried blood were splattered everywhere.

In the far corner of the bedroom was a hole where several of the floorboards had been torn up. Previous reports had said the hole was caused by the killer trying to uncover the hiding place where Fossey hid her valuables. Tarzan looked into the hole, and could see daylight coming in from below. And once again, he noticed single strains of hair, fur, on the splintered ends of the floor boards.

He stood in the middle of the room, closed his eyes and took a deep breath. He gently nodded his head in satisfaction at the vision that came to him. While other people would have felt nothing, the entire sequence of what happened ran through Tarzan's mind. The inspection of the crime scene was complete…conclusions drawn.

He next needed to ask a few questions of the inhabitants of the camp. He didn't have to go looking for them as most of them were gathered at the foot of the front porch. Word had spread and many came to see the living legend in their midst. The looks on their faces telescoped their awe. *Tarzan was real! Tarzan was here!* When he asked if any would talk with him, each clamored to be the first.

Tarzan sat on the top step and began asking questions: First general ones, then ones more specific. "What was the weather like the night Dian was killed?" "What was Jack Clayton doing here?" "Were there other outsiders in camp that day?" The staff members competed to be the first to answer, and in their rush to do so they gave Tarzan more information than he had hoped.

He looked up and saw General Zambossi striding toward him and his gathering. As he approached Zambossi began hollering at the staff, "Get back to work. Stop bothering this man. You have more important things to do. Go! Go! Go!" The group momentarily wavered, then rapidly dispersed.

The General addressed Tarzan, "You're a disruptive element. Finish your work and be gone. We do not need you here."

"I'm finished except for one question, 'Where can I find one Todd Holley?'"

The General took a deep breath and exhaled loudly, sounding like a bellowing hippopotamus. "Why do you want to talk with him? He's a nothing." Tarzan did not respond. Silence hung in the air. Finally, Zambossi spoke. "His cabin is on the backside of that ridge, but he won't do you any good. I've questioned him and he knows nothing."

"Thank you. I'll see him and then be on my way." And with that Tarzan rose, walked down the stairs, and past the General without saying a word…accidentally brushing the General's shoulder to remind him who was in command. The General nearly toppled over and started to say something, but then, for once, thought better of it. Besides, he would be rid of this disruptive source momentarily.

HOLLEY'S CABIN WAS easy enough to find. Tarzan knocked on the door, already knowing that someone was inside as his hearing picked up movement from within. A voice hollered, "Come in. I'll be with you in a moment."

Tarzan entered the dimly lit, sparsely furnished quarters and waited. A pair of legs was visible behind a drawn curtain. "Just developing more prints. Make yourself comfortable."

Tarzan stood, using the time to survey the premises. The curtain parted, revealing a slender-built man of medium height with a full head of flaming red hair. Tarzan estimated the man to be in his late thirties. He had on the rubber gloves that he used for developing photographs. "Oh. I thought you were one of the boys. They always knock. What can I do for you?" His accent was distinctly American.

"I'm John Clayton…Jack Clayton's father. I wondered if you had a minute."

"Sure. I only knew Jack for a few days, but I really liked him. He was a great subject to photograph. And walking around with his apes, well, those were shots I couldn't miss taking."

"Sounds like you took quite a few pictures of him while he was here."

"Yes, yes I did. His visit with Dian and the results they were hoping to achieve, made great photo-journalism." He paused, and then went on, "It's a shame how things ended… but I don't think for a second that Jack was involved…but then again I don't know why he disappeared that night. Just doesn't make sense."

"I agree with you…it doesn't make sense. That's why I'm here…to find that missing link." Tarzan paused to let the statement settle before asking his next question. "May I see the pictures you took of Jack? It might help in some way."

"Sure. No problem." Pointing toward the file cabinets that lined one whole wall of the cabin Holley continued, "Check the end cabinet…third drawer down. There should be a shoe box full of prints of Jack."

Tarzan retrieved the box from the file cabinet. There were nearly two hundred photos. "You're pretty prolific. Do you take so many photos every day?"

"No. BUT that day was a special one. It was the first day that the gorillas and apes were allowed to mix; before they had been separated by wire netting. It was a truly marvelous sight. Many thought the males would fight, or at least challenge one another. But they didn't. They sniffed each other for a few moments then pretty much went about their own business. It was amazing!"

As Holley talked, Tarzan thumbed through the box of photos, looking for something to jump out at him. Three photos showing Fossey, Jack and another man drew his attention. When he was through, he went back through all the photos again, and again the same three photos drew him in. He had seen the third person, but couldn't place where or when.

Tarzan turned to Holley and asked him if he knew who the man was. "Oh, one of the many visiting politicians we get through here all the time. Dian couldn't stand most of them. If they weren't asking for favors, they'd be threatening her with the thought of not renewing her visa. No visa, no project. It made her furious. The local politicians kept her on a tight string, issuing her only two-month visas. Then for some unknown reason a two-year visa came through. She was ecstatic. She no longer had to spend two or three days every two months going to the capital and arguing with the bureaucrats for her visa."

"Do you remember this one's name?" Tarzan said, pointing at the man beside Fossey. "There is something about him that is familiar, but I can't put my finger on it."

"No, I have no idea. I don't try to remember any of their names. They're just 'here today, gone tomorrow' types. Sorry I can't be of more help. If you want, go ahead and keep the pictures, after all they're good shots of your son. With Dian dead, my time is up here…the General has made that very, very clear. The sooner I'm allowed to leave the better."

"Thank you. You've been most helpful. I'll let you get back to your work." Tarzan tucked the three photos into his shirt pocket, turned and headed out the door.

Once outside, Tarzan glanced around the premises one last time then headed off into the jungle. General Zambossi materialized as if by magic, making a vain attempt at blocking Tarzan's path of progress.

"Where do you think you're going?"

Without breaking stride Tarzan said, "To visit some friends." Before the General could react, his adversary disappeared into the bush. Once again, the General had been bested, and he didn't like it one bit. His frustration kept him from finishing his thought.

It took about a half mile trek into the jungle before Tarzan found what he was seeking; a troop of twelve to fourteen gorillas, gently grazing on the tender foliage and rooting around in the ground and dead timber for juicy succulent grubs.

The lead silverback responded first, jumping to his feet, pounding his chest and letting out a ferocious roar which exposed his long yellow fangs. Tarzan stood his ground. The silverback moved in closer and repeated his display of ferocity. But when Tarzan did not move, the silverback started to sniff the air. He moved closer and sniffed again. Then in the language of the great primates he asked, "Are you Korak? You look like him. You smell like him. But you are not him."

Tarzan responded in the same guttural language. "No. I am not Korak. I am his father."

"Tarzan? Tarzan, Lord of the Jungle."

"Yes."

The silverback turned to his tribe members and spoke to them. With his encouragement, they all came forward to see the great Tarzan, father of Korak.

"We liked Korak. He was kind to us. He brought us good friends. But now they are gone. We miss Korak."

"I miss them also. I seek answers to the mysteries here. I need your help. Will you help me?" The tribe nodded their heads in agreement, and thus proceeded forty-five minutes of grunts and groans that to the uninitiated would have been meaningless, but to Tarzan were confirming answers to his beliefs of what had happened.

HE HAD THE PIECES. He instinctively knew he had the pieces. It was a matter of assembling them together. He was close, very close, but not there yet.

Who is that man? I feel I should know him. The thought kept playing over and over in his mind as he headed back to the waiting car and driver from Fossey's compound. His mind was so engrossed in the man in the picture that he did not sense the three men who attacked him. They were upon him before he knew it. One jumped on his back while another started punching him in the body. The third one held back, looking for an opening.

For most people a three-to-one disadvantage would have proved disastrous, if not deadly. For Tarzan three against one was child's play. He thrust out his right arm to the attacker in front of him. Steel fingers clamped on the attacker's vocal cords. The man could not breathe, nor let out a sound. He just dangled in front of Tarzan, his boots two feet off the ground.

At the same time, Tarzan threw his head backwards, smashing the back of his skull into the face of the assailant on his back. The man screamed in agony and slid off Tarzan's back and fell to the ground, rolling over and over, screaming in pain, blood freely streaming from his shattered nose.

The third man rushed at Tarzan, slashing his knife from side to side. Rather than falling back, as the attacker had expected, Tarzan charged him, catching his wrist in mid-air and with a quick twist broke the man's forearm at the elbow. The man crumbled in throbbing pain.

Tarzan turned to the three men cowering together and said, "Next time you want to act as local hooligans don't wear polished boots. They'll give you away every time. Tell your General I fully enjoyed his sendoff party. And, if I ever see him again, I'll return the favor." He then went on to his waiting car and told the driver to take him to his hotel.

As they drove back to the hotel, and even after he was in his room, he kept being teased, haunted, by the thought of the man he should know but couldn't remember.

He would soon find out.

Chapter 23: *IDENTIFYING FRIENDS AND FOES*

MERIEM LAID ON THE COT in Terrik's tent, waiting to find out her fate. She did not fight to free herself, knowing that such an effort would be fruitless. She might be strong but the ropes holding her she knew were stronger and efficiently tied. She had to wait for a more opportune time to escape.

After what seemed like an eternity, the flap of the tent was pushed aside and Terrik entered. His six-foot four-inch frame towered over her. She started to speak, but before she could get the first word out, he bent over her, getting very close to her face, and whispered, "Shhh. Do as I say, exactly as I say. Scream at me." Meriem looked puzzled, momentarily disoriented by the request and the language in which it was delivered – perfect English. The whisper came again but this time more firmly, "I said scream at me." So, she did.

Terrik stood up and shouted in Swahili, "So you think you are too good for Terrik. We will see about that." And with that he smacked his closed right hand against his open left hand. And then he did it again; while whispering once again, "Scream, then cry."

Meriem picked up on what he was doing and for the next five minutes the two verbally acted out a terrible rape of her. Cloth was ripped, screams bellowed, heavy breathing. She could not figure out what was going on, but knew it to be best to follow along.

Terrik moved to the front of the tent and in one move flipped the tent's flap open. Most of the camp's occupants had been gathered around listening, taking pleasure, with a twinge of jealousy, to Terrik establishing his dominance over the white woman. He looked down at them with a look of disappointment as a father would when casting guilt onto his children for doing the wrong thing. "Kwenda! Una mambo bora kufanya." *Go! You have better things to do.* He waited for them to disperse then turned back into the tent.

He went over to Meriem and said, once again in English, "I'm going to undo your bindings, and they will stay off unless you do something foolish."

She nodded in agreement. The first words out of her mouth were "What was that all about?" followed by "Do you know who I am?"

"Our little play-acting was to keep those renegades in line. My control of you transfers and reinforces my domination over them. That's what I have to do to keep a semblance of order. It was also necessary to make sure none of them will get the idea to attack you. It stamped my label of possession firmly upon you.

"Concerning who you are, yes I know who you are, Madam Clayton. Or, should I call you Lady Greystoke-in-waiting? But I'm sure you don't remember meeting me during a reception at Oxford."

Meriem was dumfounded. How could this near barbarian ever have been at Oxford, except only possibly as an exhibit. "Oxford? How can that be?"

"Quite simple. I am the son of a Bantu chief and my father, along with the local British consulate, saw enough potential in me to insist that I have a 'proper' education in the world in which we are being thrust. You see, I was being groomed to be the tribe's leader...following in my father's footsteps."

"That, out there, is your tribe? That group that attacked, killed and slaughtered my home and my people? I find that all too hard to believe. You're a murderous guerilla. No more. No less. There can be no kingdom in such squalor." At which point she rushed at him and began beating on him with her small fists.

Terrik was unphased by Meriem's outburst. Under the circumstances, and the appearances, her conclusion was reasonable. He reached out and grasped each wrist with his powerful hands and eased her away from him.

"I understand, but things are not what they would appear to be. Sit down and I will clear up matters." Without waiting for Meriem's compliance, he pressed her back to the cot and then down so that she was sitting on it.

"First, it was not my group that attacked your compound. We were nowhere near there when it happened. Plus it would not serve our purpose. The people who attacked your compound were the same people you saw guarding the scientists. My men were ready to capture them when you made an appearance. Makpek in his wisdom decided it was better to capture a white woman than to capture a patrol of our enemies and find out their location and motives. His lower brain overrode his upper one.

"From what we can tell, the patrol is part of a larger group of militants that have recently moved into the area. We think they are a branch of the Zairian army on a special assignment. Something to do with the geologists that they're guarding."

Meriem tried to process this new information. "You're saying the Zairian Army attacked us? That doesn't make sense. We work closely with their government."

Terrick shook his head. "No. What I'm saying is that the soldiers who attacked you were part of a covert group of the Zairian Army. They wear no insignia of any kind to hide their rank and allegiance. They operate very professionally and are too well coordinated to be just another rebel guerrilla group.

"We know the Zairian Army very well. It has been the prime mover in the systematic eradication of our tribe. Its direction is coming from officials at the highest levels. We seek democracy over dictatorship. We did not bribe the electorate, thus we lost the last election, and so now we are being hunted down for extermination. Before the eradification program we were nearly five thousand men, women and children. Now, I lead about three hundred people. We have divided into four different groups, in order to minimize discovery, and we are waiting for the day that we can strike back to victory.

"So, yes we do live in bad conditions, not by choice but by necessity. We can only remain in one location for only one or two weeks at a time. To stay longer would be to greatly increase the risk of discovery. We don't have the luxury of establishing better living conditions. We're nomads, constantly on the run in our own land.

"I am working with other tribes, that have been exiled as we have been, to build a coalition to overthrow the current corrupt government. With you falling into our hands, we may have a quicker way to gaining our goals."

"What do you mean by that?"

"I mean that you're a valuable commodity. You give us the opportunity to recruit the Greystoke family to take part in our cause; plus, if nothing else you are worth a lot of money, money that we can use to buy the guns and ammunition we need to fight on a more even field."

Meriem laughed. "You say you know who I am, then you will know that when my husband, Korak, and my father-in-law learn about my capture they will not leave a stone unturned in finding and freeing me."

Terrik laughed, laughed in Meriem's face. "It's obvious you have not heard."

"Heard what?"

"I think your Korak has his own fine kettle of fish."

Meriem was even more perplexed. "Will you please make some sense and stop talking in metaphors?"

He moved forward and leaned over until his face was within three inches of Meriem's, a grand sneer came over his face. "Your beloved husband is wanted for murdering Dian Fossey." He went on to tell her the rest of the news, grinding every word into her being, crushing the last ounce of feistiness out of her.

"I don't believe it! There's another explanation. There must be. There must be."

"There may be, but I don't think the Rwandans want to hear it. Fossey was too high profile. They need a culprit right now, and your Korak fits the bill because he was the last known person to be seen with her, and now he is nowhere to be found. So if you're thinking he's going to rescue you, you have another thought coming."

Meriem was silent, considering the depth of her dilemma. She knew in her heart that there was another explanation; but at the same time if Terrik's words were true, she could not rely upon Korak for her rescue. She had to handle her own salvation. She assumed a complacent air. "What do you want of me?" she looked back at him with the soft eyes of an antelope. She projected every appearance of cooperation; at the same time beginning to work out her escape plans.

"You will do as I say when around the men. Any sign of a non-compliant attitude and I will have to beat you in front of them; otherwise the men could lose faith in my leadership. They only believe in strength and any defiance on your part will be answered swiftly with the back of my hand, or worse. Have I made myself clear?"

"Yes. I will do what you say. Will I be allowed to move around within your camp, or am I 'confined to quarters' as you military poseurs would say."

The reaction was quick and stinging: a backhand slap across Meriem's face. "I said no defiance or disrespect. Try it again and next time it may be a fist, or a boot. Now do you understand?"

"Yes," as she rubbed the red splotch on her cheek. She would have to keep her feelings in check. "I will do as you say."

"Good. Now we need to..." Terrik did not get to finish his statement as there was suddenly a great shouting coming from the camp. "Stay here. I'll be back. And remember what I've said, or you'll regret it."

Once again Meriem began to ponder her fate, but this time without the hope that Korak or anyone else would be coming to her rescue. She was alone.

Chapter 24: *GRANDSON VS. GRANDFATHER*

KORAK STOOD IMMOBILE STARING at the human interloper. The human did not belong in the sacred amphitheater. Korak admitted to himself that he, Korak, was also human, but that was different. He had returned to the apes, and was now king. This other human was not of the apes. The bulls would not tolerate his presence. As king, Korak must kill this white man. Why then, was he hesitating?

The white man continued speaking, holding out his hand and moving towards Korak. The bulls behind Korak were agitated, waiting for their king to take action. He must act or be challenged. Still, he hesitated...foolishly. Men were not to be trusted. Men had rejected him as a child, driving him away with bullets and spears. He had been lucky to survive. In truth, the apes had also refused him at first. But now he was one of them. They were family. Man was not. He would kill this one now as he had killed others before. Yet still he hesitated.

The howling and snarling of the bulls surged. Several charged Jon, stopping just short to growl and beat their chests, then retreat.

Ashanti straddled a limb above, pointing her notched arrow at the heart of the man Jon had called "Grandfather." She had promised not to kill him but if the fight went against Jon, she would not hesitate to break that promise. The resulting confusion among the bulls would buy her time for escape.

Jon, on the ground, did not understand why Korak was not responding to him. Surely his grandfather recognized him, but he had not moved or spoken, ignoring both Jon and the escalating excitement of the bulls behind him.

Suddenly Korak charged and grabbed Jon tightly in his arms, bending him backwards and to one side, knocking him off balance. His human fangs sank into the neck of his only grandson as Jon's left knee slammed upward into his groin. Korak grunted, releasing Jon and clutching his groin. He stumbled backward and doubled over, pain radiating in waves through his body. Nausea rose as the waves slammed into his gut, seizing his full attention.

The bulls' howling intensified and several again charged Jon only to stop short, and retreat. One bull emerged from the group and beat his chest, eyeing his new king. Korak was vaguely aware of these actions through the red-tinged haze of his pain but could not respond. The bull bared his teeth and charged Jon. This time he did not pull up short.

Too late to dodge, Jon fell to his back in front of the charging bull and swung both feet up into the bull's abdomen, letting the bull's own momentum carry him up and over, somersaulting in the air and hitting the ground with a thud behind Jon. Normally Jon would follow with his own back somersault and land straddling his opponents' chest. Given the bull's immense advantage in strength, he opted out of that, scrambling to his feet, ready for another attack. He was met with stunned silence. The remaining bulls stood stock-still, staring at the winded and motionless bull on the ground.

Jon eyed Korak and the bulls, who quickly got over their shock, and raged and glowered from a distance. A second bull broke from the irate group stomping and snarling his anger. He appeared ready to charge when a roar from Korak stopped him.

Korak's pain had diminished and his vision was clearing. He was furious. This was his kill. He explained it to the bulls in growls and grunts. They retreated to the edges of the clearing, sidelined but continuing to growl, swagger, and charge short distances on all fours.

Korak turned to the white man who was speaking again.

"Grandfather," Jon said, holding out his right hand.

Korak shook his head, attempting to clear the fog. He would not listen. It did not matter. He charged and wrapped his arms around the white man, Jon lowered his hands to Korak's hips, stepped back, threw his left arm under Korak's right arm and pushed it up. He turned his hips into his grandfather and took them both down to the left ending with Jon straddling his grandfather's chest.

"Korak. Stop. It's me. Jon. What are you doing?" Jon wanted to shake him, force him into recognition. He leaned over and grabbed Korak's shoulders, a dangerous move and one he drilled lower belts against making.

Korak did not miss the opportunity and smashed his head up into Jon's, stunning him momentarily. Korak now had the advantage, but again he hesitated, not willing to kill this intruder. He shook his head in confusion, then pushed Jon aside and rose to his feet. Glancing at the agitated bulls, now joined by the bull Jon had tossed, Korak again realized he needed to finish the fight.

Jon rose more slowly, shaking off the fog in his brain. *This isn't working*, he thought as Korak attacked again this time from behind, locking his arms and sinking his teeth into Jon's throat. Jon shifted his right hip into his grandfather's abdomen, bent his knees and rolled Korak over his shoulder onto the ground again. Korak rose quickly and crouched, preparing to charge but waited, more cautious now. His grandson's blood dripped from his lips.

The white man was yelling. Korak recognized the words, knew they were English but pushed them aside. He did not want to hear them. His only concern was killing this man who dared to invade this sacred place. He moved sideways, circling the white man.

Jon wiped the blood from his neck and sighed. He did not want to injure his grandfather, so a strong front, side-snap, or roundhouse kick was out of the question. And his defensive moves could not go on forever. He had no doubt, now, that Korak intended to kill him. The teeth marks and blood on his neck proved that. But, Jon did not think he could kill or seriously injure his grandfather. Anyway, if he did, he would be in deep trouble with the bulls.

He had a pistol that Red Slocum had given him. That might scare the bulls off but Korak might go with them. Firing it would be his last resort. Somehow, Korak *had* to recognize him.

Jon crouched again into fighting stance and circled. Korak moved in closer, grabbing one of the big bones left by the females as he passed the drum. He had a weapon. The white man did not. He charged.

Jon moved back and to the side. Korak matched him move for move, striking out with the bone, meeting only air as Jon dodged and moved towards the drum to acquire a weapon. Korak cut him off. They danced around the circle, one or the other moving into grasp or strike. Few blows landed and those that did were glancing and of small consequence.

Jon was tiring. Something had to break this mystifying stalemate. What could he do to get through to Korak?

"Korak, Grandfather, stop this. Come back with me to Meriem!" No response.

"What happened with Dian?" No response.

"Grandfather, please." Again, there was no response and they continued to circle each other.

Korak wearied of the talk. His mind was picking up familiar words. It had caused him to hesitate in the beginning and he could not permit that to happen again. Perhaps he should call in the bulls. They were stomping and hooting in the background. It would end this impasse. He was ready to do it when Jon spoke again.

"KORAK, MERIEM IS LOST. HELP ME FIND HER."

Korak shook his head. *Meriem.* That name. That name was important. He listened, allowing his brain to make sense of the words that were being said.

Jon spoke again. "Meriem. Your wife. We are searching for her. Help us." Jon held his hand out to his Grandfather.

This was nonsense, Korak thought. The name Meriem meant nothing to him. He prepared to charge again then stopped. He was wrong. She did mean something to him. She meant everything. He knew that but not why. He could not kill the white man until he did. Korak lowered his arms.

"Speak."

Jon did not answer. Korak had spoken in the language of the apes which Jon did not understand.

"SPEAK, OR DIE."

Korak was yelling and facing Jon, so he repeated, "Meriem is lost. We are looking for her. Come with me."

Meriem. The fog parted a bit. Snippets of memories flashed in Korak's mind; a little girl holding a doll with an ivory head and rat skin torso, a little girl being kicked by a savage sheik, and Korak killing him. *Meriem* was his wife. He shook his head trying to clear the fog, trying to find memories, his mind producing only fragments.

The restless bulls moved closer to Jon and beat their fists on their chests. Korak growled viciously at them and they cowered back. He was their king.

Korak needed time to think. He looked at the man and this time saw a man who looked familiar although he could not say how. Meriem was the key. He would go anywhere and do anything for her. Of that he was certain.

Korak turned to the bulls and spoke to them in the growls and grunts of their language. "I must go with this man to find my mate. You must select a new king."

The bulls were stunned. Such a thing had not happened in their memory. No word for abdication existed in their language. They jostled and elbowed each other. *If the king left, who would be king?* Always before a challenger killed the old king and became king. There was always a king. If Korak left, there would be no king to kill. An idea unique to the ape mind occurred simultaneously to three bulls. They moved to the front of the pack, growling and snarling. *Kill the king now. Kill the intruder as well as the she in the tree.*

Korak realized he had only seconds before one of the three bulls decided to challenge him for the kingship. He moved to the center of the clearing and spoke to the whole tribe.

"I am Korak, son of Tarzan, and your king, but I am not like you. I must go with this man," he gestured toward Jon, "to find my mate and return to my own kind. You must choose a new king."

Kerkuk moved out of the pack of bulls to Korak's side. "I go with Korak," he said.

Korak welcomed the ape who had accompanied him across the plains, then turned to Jon and said in English, "Follow us, slowly. Do not run."

Ashanti dropped from the tree to move ahead of Jon. Korak was startled but said nothing. Three humans and an ape left the clearing and the moonlight. Behind them the bulls milled around growling and snarling at each other, wondering who would be the new king.

Chapter 25: *INTERROGATION-GUERILLA STYLE*

TERRIK FOLDED BACK THE FLAP of his tent and stepped out into the common area of the encampment. A returning patrol was pushing and prodding two bedraggled souls into the camp. Their hands were tied behind their backs and a rope looped around each neck ran from one to the other, with each end being held by a patrol member.

The captives were dressed in military fatigues but carried no markings of identification. Terrik approached the patrol leader. "Well, well, what do we have here?"

"Sergeant Boolonie, sir. We came across another group that appeared to be taking some kind of measurements. These along with three others were acting as guards."

"Where are the others?"

"We took them by surprise and some fought back. We captured these two and had to kill the rest. We brought back their equipment. I don't know what it does but it looked important so I thought you would know its worth and what to do with it." Having said that he raised his arm and motioned for two squad members who were in the back of the procession to come forward. Each carried boxes of electronic gear.

"You have brought us a mixed blessing," said Terrik. "We can surely get some fresh information from these two. On the other hand, the main body of their army will be sending out search parties when this group doesn't return. We may have

169

to move camp, but first let's see what these two fine specimens of humanity have to say for themselves. Bring them here."

The two captives were pushed forward until they were directly in front of Terrik. He transformed his face into a deep, deep scowl of displeasure, learned from acting courses at Oxford. The two prisoners shivered in fear. His look was so terrible that they thought they were in the presence of a jungle demon, if not in fact, Lucifer himself.

Giving them time to absorb the full impact of his performance, Terrik said, "I have need of information that you possess. Where is your main campsite? What is it that the scientists you guard are looking for? What is the size of your main body?" He paused, adjusted his face to a new, wiser-looking appearance, then continued.

"I think you know what I want, so which one of you will tell me?" Silence. "Oh, you want to be that way. Fine. We don't have the time to wait, so here's what we're going to do. The first one that answers my questions will live. The other will be hacked to death, losing hands, arms and legs, one at a time." The prisoners' ashen looks radiated their understanding.

Terrik turned to his sergeant. "Take one over there by the latrine and the other," turning in a different direction, "put him by the cook pot. That should conjure up some thoughts."

"Now for you," addressing the prisoners. "You have fifteen minutes to decide if you want to cooperate. That's when I'll come and ask for your answers." And with the wave of his hand, he dismissed them. "Take them away Sergeant."

ON THE MARK OF FIFTEEN MINUTES, Terrik ordered the prisoners to be brought back to his presence. Seconds later the prisoners hovered in front of Terrik waiting their fate. Terrik began his questioning. Each of the prisoners verbally tripped over each other to be the first to give a response.

After twenty minutes of questioning, Terrik was confident that he had all the information that the captives could provide. The army was composed of Zairian Special Forces being led by General Kanka who was making a move to overthrow Sakumbi's government. The main body of troops was encamped near the edge of the jungle, about eighteen miles east-northeast. It numbered around six hundred, the size of a mid-size battalion. The scientists were using a new method to pinpoint the underground location of deposits of gold, silver, uranium, titanium and other valuable minerals. While the General commanded the soldiers, the General seemed to take orders from another...a foreigner described by one of the prisoners as, "A nasty little man that had the darting eyes of a ferret."

Suffering from near exhaustion brought on by their capture and subsequent interrogation, the prisoners looked up at Terrik with the hope of their imminent release. Terrik looked down at them and smiled. "Thank you for being so helpful. You've performed a great service to me and my troops. It is time for your earned rewards, and that presents a problem, who lives and who dies. I guess there is only one way to resolve this."

Before anyone could react, or anticipate what might come next, Terrik drew his 9-mm Glock from its holster and shot each prisoner between the eyes. The bodies momentarily swayed back and forth and then crumbled to the ground in a pool of their own blood.

"Sergeant. Take a few of your men and dispose of these bodies into the jungle. About five miles from here should do. Then, strip them and nail them to trees. Let them be a warning to others that danger lurks in our jungle."

Terrik spat on the bodies, then turned and walked back to his tent. He saw the tent's flap flutter. He smiled to himself. "*Good,*" he thought, "*Madame Clayton had listened, if not seen, the proceedings.*" A small grin crossed his face as he strolled to his tent and the occupant inside. "*That should keep her in line... let her know I'm serious.*"

UPON ENTERING THE TENT he went directly over to his makeshift office; planks of boards resting upon two dilapidated sawhorses comprised his desk, a folding chair probably bought, or stolen, from a discount outlet store, constituted his throne. His concentration was such that he did not even acknowledge Meriem's presence, with which she was just as happy. She shrank into the shadowed far corner of the tent. It was not that she was afraid of this hideous beast that held her captive, it was just that she wanted him to *think* that she was afraid of him.

The desk was piled with maps which Terrik spent the next several minutes studying. Knowing that the camp had to move, he weighed the pros and cons on where to relocate. Should he move farther into the jungle away from the enemy's main camp; or, should he move closer in order to put his small army in the position to launch a surprise attack?

It took a half an hour for Terrik to decide he would move the camp to a well-hidden area within two miles of the enemy's position. It had dense growth and was backed by a canyon that would keep the enemy from surrounding his forces should by chance they be discovered. He looked up from the table, looking across the tent space to Meriem.

"We're moving our camp. But you won't be coming with us."

Chapter 26: *LATE NIGHT REVELATIONS*

TARZAN SPENT AN UNSETTLED NIGHT. Normally he could easily fall asleep, but the image of the other person in the picture with Jack and Dian Fossey kept haunting him. He knew the face. But as hard as he tried he could not attach a name to the face in the photograph.

Ultimately, he fell into a fitful slumber; his body forcing him to surrender to its needs. While he slept, his unconscious mind produced thousands of past images, comparing them to the image he was trying to identify. It looked at facial shapes, facial characteristics, down to even the shape and size of the lips, nostrils and eyes, even the spacing between the eyes. Once a discrepancy was found, the image would be discarded and the next image pulled forth. The process continued nonstop while Tarzan slept.

At 3:30am Tarzan sat straight up in bed. The image found. The face remembered. The name recalled. *But, how was it possible?* Tarzan had seen him killed many years before, being shredded to pieces by the claws of Sheeta. As he shook the sleep from his head, the truth came to him; the person in the picture had to be a descendant. Based upon the estimated age of the person in the photo, he was probably a grandson. The name of the man was different. Chertok, not Rokoff. That could be explained in any number of ways. The scent he could not identify in Fossey's cabin compared closely to that of his former arch-enemy.

Even though it was the middle of the night, Tarzan did not hesitate to pick up the phone and have the hotel operator put through a call to the British Embassy in Zaire. A secretary answered.

"I need to talk to the ambassador."

"I'm sorry but, at the moment, the ambassador is not available."

"Then make him available. Tell him it's Lord Greystoke."

The title got the attention needed. "Yes sir. He said to wake him if you called. Please hold. I'll get him right away."

The right away turned into seven minutes before Ambassador Garner came on the line. "Don't you ever sleep? Do you know what time it is?"

"Yes, to both. Now I need you to check out in *extreme* detail the lineage of one Vladimir Chertok. If I'm right, he's the key to resolving everything."

"Aren't you going to give me any more details to go on? You're already pushing your luck."

"Trust me...one more time. I don't want to tell you more because I don't want to skew the search. Just check him out and get back to me. If I'm right, I'll also need to be on the next plane to Moscow. I await your call." With that, Tarzan hung up.

On the other end, Ambassador Garner looked at the receiver and shook his head from side to side, half in wonderment and half in disbelief. His old friend was pushing the window of their relationship, especially with the latest disquieting news he had received from London. With a shrug of his shoulders, Garner hung up the phone and headed to his office to do what he could to help a friend in a dire strait. Morning was starting early....and it was going to be a very, very long one. As he walked to his office he thought, *"What are good friends for if one can't offer help when a friend needs it? And if there is any friend that needs* my *help, John Clayton surely qualifies."*

IT WAS NEARLY NOON before Garner got back to Tarzan. "I have what you wanted, but I don't see how it will help. The Home Office is getting brutal about why you haven't been put into custody. I've stalled as much as I can."

Tarzan ignored the custody comment. He went to the heart of what he needed to know. "What did you find out?"

"Vladimir Chertok is the only son of Ivan Chertok and Helga Polenski. Ivan's parents..."

Tarzan interrupted. "Who were Helga's parents?"

"The mother was Deniska Vokolesky. She was married to Commissar Vokolesky when Helga was born. She was previously married to...."

Tarzan didn't let him finish. "Is she still alive?"

"Yes...living in Moscow."

"Just as I thought. Do you have an address?"

Garner gave him the address then asked, "What do you mean when you said, 'Just as I thought'?"

"I'll explain later. What about the flight?"

"Bad news. No way. As of twenty minutes ago the Home Office has issued a "find and detain" order on you. It's not safe for either of us to talk any more. As it is, I'm calling you from a clean phone from my club. Be careful my friend. You're trolling in very dark, deep waters. You're on your own."

The line went dead. Tarzan was on his own in a jungle not of his choice.

TARZAN IMMEDIATELY placed a call to Paris. It was answered on the fourth ring by a male voice. "Residence D'Arnot."

"Paul. John Clayton. I could use your help."

"From what I read in the papers you most assuredly need my help."

Paul D'Arnot was the first white man that Tarzan had met. At the time D'Arnot was a lieutenant in the French navy. Tarzan had found him in the jungle and nursed him back to health. They had remained life-long friends. D'Arnot's military career had grown into the diplomatic arena where he eventually became one of the elder statesmen of France. In quiet corners, he was oft times referred to as "the power behind the presidency" because of the weight of judgment that French leaders placed on his astute knowledge, international diplomacy and political awareness.

It took the next twenty minutes for the two longtime companions to update each other on the past events and the current situation. It was obvious that Paul was well-informed and had already begun to be proactive on his friend's behalf.

"I need to get to Moscow. Do you have a way?"

"Yes…Most certainly. As you know I still have top security clearances, plus, as you also know France has many business arrangements with the Soviet Union." He chuckled and said, "We French, we will trade with anyone!

"From where you are, you are about forty-five minutes away from a private airfield that is twenty minutes beyond Kinshasa International. By the time you get there, there will be a Mirage jet waiting for you. It is not Air France, but under the circumstances I'm sure you'll find the transportation acceptable. You have your passport and other necessary papers?"

"Yes."

"Good. You will need them for clearance. In Moscow, there will be no questions asked. You will be taken to our embassy where there will be the papers necessary to successfully change your identity. We need to be on the safe side. Don't know what your nasty British countrymen might try to do with the Russians to detain you."

"Thank you, Paul."

"Most assuredly…Keep in touch. Let me know if you need anything else. *Bonne chance, mon ami.*"

Each hung up.

TARZAN SHOULDERED his backpack and headed to the taxi stand. Three people were ahead of him. As he waited two men came up behind him. He paid no attention to them until they started crowding into him, casually bumping him.

As he got to the head of the line, just as the waiting taxi's back door opened, the men behind him rushed forward grabbing each of Tarzan's arms and at the same time pushing him into the taxi. Then things happened simultaneously.

Tarzan recognized that the driver was not your typical African taxi driver. He was white and wore a shirt and tie. Rather than resisting he stepped forward, pulling the two assailants with him. At the last moment, he ducked his head under the taxi's top and rolled his shoulders forward. The two men smashed into the top of the taxi. Both slumped to the ground, unconscious. Tarzan grabbed each man by his belt and tossed them into the cab. He looked at the driver and said, "Drive…Now… unless you want to join your friends." Tarzan slammed the taxi door shut as he stepped out and the taxi roared out of the lane into mainstream traffic.

Tarzan turned to the stunned concierge of the taxi line and said, "I'll take the next one. That one was too crowded."

The speechless concierge hailed the next cab inline in due haste. He didn't know what was going on and did not want to find out.

Forty-five minutes later Tarzan arrived at the secluded airfield, and true to D'Arnot's word, a French Mirage jet was waiting for him. He generously tipped the cab driver, reminding him that he should forget where he had been. The driver looked at the pound notes, aware of the favorable exchange rate to the Rwandan franc, and was happy to have a lapse of memory.

Tarzan walked over to the hangar where the pilot of the Mirage was standing, in conversation with another gentleman who was dressed all in white, in stark contrast to his dark native skin; obviously, a government representative. Introductions and courtesies were exchanged. Then the representative asked to see some identification. Tarzan handed him his British passport with several hundred pounds purposely tucked inside it. After a courtesy glance, the passport, sans cash, was handed back with the words, "Have a safe journey."

The representative turned and walked away. The pilot nodded toward his plane, and then walked toward it. Tarzan joined him. Next stop...the Soviet Union.

Chapter 27: ESCAPE TO CONFRONTATION

TERRIK CROSSED THE TENT, GRABBING Meriem by the arm, pulled her to her feet and propelled her outside. She didn't resist. In his roughness, he did not feel Meriem remove his knife from the sheath that hung at his side. His mind was concerned with more important, more immediate matters.

"Makpek, come here!" The beckoned looked across the campsite to see who was calling. Seeing it was Terrik, he immediately stopped what he was doing and ran to Terrik's presence. He did not want, nor did he need another reprimand, especially in front of the rest of the men.

"I have a special assignment for you, one that you must be most careful in fulfilling. Do you think you can do this for me?"

"Yes, most certainly!" was his immediate response even though he had no idea what the assignment might be. He squared his shoulders, making him seem a little taller. He was back in Terrik's favor. He couldn't be happier...until he heard the assignment.

"Good. While we're moving the camp, I want you to take Madame Clayton to the safe house on the river. I don't want her placed in danger... nor hurt. She's a valuable asset. Her family will pay a great deal for her safe return. She can bring many Zaires. Keep her safe. Is that clear?"

"Oh yes. Oh yes. Most clear." Makpek struggled to keep his inner joy from showing externally on his face. He would have the woman alone again, and this time he would get his desires fulfilled. This time there would be no interference. No Terrik. She would feel the full thrust of his manhood, the strength of Makpek.

"Excellent. Now get your things and come back here. She will be ready to go when you are. She doesn't have very much to pack." He laughed at his little joke, as he looked at the tattered clothing that clung to Meriem, clothing that barely covered her.

Terrik watched Makpek scurry off to collect his necessities, and then he looked down at Meriem. "I can still see fire in your eyes. Don't even think of trying to escape. It would do you poorly. Try to run and Makpek WILL kill you. Behave and everything will be fine."

Meriem remained silent, striking a most complacent, obedient posture. Terrik misread her passiveness as a sign of agreement when in truth it was her disguise of waiting for the right moment to strike.

THE TRIP THROUGH THE JUNGLE to the river was uneventful. Meriem remained complacent as Makpek forged ahead. The fact that her hands were tied in front of her and that a noose hung loosely around her neck — the other end being held by Makpek — made compliance very easy. She was biding her time, holding her energies, and the stolen knife, in reserve for the best time to strike.

It took two hours before they reached the river. Meriem noted the river was nearing the top of its banks and was churning up brown muck from the insurgent runoff of the snow-capped peaks far to the north. There would be no trying to transverse it. The river offered no means of escape.

Makpek pushed Meriem along the riverbank to a small side pool that was relatively calm. A short distance from it was a small cabin, more of a shack than a cabin that was virtually hidden from view until one was upon it.

He said, "Welcome to OUR new home," as he removed the noose from her neck. He left her hands tied in front. "There is no place to run. We have it all to ourselves." He laughed in anticipation of the fulfillment of his fantasy.

Meriem understood the full meaning of his words. She read the heat of his desires in his eyes. He wanted her and he wanted her now. He stepped toward her. She moved back and to the side, towards the pond. He moved closer to her. She moved closer to the pond. She had a plan, but it would be difficult with her hands tied. She would just have to let events play out, and hope that whatever happened was for the best.

"Now that is not the way to treat your new master. You should welcome me as I'm here to take care of you. You in turn should take care of me." His eyes flared with desire. His body began to shake with anticipated fulfillment.

He lunged at her, but she sidestepped him, and at the same time swung her right leg out to drive her foot into the shin of Makpek's left leg. He stumbled forward, trying to regain his balance. He failed. He tumbled headlong into the pond. He turned and pulled himself up from the muddy bottom. He was drenched in mud from head to toe. He wiped his hands on his pants, then wiped the mud from his eyes. If looks could kill, his glare would have cut her down. He couldn't believe what he saw. Meriem, a woman ablaze with anger, holding an eight-inch knife in her still tied hands. She was crouched in a fighting stance, waiting for his next move.

His grimaced face broke into a broad grin, and he rolled back his head and laughed. "Oh my, I'm too afraid for words. You look so threatening there. You really are ready to battle. Good! I like my women feisty."

He took a step forward to see what she would do. Meriem stood her ground, swaying back and forth, never taking her eyes off him. Something moved under the water around

Makpek, but he was too intent upon attacking Meriem to notice. He reached behind his back and pulled out a 15-inch machete. "You have a knife. Well, I call this a weapon. Drop your toy before I have to cut it away from you." He paused, then continued, "Although, I've never had sex with a one-armed woman. That might be interesting." He started to laugh again but before it came out of his mouth there was a splash around his ankle and his grin turned to a grimace. Instead of a laugh, terror flowed out of his mouth. "Ahhhgh! Ahhhgh!"

The water trashed with turbulence. Makpek began losing his balance. He flailed his arms to keep upright. The effort had only momentary success. He fell back into the churning water. It was only when Meriem saw the silver body and large tail fin did she see the catalyst to the action. It was a giant Goliath Tigerfish, a distant relative of the piranha, capable of killing a man. It must have been in the pool taking a momentary rest from the mainstream fast-moving flow of the river. Makpek's splashing had roused it and the silver bracelet on his ankle had created enough interest for it to attack.

Makpek's kicking and flailing of his arms sent streams of water four to five feet into the air, only intensifying the tigerfish's attack. The water became blood stained as the fish remained clamped on its victim. More large tail fins came into the pond attracted by the blood. Within moments the brown cast of the pond had turned crimson, the thrashing of the water reduced to ripples, followed by a return to tranquility. Makpek vanished, never to be seen again.

Meriem was once again free. Free to find Korak. The feeling was exhilarating.

In the excitement, she had forgotten that her hands were still tied. At first, she tried to maneuver the knife in her hands to a position where she could cut the binding cord. After several minutes of frustration, including dropping the knife twice, she hit upon a better plan. She walked over to a nearby Yuka tree, turned the blade-side of the knife up, and plunged the point of the knife into the tree's trunk. Pressing her right hip against the handle of the knife in order to provide better stability for the knife, she twisted her body so her bound wrists would be over the blade. She positioned the blade between her two hands and began to slowly move the restraining bindings against the blade. Individual strands snapped until the bondage gave way and her hands broke free.

She backed away from the tree and the embedded knife, rubbing her wrists to regain full circulation in them. Now she was truly free. She pulled the knife from the tree and turned to go to the cabin to see what supplies she could use on her renewed journey. Before she could take a step, she stopped in shocked disbelief.

"Very good, Madame Clayton. That was most entertaining, plus you saved us the trouble of disposing of your, how should I say…your escort." It was the voice of the lead man of the four armed men standing in front of her. They had obviously been in the cabin all the time.

"Ah, I can tell by the look on your face that you are disappointed in your new surroundings. Let me reassure you that you are safe with us. No harm will come to you, at least not from us. You may not know it but there is a grand reward for your safe capture, and we intend to collect it."

"A reward? For my capture? I don't believe it! Who is offering such a thing? Your fatigues speak nothing about who you are or your associations. Who are you?"

"You need not worry yourself about who is offering such a reward." Changing subjects, "We are soldiers of the new revolution, freedom fighters for the new government."

"Then you're the people who attacked my home? The people who killed my friends? The people who slaughtered our livestock? Are you those demons?" Bitterness rested on each letter of each word. She lost all control of her senses and the situation she was in!

"We were only following commands because those who objected were shot on the spot. We chose to live. Do not hold it against us. We are only tools in their hands. We must do as told…or suffer the consequences."

Thrusting her hands on her hips as the only act of resistance available to her under the circumstances, she said, "And who are these people that have such a command over you? I would like to meet them."

"Oh, you will, you will."

The air hung heavy in silence. Meriem said nothing, but retained her hostile body position. Hearing no response and seeing her continued hostility the lead soldier said, "So, would you like to travel peacefully with us, or will you have to once again be bound up like a pig being led to market? The choice is yours. What will it be?"

All of Meriem's resistance evaporated. While she wanted to stand and fight, the words of her father-in-law resounded in her head, "There is a time to fight, and there is a time to wait to fight. Save your energies for the time to fight." Heeding Tarzan's words, Meriem dropped the knife and said, "You'll have no trouble from me, but before we go can we have something to eat? I'm starved."

The four burst into smiles, not because of Meriem's cooperation, but because each could see the great reward waiting for them. And, like most men, each counted their share to be greater than the others.

After a quick meal, Meriem and her four captors set out to meet the person or people behind the assault on the Claytons. She didn't know how or when, all that she knew was that she would find a way for escape and revenge.

Chapter 28: *GORILLAS VS. GUERILLAS*

THE JUNGLE IS TREACHEROUS AT NIGHT, especially at ground level. Hunters gifted with night vision seek easy prey and it is only the brave or foolish humanoid that tempts fate on the ground. The three humans and the ape had little choice. The sacred amphitheater had ceased to be a place of sanctuary for Korak and Kerkuk, and had never been for Jon and Ashanti.

Travel through the trees was fastest and safest, and the ape had no objection. Jon and Ashanti, however, had never traveled that way and there was neither time nor moonlight to teach them. The full moon was approaching the horizon and would soon set.

Korak was surprised at Jon's inability to use the trees in this manner and he began to question the young man's story. Surely his own grandson would be able to race through the canopy.

"We need a ride." Korak said once they were away from the clearing. He cupped his hands and sounded a call into the jungle night. An answering call came quickly. "Come. There is a trail over here." He took Ashanti's flashlight and set off.

Korak was still foggy. He felt like he was walking through a mist where pieces of memory faded in, and then as he reached for them, faded out again. He was not sure who this young white man was but he had information about Meriem and that was sufficient for the moment. Of the trail, he was certain. It was well used by both man and beast. Within

moments the sounds of something large thrashing and trounc-
ing vegetation could be heard coming their way. Korak smiled.

The gleaming eyes and gray trunk of Tantor revealed
themselves in the glow of the flashlight. Jon and Ashanti
jumped off the trail as he brushed past them. Korak laughed.
"Tantor is friendly. He is our ride."

At a word from Korak, Tantor raised his back leg and
lightly twisted his tail, forming two steps that Korak used to
climb onto the elephant's back. Jon and Ashanti watched in
apprehension as Korak settled behind the big ears and turned
to the others.

"The back leg and tail is easiest. But Tantor will also
lift you up with his front leg if you prefer."

Jon turned to Ashanti and shrugged. "After you," he
said, waving his arm towards the raised back leg. Ashanti
frowned then stepped on Tantor's leg and clambered to the top.
Jon quickly followed. Only the ape declined, preferring to make
his own way through the high canopy.

Korak used Ashanti's flashlight to spot adjoining trails
and directed the big elephant toward the village. The three
humans were safe up top, swaying with the lumbering elephant's
passage through the jungle. Only a desperate predator would
attack a full-grown elephant that could stomp it into mush in
moments or impale the attacker with his tusks. On this night,
none felt inclined to try. Even Numa, the king of beasts, found
sustenance in other prey.

Korak rode Tantor in front and picked Jon's brain. He
was incessant and demanding, asking the same question in
different ways, repeating them over and over. Jon knew he was
being interrogated and that Korak did not believe him.

For Korak, the fog continued to clear with only tanta-
lizing tidbits of memory. He recalled, as far as he could tell,
most of his life in the jungle and with Meriem. He remembered
his parents, Tarzan and Jane. He had no memory, however, of

his son Jackie, or his supposed grandson, Jon, now seated behind him. He was frustrated.

It was worse when Jon told him about Dian Fossey. He had no memory of her and now, this young man informed him he was wanted for her murder. He could not deny what he could not remember. He had killed many men in the life he did remember, but only when he had no other alternative. It was the way of the jungle he had learned from Tarzan; when there was no escape, kill or be killed.

As the night progressed, bits and pieces about the compound came back to him. Off in the distance, a lion roared, and suddenly a specific memory rose clearly in his mind. Korak turned and flashed the light past Ashanti into Jon's face.

"Jonny," he said, and then returned to facing forward. "Now I remember you. You were that little pipsqueak that got away from Nubiby and met up with Numa. Your father and I had to pull your young butt out of the fire. What were you seven...or eight?"

The lion, Jon thought. *Of course, he would remember that.*

"That was quite a performance. You weren't around much after that. Lion put the fear of the jungle into you, did he?"

Jon didn't answer. This was not a conversation he wanted to have, ever, but especially now in the presence of Ashanti.

"Jonny, you still back there?"

"It's Jon, Grandfather."

Korak paused, grinning to himself. "Yes, I suppose it is."

They continued in silence, swaying atop the plodding elephant. Korak relished the returning memories streaming through his mind, and, towards dawn, finally remembered that he had not killed Dian Fossey.

Dawn came swiftly. In another hour, the trail turned sharply and Korak spoke softly to Tantor, who stopped and allowed them to dismount. Korak stepped on a raised front leg and was lowered to the ground. Ashanti and Jon followed suit. The ape appeared, gliding down from the treetops. The village was close by and Korak led the way as Tantor departed down the trail trumpeting as he went.

They could smell the Waziri's cooking fires before they saw the huts. Suddenly men with machine guns slipped out of the foliage and surrounded them. The guns were quickly lowered when they recognized Korak, and escorted the party into the village.

Masamba, one of the Waziri who had left the compound with Jon's group two days prior, had found news of Meriem. He and Tafiri had come across pygmies who claimed to have seen a white woman fitting her description being taken to a guerrilla camp a few kilometers from the village. The two had returned to the village where Masamba had stayed to wait for Jon. Tafiri and several Waziri had gone to find the camp, and to follow it if necessary. Guerrilla camps were notorious for moving around.

Korak and Jon conferred with the village chief. The chief had sent warriors on reconnaissance in the days after the destruction of the Clayton compound but they had found little information – the perpetrators appeared to descend suddenly as if from nowhere, and then disappear as quickly into obscurity. The Waziri buried their dead and began to search for survivors, while making ready for war.

The chief first thought the local guerrillas were involved, but after his and the other chiefs' warriors interrogated all the small camps of rebels hiding in the jungle, he discovered they too were surprised at the attack and very open with their information. They were supremely aware of the Claytons' power, not to mention the benefits reaped by their presence. It appeared, the chief thought, that an outside player had arrived, a very secretive player. There were rumors of a large military encampment but no one could say what military. Waziri warriors were combing the area for any sign of it but so far had found nothing.

While they were talking, Tafiri had radioed back that they found the guerilla camp, and the rescue of Meriem again became the priority.

Several hours later, Jon, Korak, Ashanti, Kerkuk, Masamba, and a band of Waziri met up with Tafiri's men in a small natural clearing several hundred yards off an elephant trail. The guerrillas were less than half a kilometer away. Korak and Kerkuk took to the trees to get a read on the camp.

There was no sign of Meriem but Korak thought he recognized one of the guerrillas. He then considered just walking into the camp, but they were heavily armed and possibly held Meriem captive. Though his blood boiled at the thought, Korak would never endanger her. He opted for a tactical approach.

When they returned to the clearing, Korak drew a scratch map in the dirt showing the location of sentries and he and Jon plotted the operation. They would wait for morning and go in at dawn when the sentries were most likely to be drowsy, if not asleep, and the others in the camp off guard. Korak radioed back to the village. He wanted a few more villagers with guns.

Just after dawn the next morning, the Waziri surrounded the guerilla camp. The sentries were either surprised by a man and an ape dropping out of the trees on top of them, or rudely awakened with the muzzle of an AK-47 tickling their noses. At a whistle from Korak, the Waziri moved swiftly into the camp, guns ready. There was no need, really, as the camp was asleep, one lone man up and feeding a fire.

Korak fired his revolver in the air. The guerrillas jerked awake and grabbed for their guns; then, grasping the situation, slowly let them drop. Their leader burst out of his tent, yelling at his men, then stopped abruptly seeing the circle of Waziri. He recognized Korak immediately. He sighed and lowered his gun.

Korak also lowered his gun but signaled the others to remain ready. He and Jon approached the leader.

"I know you, Terrik isn't it?" Korak said.

"It is. And you are Korak, son of Tarzan and a Clayton. Why are you here? We are not the ones who attacked your compound."

"That may be. Or it may not," Korak said. "I am looking for my wife. Have you seen her?" Korak watched the leader closely noting how his eyes shifted at the question. *He's going to lie*, Korak thought.

Terrik considered professing no knowledge of her, then thought better of it. The Claytons were powerful and likely to discover she had been here. They would not know his plans of course. He decided part of the truth was his best choice.

"She was here. We found her in the jungle, lost. I sent her to a safe house by the river…a day's journey from here. My man has not returned or called in. He must have been killed. She was alive when she left here, but I suspect I know who has her now."

Korak's first urge was to kill him. He handed his gun to Jon thinking how much he would enjoy squeezing the life from this scum. Then, Jon's calming hand on his arm stopped him from doing just that.

"Granddad, later might be wiser."

Korak stopped. Jon was probably right. He took his gun back and leaned into Terrik's face. "Tell me everything you know about those who took her. Leave nothing out."

Chapter 29: *KORAK CAPTURED*

JON FOLLOWED KORAK INTO THE CANOPY. They were bound for the Zairian Special Forces encampment. Terrik's information combined with reports from the local Waziri chiefs had led them to believe that these were the attackers of the compound as well as the captors of Meriem. Terrik was certain of their identity. He had once trained with those forces.

Jon had never traveled through the trees, but Korak had agreed to teach him. He silently thanked his father again for his martial arts training. His balance was superb and necessary at heights 200 feet above the ground as he moved from tree to tree, stepping or swinging onto branches that dropped, swayed, and bounced. Black and white Colobus monkeys followed him for a way, chattering constantly. *Cheering me on,* he thought. *Or, perhaps just laughing.*

Korak had demonstrated the rudiments of canopy travel and stayed long enough to see that Jon had the basics. Then he sped ahead through the trees toward the camp. Jon and Kerkuk followed at a slower pace, Kerkuk's keen senses keeping them on Korak's trail.

The jungle thinned out and the canopy lowered as Korak approached the plains. The army camp was well camouflaged in the tall grasses. He would not have found it had he not known where to look.

Korak stopped in a fifty-foot tree that provided a view of the base and waited for Jon and Kerkuk. He focused the binoculars he had borrowed from Terrik on the camp. It was an amazing job of concealment. The camp was virtually invisible in the eight-foot tall elephant grass. The tents were dyed to blend in with the grasses. Even the jeeps and trucks were painted to conform. A helicopter sat idle off to one side, its blades drooping like wilted leaves. He could see no sentries but assumed they were there. An army careful enough for this kind of concealment would post sentries. *Where were they?*

He scanned the patches of trees scattered over the plains, all at least fifty yards from each other. A flash of sunlight grabbed his attention and he brought the binoculars back to a tree on his far left. Another glint and he found the source. A man with a rifle across his lap straddled a low branch, legs drooping like low hanging fruit. He could not make out the gun. This would not be the only sentry.

By the time Jon and Kerkuk arrived, he had found five other sentries. There was one near them on the jungle floor and they counted themselves lucky not to have stumbled on him. Korak did not believe he could enter the camp in daylight without being detected.

They had seen enough and returned the way they had come, Jon making better time, almost keeping up with Korak by the time they reached Terrik's camp.

Korak drew a map in the dirt showing Terrik the basics of the camp. Fifty tents were pitched in a rectangular shape with the biggest tent, ten times the size of the others, in the center. He thought this was probably the mess tent. There had been no cooking fires. There was no fence. He figured four men per tent and estimated 2000 men inhabited the camp, although he had seen only twenty or so moving around.

"A surprise attack in daylight is impossible," Korak said. "The camp is too far from the jungle and the sentries are well-placed. The grass will not protect us."

"A night attack, then," Terrik said. Korak shook his head.

"We do not know where Meriem is or if she is there for certain. Nor do we know for certain how many men they have. It would be folly to attack now. They might kill her."

"Not if we attack from within. We have more than a hundred men with your Waziri here now, and ready to go. The soldiers in that camp are protecting several sites being used for some type of scientific research or exploration. My men can easily attack the outlying sites, where their security is minimal, no more than three soldiers at each. We can use their trucks and uniforms to gain entrance to the camp and attack from within and outside at the same time. As your Waziri arrive, some can be deployed to these sites alongside my own men."

"No. I won't risk Meriem. I will sneak in at night. If I can rescue her, I will. If not, we will have more information. Do not attack. Do not alert them until I have Meriem. And do not use the radios. If they capture any of your men or the Waziri they will have their radios. I need total surprise."

Terrik was opposed. He had recognized the camouflage worn by his captives. It was camouflage given to the Zairian military years ago by the Russians, but had never been issued. He was certain of this as he had once been an officer of the Zairian military. That was before the President Joseph Pelo Sakumbi, in a pique of paranoia, accused Terrik's commanding general and officers of coup plotting. They had been stripped of all rank and privileges and sent back to their villages.

There had been no plots. Banishing them to their villages was a mistake. There were no opportunities in rural Zaire save subsistence farming and hunting. Many of the men immediately joined guerrilla groups or became poachers. There were plenty of both kinds of groups from which to choose. Terrik had resisted until his village was destroyed by the army for which he had once fought. He never knew why, but suspected Sakumbi's hand as several other villages of disgraced army officers had been simultaneously targeted, including that of his commander. Terrik's village had been wiped away, his family slaughtered. Six men of the village survived because they were away rebuilding another village on the night of the attack. Four of them were now part of Terrik's band. There would be an attack and there would be vengeance.

He wanted to do it immediately. He didn't much care if Meriem was there or not, although he was wise enough to not speak that thought. He suspected, incorrectly, that once Korak rescued Meriem, he would be less inclined to attack and Terrik would lose any influence with the Waziri, whom he knew were intent on vengeance. He pretended to agree with Korak, silently vowing to send patrols to those scientific sites after Korak left. But Terrik was not inclined to delay his retribution.

Korak, Kerkuk, Jon and Ashanti – because she refused to be left behind – returned to the Zairian camp just before dark. They stayed high in the canopy, Ashanti trailing, aided by Kerkuk. Ashanti was determined. If Jon could travel through the tops of the trees as an ape did then she certainly could master the technique as well. She was slow, however, slower than she had imagined she would be. Kerkuk grabbed her more than once and carried her when the vines were sparse or the branches far apart. She resisted the first time, pushing and punching him, refusing to be helped, until she came close to falling and was saved only by the swift wrapping of a furred arm around her waist.

They arrived in the early morning, and waited in the top of the canopy until dark and the camp was quiet. They watched flashlight-carrying sentries exchange places, allowing them to pinpoint all the guard posts.

Korak, finally satisfied that the camp was asleep, dropped to the ground. He was clad only in loincloth. He carried an AK 47 and three knives, two for throwing and one for hand-to-hand combat if it came to that. He crept slowly through the tall grass staying close to the ground. The camp had no fence. He reached the first tent and slunk slowly around it. The center part of the camp was deserted.

A sentry stood beside the entrance to a tent directly behind the mess tent, granting some importance to it. Perhaps he guarded a weapons cache or a commander's tent, or perhaps a tent of captives. Korak moved back out to the grasses and around the camp past the sentry. He saw no other people. Once he was well past the sentry he moved silently through the camp to the back of the tent. He lay flat on the ground and attempted to raise a piece of the canvas but it was staked firmly to the ground. Finally, he pulled a knife and slashed an opening. He opened the slit slightly to see inside, then wider. Suddenly a flashlight clicked on and Korak found himself looking directly into the barrel of an AK-47.

Behind him, he heard, "Welcome to our camp, Mr. Clayton. I have been looking forward to this meeting."

Korak rose to his feet and turned to face the voice. He did not recognize either of the two men standing before him. The one holding the gun was white, possibly European. His accent was Russian. The other man was African. Behind him, he felt someone taking his knives, gun and binding his hands.

The Russian spoke to the other man. "Is this the man you are looking for?"

"No. The one I want is young."

Korak was taken to a tent at the back of the camp where he was pushed into a chair and his hands tied behind it. Another European entered. Korak immediately recognized him - Vladimir Chertok, the Russian official from Dian Fossey's cabin - her killer. Enraged, Korak launched himself from the chair, slipping his arms up and over the chair back, and shoved his shoulder into Chertok's chest.

Fortunately for Chertok, four guards entered just as the two hit the ground. One of the four yelled for help and Korak was soon chained to a metal post on the floor. The chain terminated in a tight metal collar around his neck. His hands were tied behind him and his legs bound tightly together.

Chertok had risen slowly, dusting himself off.

"Jack Clayton," he said, then kicked him in the stomach. Korak grunted.

"You should be in jail. How did you avoid that?"

Korak did not answer. Chertok dragged a chair over to his captive and straddled it. He looked down at Korak and smiled.

"Well, Mr. Clayton?"

Korak remained silent.

"I see. We will persuade you to talk if you insist. It is unimportant how you avoided the Rwandan police. I shall turn you over to them in due time. What I want to know now is the location of your grandson and your father. They are the only remaining Claytons, on the loose, shall we say."

Korak absorbed this information. It meant Meriem was probably here and Jane as well.

He broke his silence. "You have Jane and Meriem." It was a statement…not a question.

"I do. I do. Not far from here. And I assure you I shall not hesitate to … use them."

"You have made a grave mistake. Neither Tarzan nor I will rest until we have them back and you are dead."

The Russian laughed. "Yes. Your devotion to your mates is legendary, as are your abilities. But I would say, at the moment, those abilities are a bit restrained." The Russian was enjoying himself. He only wished his grandmother were here to enjoy it with him. Korak was silent.

Chapter 30: INSIDE A CERAMIC CELL

JACKIE CAST A LONG LOOK back at Ian as the guards led him away from the processing center to his new temporary residence, a cell in The Old Bailey courthouse, which along with the built over Newgate Prison was the center of the criminal justice system in Britain since the 16th century. They passed through one iron door to enter a corridor lined with other iron doors on either side. They had entered the "cell block." They passed doors that were closed, hearing an occasional shuffling noise coming from behind.

Then they stopped in front of an open door. It opened onto an eight by ten-foot room whose floor and walls were entirely of white four by eight-inch ceramic tile. The tile climbed the twelve-foot wall and spread across the ceiling. There was one ceiling-mounted light fixture holding two glowing fluorescent tubes. It too was white and encased in a wire mesh. There was a camera in each corner providing the guards a total view of the cell and occupant at all times.

The floor was not level. It had a three percent slant down from the outside walls to the center where a drain resided. Jackie surmised the cell was designed that way so it could be easily hosed down. Its design made Jackie wonder if, besides the cell, the residents were hosed down in the same way.

The only adornments to the room were a steel toilet in a corner; a steel sink the size of a drinking fountain; and a ceramic projection from the wall. By the fact that there was a folded blanket resting at one end Jackie correctly surmised that this was for all given purposes a bed. "This is your new home," said the lead guard. "Make yourself comfortable. You'll be here a while."

Jackie couldn't believe the starkness of his circumstances. He stood in the doorway as his eyes swept the room left to right and then back again. He thought, "*From penthouse to penal house in short order.*" He raised his handcuffed wrists to the lead guard and said, "At least take these off."

The guard snapped back at him. "Get this straight. Right Now! You don't give orders here. You take them, from me, or him," pointing at the other guard, "or anyone else in here. You may have been a big cheese out there, but in here, you're nothing. Don't say another word."

Jackie, momentarily stunned, quickly recovered, realizing this was not a time or place to argue. He shuffled over to the bed and sat down. The lead guard turned to the other guard, held out a key and said, "Here, go ahead and take off his cuffs… and the shackles."

When the other guard finished, the lead guard said, "You better take that leg brace off too. Don't want him to get any grand ideas about using it as a weapon on one of us."

"Don't. Please, don't. You took my wheelchair and my cane. How am I going to walk? I NEED THE BRACES!"

The lead guard moved forward, bent over Jackie, swung his right arm, hand balled into a fist, in an arch as if he was about to deliver an upper cut to his ward's chin. The fist stopped just shy of Jackie's face. "I TOLD YOU, you don't give orders, WE DO. Next time my fist might not be able to stop so quickly. The braces comes off! Guard safety comes before your comfort."

The other guard quickly removed the braces without any further resistance from Jackie. He gathered up the shackles, cuffs and braces and headed out the cell door. The lead guard followed, pausing at the cell door to say, "If you need anything, just ring for room service, your Excellency," sarcasm dripping from his every word. The iron door banged shut, followed by the slamming of the three deadbolts into place and finally the click of the lock being engaged. Jackie was alone…to ponder his fate.

THE FIRST NIGHT held little comfort. While the overhead light was dimmed, it wasn't extinguished. It seemed the lower the brightness, the more intense the buzzing it generated. The raised slab, jokingly called a bed, was cold and hard, the blanket scratchy. Everything was compounded by the small slot in the door being periodically opened, metal grating on metal. It seemed its opening was synchronized with his every attempt to close his eyes.

Jackie had heard the first moments of confinement in a penal system were aimed at demoralizing and dehumanizing prisoners. The goal was to break any hostility or latent resistance the prisoner might have as quickly as possible. Hearing about it and experiencing it were two different things.

At a little after nine in the morning Jackie was awakened by the "peek-a-boo" slot scraping open and rapidly slamming shut, immediately followed by the deadbolts being disengaged and the definite opening of the lock. He sat up not knowing what to expect next.

The door swung open. Two guards stepped forward, followed by a third person. "You have a visitor." They moved aside and Ian stepped forward.

"I thank you gentlemen. We'll require a few moments of privacy. Please be sure the audio and video are turned off for the duration of my visit." Having concluded, Ian struck his most lawyerly imposing of poses and stared at the guards. Each guard looked at the other, shrugged their shoulders as if on cue, and withdrew from the cell, closing and locking the door behind them.

Ian walked over to Jackie. "How are you? You look hellish."

"I feel like it. Every time I started to fall asleep they'd do something to keep me awake. They're a bunch of…."

"Don't say it. They could be listening."

"Okay." Looking at the ceiling cameras, "I understand." Jackie changed subjects. "What have you learned about WHY I'm in here?"

"First off, I've gotten them to expedite the Committal Procedure on the charges they're planning to bring. Not only are they not pretty, they're outrageous at the same time."

"Give me the worst."

"You're going to be charged with high crimes against the crown."

"WHAT?!"

"You heard me. In essence...Treason."

"On what grounds?" Jackie was practically screaming. He couldn't believe what Ian was saying.

"Their claim is that The Trust, with your knowledge and consent, has been funneling monies to various terrorist groups...the most important one, in their eyes, being the IRA." Jackie started to interrupt, but Ian held up his hand to stop him. "There's more. They claim that they have rock-solid evidence, and a star witness. When I asked who, they wouldn't say."

Jackie's business mind kicked in. He forgot his circumstances and focused on the situation. "But who *is* their witness? That's the key! Where's the so-called paperwork to back up their claim?"

"They won't say now. But they'll have to produce it all at the Committal Procedure."

"When?"

"Because of the serious nature of the charges, and because we want to deal with it in a most expeditious manner, we've mutually agreed upon holding it next Monday. At which time I expect we can get you out of here and put all this nonsense to rest."

"Why do all barristers use a dozen words when you can use two." He didn't wait for an answer. He already knew the answer, barristers and all attorneys liked to hear themselves speak. And the more multi-syllable words used the better. They continued their conversation for several more minutes, trying to set strategy for the forthcoming hearing.

The guards returned. It was the lead guard who spoke, "Time's up."

Jackie looked at Ian. "What do we do in the interim?"

Ian stood up, looked at Jackie and said, "You sit and wait until the hearing while I go save your neck. Hopefully the Committal Procedure will be the end of things. If it isn't, we'll at least know which way to go. Get as much rest as possible. Do what they tell you. Get focused." Jackie nodded his willingness to comply.

As the cell door swung shut, Jackie began to refocus his thoughts. He had the fight of his life ahead of him and he knew he had to be ready. His family's honor, and fortune, rested upon it!

AFTER THE FIRST DAY events fell into a routine. The sleep deprivation and other harassment stopped. Other than normal day-to-day matters - delivery of meals and routine inspections - Jackie was left to his own means. At first, he sat for hours on his bed thinking what he could do, thinking who might be behind the scheme to destroy The Trust, thinking whether Jon had somehow lived, and where Tarzan, Jane, Meriem and Korak might be, and why he hadn't heard from them.

The thinking was driving him crazy. He soon realized he needed to balance his thinking with physical activity. He set about to strengthen his crippled leg. He thought it hopeless, but at least it was an activity. He paced the cell, stepping forward on his good leg then pulling his bad one forward, firmly planting it to allow the good leg to come forward. At first, he leaned against the wall for balance. Then he tried stepping away from the wall. The first time he made it three steps before collapsing.

He crawled over to the bed, pulled himself up and started over again.

He supplemented his feeble walks by sitting on the bed and lifting his bad leg with his arms. Slowly he felt strength flowing into the muscles. He tried to do leg lifts without the assistance of his arms. On the first try, the foot barely cleared the floor. One would have been hard pressed to pass a piece of paper between the sole of his foot and the floor. He didn't let that discourage him. He tried again and again until he could raise the leg level with the bed. He worked himself to near exhaustion before stopping. And once rested, he attacked it again. He became a man possessed.

In the end, he had worked out a routine. He would rise before the morning meal and do leg lifts until he was soaked in sweat. The time after eating breakfast he spent thinking, letting his meal digest; then he would once again commence with his walking. Think. Exercise. Think. Exercise. That became his everyday regimen from early morning into the late hours of the night.

THE DREAMS STARTED the very first night. Not full-length dreams. More like flashbacks, flashbacks to the traffic accident that crippled him...the one where Irene died...the one that would forever haunt him. If he had been more careful... had he not had that extra drink...she'd still be alive. Her death was HIS fault, his burden for eternity. His crippled leg the forever testimony to his carelessness.

The first flashback was more of a blur than detail. They were returning from Jon's high school graduation. For no apparent reason the car suddenly swerved out of control. He tried to straighten it out. He failed. It smashed into the rock wall that comprised the inner edge of the road. He heard the crunching of metal, followed by sirens. Later, sometime later, he was told Irene was dead.

The second dream brought out more details. Irene and Jackie had been arguing over Jon's public schooling, where he should go for his next stage of education. Jackie said Jon should have a say. Irene disagreed. Then the crash and the same details repeated.

It was the third night and the ninth flashback that full disclosure happened. They were driving away from Jon's graduation, leaving Jon to continue to celebrate with his friends. Jackie and Irene were headed back to the house in the mountains that they had rented for their brief stay. The road was slick from an earlier rain. Both Jackie and Irene had too many drinks. Little was said until Irene brought up where Jon should continue his education. Irene was insistent and when Jackie said Jon should have a say in where he should go, Irene began shouting; how he never agreed with her, how if she said black he would say white. Jackie couldn't placate her. She was out of control, her drunkenness sending her over the proverbial edge.

Suddenly Irene was beating on Jackie's shoulder with both fists, cursing him, his family and their way of life. The car entered a curvy section of the road. Jackie pushed Irene away, back to her side of the car. She became a hellcat. She lunged back at him. Her right hand grabbed the steering wheel. Jackie pushed her back again. He tried to slow down, to get off to the side of the road where he could talk some sense into her. As she fell back she maintained her grip on the steering wheel. The turning force ripped it out of Jackie's hands. The front end of the car bolted to the right smashing into the granite rock wall that made up the right-hand curb. It ran up the side of the wall and then rolled over, sending the occupants flying. It rolled a complete three hundred sixty degrees, miraculously landing upright. Three tires blew out. Jackie was groggy. He looked over at Irene. She wasn't moving. Then he passed out. The next thing he remembered was the arrival of the ambulance followed by the news that Irene was dead... her neck broken.

The revelation was electrifying for Jackie. He *hadn't* killed Irene; HER reckless behavior had caused the accident...

not his. She almost killed him. It was *not* his driving that had caused the accident. She had. It was a moment of revelation that freed Jackie from his guilt. Jackie was transformed...freed from the chains of the past.

The next morning Ian arrived to see a totally different person than he had seen prior. Ian had to take a second look. The angry person Ian had become so accustomed to was gone. Ian couldn't help but comment.

"Jackie. You've changed. How? Why? What happened?"

"For now, let's just say I had some good news. Nothing related to this ...Just good, very good news of a personal nature." Jackie quickly changed the subject.

"Do I have to go into court looking like this, and in handcuffs?"

"No. I brought you a suit that Louise picked out from your closet. By the way, she's doing a grand job of keeping everything on an even keel. And no, there won't be any cuffs or shackles. I've talked at least a modicum amount of sense into the opposing Queen's Counsel.

"So, tomorrow we end this cesspool of malicious accusations and get you back to the real world. Or, have you found happiness in these humble surroundings?" Ian laughed at his own joke, his belly oscillating up and down like a "Slinky" tumbling back and forth from hand to hand.

Jackie frowned. "And I pay you for this?" Then he broke into a sly smile. "Get me out of here tomorrow and you can have my next-born child. I'm ready to leave." And with that Jackie rose up from the bed and walked across the floor. It was a slow walk, emphasized by a pronounced dragging of one leg, but it was a walk.

Ian looked on in disbelief. For once he was speechless. Jackie nearly burst into laughter at his silent barrister. "Pick up your bulging body and go do your thing. I'm ready to be extricated. I'll see you in court tomorrow...and you better be good!"

"You will indeed see me in court and I will be more than good, I'll be supreme. Start packing your bags." Ian walked over to the door, pounded on it twice and shouted, "I'm ready. Let me out." Within seconds the door opened and Ian stepped through it. As he walked down the corridor, past the other cells, he thought to himself, "*I better be supreme if Jackie is ever going to see more than four walls.*"

Chapter 31: *JUNGLE FULL OF GUERILLAS*

BACK IN THE CANOPY, Jon and Ashanti could see movement in the camp. It was too dark to see details but there was too much noise to be due only to Korak.

"I think he's caught," Jon said.

"I think you're right. Now what?"

"You stay here with Kerkuk in case Korak returns. I am going back for Terrik. I begin to like his 'Trojan Horse' idea."

"You want to attack this place?"

"No. Not really. If you have a better idea, now would be the time."

Ashanti sighed, and shook her head.

The gibbous moon was bright enough for Jon to find his way back to Terrik's camp through the treetops, although it took him considerably longer than one of his grandsires. Nevertheless, another generation of Claytons traversed the high canopy of the jungle.

An hour later a helicopter passed overhead traveling from the direction he had just come. He watched its path toward the mountains until it disappeared. He then continued on, arriving back at the campsite shortly after dawn.

Terrik was thrilled to finally have an attack in the works. The patrols he had sent out earlier had returned with two trucks and miscellaneous supplies, including several guns and ammunition from the science camps. He ordered his men to pack up. They followed Jon and the Waziri back to the enemy camp, arriving in the late afternoon.

Jon moved ahead and called to Ashanti with birdcalls she had taught him. No response. After several attempts and no answer, he took to the trees but she was not where he had left her. Nor was Kerkuk. He looked out to the plains. The camp was gone. He was astounded and returned to Terrik.

The whole group then walked out to the campsite. Nothing was left but imprints in the grass where tents had stood. Tire tracks led toward the mountains.

"Where is she? Did they get her? Did she follow them? And where is Kerkuk?" Jon paced the empty camp frustrated at the absence of information.

Terrik, frankly, did not care. She was a woman, not his woman, and a pain in the ass besides. Good riddance. He was equally glad to be rid of the ape that intimidated his men.

He shrugged. "If we leave now we can reach the mountains tomorrow latest. The PRP operate from there and they have no love for the General either. They know everything that goes on in the mountains. If the army went there they will know."

"Who are the PRP?"

"A well-financed and entrenched resistance movement in the Ruwenzori Mountains which is where it looks like these guys went. They have been around awhile, fighting Sakumbi, and foreigners. They are good. And they will not like Russians encroaching on their game."

"How do we find them?"

"I'll send runners but they will find us. They won't be happy to see you though. They don't like white men. You stay out on the plains with your tribe and I will negotiate for both of us." He motioned to several of his men and walked over to confer with them.

Jon watched him go and shook his head. This was not going well. Nubiby appeared beside him. "I don't trust him."

"Nor do I." Jon said. "He will not be going in alone. Are you familiar with the PRP?"

"Some. They fight for a socialist state. I have heard they are a good fighting force. They are disciplined, unlike those around us. They operate mostly outside our territory – in the mountains. We have had little contact."

"Send a runner to the village and tell the drummers to let the compound know where we are going. Then come back. I want to know everything you know. And keep an eye out for Kerkuk."

They gathered their forces and the stolen trucks and followed the tire tracks for some ways, then veered off to the south closer to where Terrik thought the PRP had a base. He sent out runners in several directions. Jon insisted on sending Waziri with them. Terrik refused.

"If the PRP don't recognize the Waziri they will shoot first."

Jon acquiesced but quietly sent the best Waziri trackers he had out to follow them.

Then they waited. The next morning at dawn two of Terrik's men returned with the grisly heads of the two Waziri Jon had sent to track them. The PRP would negotiate only with Terrik. No one else.

"I told you so," Terrik said.

Jon and the Waziri with him were incensed, but there was little they could do in the short term. This score would be settled later. Jon held firm. Terrik was not going without him.

THEY MET THE PRP in a small valley well to the south. Jabari, the leader, was tall and dressed in the camouflage of the FAZ, the Zairian army. At Jon's raised eyebrows, he said, "They run easily. Leave lots behind." He shook Jon's hand.

"Glad to meet the great grandson of Tarzan." Jon shot a glance at Terrik who was stone faced. "Terrik tells me you have issues with the elusive army. Come. We will talk." Jon was now confused. This was the guy who ordered two Waziri beheaded. He seemed way too friendly to be that hostile towards them. But he went along for the moment. He needed the information.

Jabari led them deeper into the valley to a small waterfall and pool where his men had set up camp.

"We are safe here," Jabari said. "I have sentries in the hills surrounding us watching wherever that army is. We will know if anyone approaches. Let your men enjoy themselves." Both Jon and Terrik released half their men in shifts. The others they kept on guard, neither side trusting Jabari and the PRP to protect them.

Jabari's group had several camps throughout the mountains but there was one blind valley that they left alone. They thought the headquarters of the elusive army camped there. Whoever they were, they were vicious and protected by witchcraft. Several of his men had been caught doing recon and had been skinned and left hanging upside down at the entrance, their skins nailed to the trees. The men were certain it was witchcraft and would not enter that valley.

"Witchcraft." Jon sighed.

Terrik said, "You are a fool to take witchcraft so lightly. The ancestors will speak and you might not like what they say."

"They aren't my ancestors."

"Perhaps, but you are in their land. You cannot win without their approval."

Jabari nodded his head. Jon raised his hands in surrender and the discussion continued. In the end, Jabari was most interested in the General heading the army. Many of his men were from villages attacked by the General and sought revenge for loved ones killed. Their headquarters appeared to be in a cave halfway down the valley just north of his own camp. Most of the army camped out in the plains close to the entrance, when it was there. And it was there now.

It disappeared on occasion for sometimes weeks at a time. The Africans were not from tribes in the area. Plus, there were many white men as well. The force was well provisioned with weapons and supplies – food, clothes, equipment. He was certain they ran extensive reconnaissance and would be tough to surprise.

They had also seen helicopters going and coming. Jabari had one other interesting piece of information that answered questions. He showed them a pair of Russian-made night vision goggles taken off a sentry they had killed before the ghost army put up the witchcraft signs terrifying his men. *This is how they caught Ashanti*, Jon thought.

Jon gathered his Waziri and laid out his problem. He was going into the valley to investigate the cave and needed volunteers to accompany him. Terrik's men refused to enter the valley. Of the twenty Waziri with him, Jon chose two to accompany him: Nubiby and his son, Zuberi.

Nubiby said he had not allowed Jon to go anywhere alone in Africa for so long that it was impossible for him to do so now. And Zuberi would not let his father go without him. Jon sent the remaining Waziri to inform their gathering tribesmen of the army encampment at the end of the blind valley. This was their target. Terrik and his men left to scout the area where the approaching battle would take place.

Jon, Nubiby and Zuberi set off before dawn for the valley. Moving fast, they reached the valley in mid-morning. Jon and his companions moved up into the forests to the ridge across the valley from the cave. The valley was narrow, less than a quarter mile across.

As they crossed over the ridge of the valley, Kerkuk and several apes suddenly emerged from the undergrowth. Kerkuk grabbed Jon's arm and began dragging him back up a path. Surprised, Jon jerked his arm away and stepped back.

"What are you doing?" Kerkuk raised his head and growled in response. The apes had not devised the "*C'mon, follow me,"* arm wave. Kerkuk walked away, stopped, and looked back at Jon. When Jon didn't react, Kerkuk took several more steps and looked back again. This time Jon understood and the three humans followed the apes up the path.

Kerkuk led them onto cliffs overlooking the valley. Across the valley, Jon could see similar cliffs covered in vegetation. Several trees grew at angles to the cliff. Hanging vines and drooping ferns partially obscured the entrance to a cave. He saw no obvious trails to the mouth but they could be hidden.

Jon watched for a time, finding and observing the sentries. A helipad was clearly marked out on the valley floor. This was probably the destination of the helicopter he had seen the night Korak was captured. There was a good chance Korak was in the cave and possibly Ashanti as well. Kerkuk's excitement and insistence on bringing Jon to this spot argued for that conclusion. He walked over to where Kerkuk and the other apes were munching on leaves. Jon took his arm, pointed at the cave and asked, "Korak?" Kerkuk jumped up and down grunting "unh,unh, unh." Jon had his answer.

Evening light was approaching and they did not want to be near this ridge after dark. Kerkuk, however, had other ideas and jumped up and down in front of Jon, conveying in grunts, growls and gestures that he had something else to show them. It made no sense to Jon, who listened then moved around him and continued walking. Kerkuk moved in front of him again. Jon moved to go around him and Kerkuk jumped to block him. This time other members of the tribe formed a group behind Kerkuk.

"Kerkuk," Jon said, "there is nothing else to see." Kerkuk raised his head and roared.

Jon again tried to go around the apes but Kerkuk's long arms wrapped around his body holding him in place.

Jon struggled but could not free himself. The other apes blocked Nubiby and Zuberi from helping.

Jon looked at Nubiby and shrugged. "Let's see what he wants."

Jon relaxed his muscles and said. "OK, Kerkuk. Show me." Kerkuk released him and knuckle-walked to a nearby anthill. The three humans followed.

"Do you know what he means?" Jon asked Nubiby, who shrugged.

Jon turned to Kerkuk." It's a great anthill, Kerkuk, but…?"

Kerkuk stared at them with his head tilted and teeth bared, the ape equivalent of hands on hips. Then he grabbed a handful of the anthill and threw it at Jon who jumped back brushing dirt and ants from his clothes.

"What are you doing?" he asked, almost shouting the words. He picked an ant off his neck and tossed it to the ground. "What is it? What do you want?"

The apes around him hooted. Nubiby and Zuberi chuckled. Jon stared at them, incensed, then glanced at the anthill. One part of it was now open to scurrying ants intent on repairing their home and tunnels. *Tunnels?* A big grin slowly stretched across Jon's face. *Tunnels!*

"I know what he wants," Jon said, and then he explained it to his companions.

Chapter 32: THROUGH THE BACK DOOR

THE THREE HUMANS FOLLOWED the apes along the ridge, crossing the plateau at the end of the valley and on to the other side. It was late afternoon when Kerkuk stopped and took to the trees. Jon followed. He scanned with binoculars until he spotted a sentry at the base of a tree. He watched for a long time. At dusk, a bush near the sentry's tree rose above the ground spewing light into the twilight. Two men, one after the other, rose out of the light like apparitions. The sentry climbed down from his tree and, across the clearing, another sentry dropped down from the lowest branch of a tree. Jon was surprised. He had missed that one. The four exchanged words and the new men took to the trees while the old sentries disappeared into the hole pulling the bush down into place behind them.

Jon had seen enough. The new sentries had night vision goggles. He moved the group quickly back towards the end of the valley.

They spent the night with the apes sleeping in the lower branches of the mountain trees and headed back to the PRP compound at dawn. Kerkuk and his new clan remained behind.

THE DAY WAS SPENT planning their two-pronged attack. Jon, Nubiby and Kuberi would enter the caves through the sentry hole Kerkuk had discovered while Terrik, the PRP and the Waziri engaged the bulk of the enemy camped on the plains, hopefully drawing out the soldiers from the cave. If not, at least their attention would be diverted. Jon sent several Waziri to

214

the surrounding villages to recruit as many warriors as possible. They were well outside Waziri territory but no less affected by this army encampment. Two other Waziri left to update their massing tribesmen. These two were also tasked with sending drum messages to the compound. Four additional Waziri raced back to the compound to be sure the information of their whereabouts and intent was received. His father and great grandfather could well be there by now, and the drums, while fast, could not convey the details he wished them to know.

Before Jon, Nubiby and Zuberi left the next morning for the tunnel entrance, Jabari pulled Jon aside for a private conversation. Nubiby saw Jon stiffen, nod, and return to the group.

"What was that?" Nubiby asked.

Jon hesitated then said, "He says that he did not behead our Waziri. Terrik did."

Nubiby nodded. "I am not surprised. Do you believe him?"

"I do. Korak was certain Terrik lied about Meriem. I think this is the truth. A score to be settled later."

They reached the area of the tunnel entrance mid-morning. The tunnel entrance was out in the open – they could not approach it without being seen by the two sentries posted on either side of the clearing.

Jon took Kerkuk and the apes a few trees away and gestured to them to make a ruckus. Kerkuk quickly got the idea and conveyed it to the others. The apes enjoyed themselves immensely, howling, chest beating and making general mischief. The sentry stood up on his branch to see what was going on giving Nubiby a clear view. The twang of Nubiby's bow was the last thing the sentry heard. He dropped to the ground, his throat impaled by an arrow. Zuberi dispatched the sentry on the other side of the clearing in a similar fashion.

They grabbed the radios and searched the bodies. Nubiby and his son donned their uniforms as Jon attempted to convey to Kerkuk that he wanted the apes to go to the front of the cave in case they were needed for another diversion. He was not at all certain Kerkuk understood.

THE MEN DROPPED INTO the hole that marked the rear entrance to the cave. Daylight disappeared and within a few feet they felt the cool natural air conditioning of the underground. Their flashlights revealed a tunnel not quite tall enough for them to walk upright. Hunched over with Jon in the lead they followed it a short distance until it opened into a larger chamber. The flashlights revealed a small house-sized room dotted with stalactites and stalagmites. The twenty-foot ceilings fluttered at the onslaught of light. Dark shapes dropped and dove toward the lights. Jon threw up an arm to cover his face as the shapes pelted his head and body. It felt like a hundred birds beating him with their wings.

"Turn off the lights," he yelled, crouching on the ground and flicking off his own.

They plunged into darkness so black they were disoriented, unsure of up and down. Nubiby fell onto his side in a fetal position. Zuberi fell backwards and found his back against the cavern wall. Jon dropped to his knees and hunched down covering his head with his arms. Leathery bat wings thrashed against them flinging gusts of chilled air as the bats vented their fury and fear at being disturbed. After an interminable time, that was only minutes, the bats calmed and returned to their roosts.

After that, Jon, Nubiby and Zuberi kept their lights trained on the ground or low on the walls of the cave. The chamber's only exit led into a tall passageway. They followed it, encountering several cross passages. Footprints or chisel marks on the cave walls indicated the way. Twice they crossed deep pits on narrow two by fours. Further on, they were forced to bend down and crawl for a distance taking it on faith that the passage went somewhere.

Finally, they came to a metal door across the passage-way that no amount of pushing or pulling could move. At least they felt they were in the right place. Why else would there be a door?

Nubiby keyed a radio and spoke Swahili into it slurring his words, saying he had been mauled by an ape and was at the door at the back of the cave. The response asked him to repeat and clarify. Jon rubbed rocks on rocks simulating crackling and Nubiby pleaded again. Finally, the door began to open spilling light into the passage. The cave beyond was wired.

Nubiby bent over in the passage, one hand on the cavern wall and head down as if injured. Jon and Zuberi crouched behind two boulders as two guards came out with flashlights. Nubiby groaned loudly and collapsed to his knees, head almost on the ground. One guard flashed his light casually around then went to Nubiby when he groaned again. The guard spoke to him in Swahili. Neither guard had their weapons ready.

Nubiby abruptly grabbed the legs of the guard in front of him and jerked them back towards him. The guard toppled onto his back with a loud grunt. Nubiby sprang on top of him, slitting his throat before the grunt was complete. The other guard who had started to bend over to assist Nubiby was star-tled at his companion's sudden fall and then shocked as he was immediately tackled from behind. Zuberi kept the door ajar while Nubiby and Jon bound the hands and feet of the semi-conscious guard and then raised him to his feet. A gun in his face and the body of the other guard guaranteed his silence.

"Ask him where this passage goes."

Nubiby complied and got no answer. The guard stood stoically before them still somewhat in shock that attackers had appeared from the depths of the cave.

Jon grabbed the guard from behind and held a knife to his throat. "Ask him again."

The guard sputtered an answer. "He says it leads to the main cave."

"Ask him how far, never mind. Zuberi, check out the other side of the door."

Zuberi cracked the door wider. "There's a hall – short. Twenty feet maybe. Then it turns left I think. No people. No cover either."

"Ask him what's down the hall."

Nubiby complied. "He says nothing for some ways. It curves around and branches out."

"Ask him where the hostages are."

"He says he knows of no hostages."

Jon increased the pressure on the knife and drew blood. He was rewarded with a stream of Swahili.

"The women are in a dead-end passage off the main chamber. He doesn't know where the man is." Jon increased the pressure. His captive struggled and choked, pleading in another string of Swahili.

"I think he really does not know, Jon. And he used the plural for woman. There must be more than one."

"Ask him how far before we run into people. Tell him he goes first and dies first if we see anyone." Jon tightened his hold on the guard.

"He says there are few people in this area. No one expected this entrance to be found. That is why there are only two guards. He says he will take us to the women."

"Ask him how many women."

"He's not sure. Two he knows of, but maybe three."

"Three? Is he certain? Ask him if there are other entrances."

"He says they found three other ways in and out of the caves besides the main chamber onto the valley. But they are more treacherous than this one and have been sealed off with rocks."

Jon stepped away from him then and held his gun in front of the man's face while Nubiby untied his feet.

"Tell him this gun will be pointed at his head and if he has lied, he will be the first to die." Nubiby delivered the message. The captive's eyes grew round and his shoulders slumped, but he nodded.

Zuberi took the lead walking around each corner as if he belonged there. The captive followed with Jon's hand on his shoulder. Nubiby brought up the rear, lagging behind, listening, then catching up. They passed several cross passages but each time the captive indicated straight ahead. Finally, he directed them into a dark depression in the rock to the left, and spoke to Zuberi.

"He says the main chamber is just ahead maybe twenty feet."

Nubiby ran up, then, and almost passed them. Jon grabbed his arm and brought him into the depression. Zuberi slunk towards the main cavern, hugging the wall. Suddenly, he turned and ran back to the depression.

"Someone comes," he said.

"How many?"

"Not sure. Maybe three or four."

They pressed up against the walls of the depression. Jon held his knife at his captive's throat.

They heard advancing footsteps then four men passed the depression speaking a dialect none of the three recognized. When they were out of hearing range, Nubiby asked the captive who they were.

"He says they are of the other tribe, the Kibuli, and speak only their local language when alone. He does not understand it."

"The other tribe? No. Don't ask. Just – where are the women?"

The captive's directions led them into the main chamber, which was stunning in its enormity. They stared up at the rugged ceiling six stories above them. Half of the cavern was filled with military equipment. Stacks of wood and other materials sat in the center of the open space that could have held two football games simultaneously. Two passages led off to the left. The captive told them the women were down the passage closest to the cave entrance.

The cave entrance was an impressive two stories tall and half a football field wide. They could see through the hanging vines across the valley to the cliff from which they had conducted their first surveillance. A group of five or six men clustered at the opposite end of the cave entrance, talking excitedly and pointing to the right towards the canyon entrance.

"Terrik and the Waziri I think, stirring up trouble," Nubiby said with a grin.

"Let's hope," Jon led the group down the left side of the main cavern and into the passage. They saw no other men than those at the entrance.

The passage was not lit but there was enough light from the main chamber to see a short distance. After that they went by sense of touch and short bursts of their flashlights, Nubiby on one side, his son on the other. They came to a solid metal door installed on the right and were contemplating how to get in when they heard footsteps coming their way. They melted into the darkness further down the passage, scrunching up against the walls. Jon held his knife tightly to the captive's throat.

Two Africans in uniform silhouetted by the main chamber's light approached. One held an AK-47 and opened the door with a key. He waited by the door pointing his rifle inside while the other man entered with a tray. Jon whispered to Zuberi who took the captive maintaining a knife at his throat. Jon and Nubiby approached the door silently and waited for the second guard to return.

The second guard appeared and turned toward the main chamber as the first began to close the door lowering his rifle slightly in the process. At that point, Jon silently took him from behind, jamming a knife into his throat and cutting his windpipe, stifling any noise he might wish to have made. Nubiby was equally quick and quiet. They dragged both men into the room and were shocked to find a man sitting on the floor, his right leg chained to the wall. A tray lay beside him on the floor. He watched the proceedings passively. Jon and Nubiby dropped their respective kills on the floor and he spoke.

"You're late."

"And you're chained to a wall, Grandfather."

Korak smiled and looked his grandson up and down. *Perhaps Mubuto was right and Jon was not lost to them.*

Nubiby went to the door and signaled his son that all was well and to enter.

Korak stood and Jon could see the steel post imbedded in the stone wall to which the chain was attached. It was two feet off the floor and bent up at a thirty-degree angle to the wall.

"If you gents will help, I think we can pull this thing out. I've been working on it but it's defiant."

They pulled on the post together with no luck. Zuberi pushed it back and forth in its hole to loosen the stone's grip. This maneuver had some success and when next they pulled in unison, the wall gave way with a sudden crack and sent the three backwards into the opposite wall.

They sat on the floor together and laughed.

"You're losing your touch, Grandfather. Meriem could have handled that easily."

Korak grinned at him. "Where is your Grandmother? You should have found her first."

Jon looked at Nubiby who shrugged.

"We don't know. We thought she was in here." Jon said. He pointed at the captive as if the answer lay with him.

Korak stared at the captive guard, who began to tremble and whine in Swahili. Korak listened for a few seconds and said, "He is incoherent. We will have to find her ourselves... and Jane also."

"Jane is here?"

"Yes. Chertok confirmed it."

"Chertok?"

"The son of an old enemy. It's a long story. For later."

"Tarzan?"

"Still out there, according to Chertok. We need to be ready."

"For what?"

"Never mind. Tell me what you know of this cave."

Chapter 33: SISTERHOOD

MERIEM SPENT THE SECOND DAY in her cave cell. Her captors had ungraciously acceded to her request for a table, chair and writing materials. She was grateful at least for that.

The first day, Meriem had spent a considerable amount of time searching her enclosure for a means of escape but could find none. The walls were uneven metamorphic rock, in some places only inches above her head. There were no windows and the door was steel, its frame embedded in the rock. She thought it would take explosives to get it out. She considered the hinges for a while but they also were heavy duty and she could not budge them.

Once she had exhausted all plans of escape she considered the blank paper. Apparently, she had plenty of time to kill. Her captor had indicated she would be there awhile. *How long was 'awhile'? Was she being held for ransom?*

She and Jane had thought to write a memoir once but had never got to it, spending all their time with their mates or in the running of the compound and their charitable organizations in central and eastern Africa. Maybe now was a good time to start. At least it would help her pass the time.

She was contemplating the blank page when she heard the metallic grating of a key. The door opened outward and as always two men with guns entered first and motioned her to move to the back wall, a result of her little escape attempt from the tent in the camp. She had rushed the lone man bringing her dinner and had nearly succeeded in reaching the jungle.

After that they kept her tied up until they brought her to the cave.

Someone was shoved into the room between the two guards and fell to the floor. She was a familiar figure. Meriem stood, shocked, elated and remorseful.

"My Dear," she said and rushed to help the new woman to her feet and engulf her in a hug. The guards backed out of the cell and they heard the door lock.

"Meriem, Meriem, you are alive. We were so afraid," Jane hugged her back.

They sat on the cot holding tightly to each other, sharing information. Meriem knew nothing of her family except Korak. She had been held in a tent close to where he had been questioned and had overheard his statement that Jane was also in the camp. The Russian had agreed but as Meriem had not seen Jane she assumed the Russian had been bluffing.

As to the others in her family, Terrik had not known anything and her new captors refused to enlighten her on what they knew. She suspected they knew a lot. She had heard the Russian, the General and the Chief discussing the situation in the camp where tents do not afford great secrecy. When they spoke Russian, she was lost. Only when the Chief was included could she catch bits and pieces as they spoke French at those times. The Chief was intensely interested in someone in her family. She thought it was her grandson, Jon, but that surprised her. She had seen his plane disappear into the trees and heard the explosion. She had been certain both Jackie and Jon were dead. If the Chief was looking for them, perhaps they had survived. She tried not to get too excited, too ahead of herself. She could not bear to lose them twice. And now here was Jane, always still 'My Dear' to her.

Meriem gave Jane a synopsis of the attack and her subsequent escape and capture. "I saw Jon and Jackie's plane go down. I assumed...do you know...?"

Jane smiled broadly. "They are both alive." Meriem jumped up, pumped her fists in the air and shouted "YES" to the rock walls. *They were alive!*

Jane laughed. "Come. Sit. There is more. You will be amazed. But we are all still in deep trouble. There is much yet to be done."

Meriem sat back down on the cot and Jane told her the story as far as she knew it. Jackie was not on the plane. Jon was lost and then found in the jungle, killed a witch doctor and was now looking for them. Korak was accused of killing Dian Fossey and had disappeared. The Trust was under financial attack and could be lost. Tarzan was in Russia pursuing a trail. The whole thing might be a legacy of an enemy long dead. Meriem's mouth fell open at "Jon was lost in the jungle" and remained so to the end of Jane's tale.

She closed her mouth and stared at Jane. "Korak killed Dian…. No…he would never…. Oh god, poor Dian. They finally got her. And Jon…. A witch doctor?…Jon never killed anyone… Jackie will be horrified. Jane, what is happening?"

Jane said, "So, how do we get out of here?"

MERIEM AND JANE settled down to consider their options. They did not like sitting on their haunches waiting for their men to come for them. The possibilities were limited and taking out the guards seemed to be the only way.

Their plans were not going well when the key clicked in the lock again. Both women's heads turned toward the opening door. It was the same scenario. Two guards pointing AK-47s at them as a third walked into the chamber with what appeared to be an undulating tan rug thrown over his shoulder. The occupant of the rug was calling him the vilest names imaginable in Swahili.

He tossed the rug on the floor and they could see a woman's head on one end still yelling at her captor as he walked towards the door.

"At least untie her," Jane said.

"Not that she-cat. I'd rather skin her and tan the pelt. She's not human."

Jane and Meriem had been concentrating on the new arrival but now looked up at the guard. His face was crisscrossed with deep parallel red and purple gouges. He looked as though his head had been tied in a bag with a furious feline. Then the door clicked and they were alone.

They bent to untie their new cellmate. It took some time pushing, pulling, and maneuvering rope and body parts but finally she was free. When she finally stood before them she was striking. Her eyes were deep blue, almost black, and her hair was braided and pulled back. She was tall, almost six feet, but her face was the feature that caused Meriem and Jane to stare. Small bead like tattoos in graceful curves, and whorls accentuated her eyes and sensuous mouth, although at present that mouth was hard as the rock surrounding them.

Ashanti was the first to speak. "Which one of you is Meriem?" she asked in French.

Meriem and Jane were stunned. *Who was she?*

"I am. And you are?"

Ashanti smiled. "I am sorry. I am Ashanti. We have been looking for you."

"We?"

"So sorry. I mean Jon. Your grandson. He speaks so much of you. He is determined to find you."

"You know Jon? Where is he? When did you see him? Is he okay?" The string of questions continued until Jane rested a hand on Meriem's arm and she relented.

"Let's sit down and start at the beginning," Jane said.

Ashanti took the chair and Meriem and Jane the cot. Ashanti told her story. Meriem and Jane gasped in unison, Meriem covering her mouth with both hands, as Ashanti replayed Jon's duel with the witch doctor and their subsequent escape in the jungle. This was repeated when she told them of the Dum-Dum ceremony and the battle between Jon and Korak.

When she was done, Meriem and Jane looked at each other and each mouthed the name Mubuto. The sage's predictions had been true. Jane and Meriem had been concerned for years about Jon's disinterest in the jungle. They were afraid he was planning a career outside the family and outside of Africa. Mubuto had assured them the jungle would not let him go.

"He can't go back now," Jane said. "He won't. I'm sure of it. Jon will stay in Africa now. He will work with the family."

Meriem looked doubtful. "I don't know. Once a Clayton sets his mind …." She let the sentence trail.

"Yes. But Jon did not choose to leave Africa. He was taken. Mubuto is right. I tried so hard when Korak was small to keep him from the jungle and this life. All to no avail."

Ashanti raised her eyes and looked from one to the other.

"But you might have succeeded if Korak had not run away with the ape to the jungle at such an early age. He was only eleven, wasn't he?" Jane nodded her head. Meriem continued. "Korak was still a child and learned to love the jungle as a child. Jon is an adult now and though he has not said, from all appearances he has made up his mind. I fear we have lost him." Meriem sighed and bowed her head.

"Meriem, the jungle is in their blood. All of them. Tarzan, Korak, Jackie, and now Jon. I do not believe we have lost him. I will not."

"Jon? Are you serious?" When both women nodded, Ashanti continued, astonished. "He is not of the jungle. He is lucky to be alive. He is stupid white man….oh…." She raised a hand to her mouth.

Meriem and Jane again exchanged looks and small smiles. Mubuto, the canny dog, had found a way. Ashanti would return Jon to the jungle and his family.

Chapter 34: UP ON CHARGES

THE OLD BAILEY HAS BEEN the central criminal court of Britain since the 16th century, the current building having been built in 1902 over the ruins of the Newgate Gaol. It is where crimes of the highest nature are tried. It was where Jackie's case was to be heard.

Jackie stood at the bottom of the circular staircase that led from the prisoner waiting area to the dock where the accused faced their fate and judgment. The nudge on his shoulder told him it was time. He ascended the fourteen stairs in a slow deliberate manner, shaking off any assistance from the accompanying guards.

At the top of the stairs Jackie stepped into the dock that overlooked the floor of the main chamber, the pit, where the bull terriers of the Law, the Crown's prosecutor and the defendant's barrister, would battle for supremacy over the other, with justice being a secondary after-thought by-product. The public gallery area was empty. The Crown had requested, and the court had complied, that the public not be permitted into the Commitment Procedure, due to the nature and severity of the charges.

To the right and center of the prisoner's dock was the Lord Justice's domain. It was strategically located to hold the focus of all participants, while its raised position subliminally told all that the sitting judge ruled supreme.

The banging of the Clerk's staff announced the beginning of the procedures. Everyone rose. The curtain to the left side parted and the Recorder of London, the most prominent judge in the Crown's judicial system, entered. The Bailiff shouted, "Hear ye, hear ye, hear ye. The Crown Court of Britain is called to order, Lord Justice Bloweather presiding."

Lord Justice Bloweather emerged from behind the curtain, took his seat beneath the Royal Coat of Arms, shuffled some papers, looked over his half-lens spectacles, and waved an arm indicating for all to be seated. He looked toward Jackie, then into the pit below him, making sure that all eyes and ears were upon him.

"We are here today for a Commitment Procedure to determine whether there are sufficient charges against the defendant, Jackie Porter Clayton, to justify a trial. The Clerk shall read the charges."

The Clerk stood, held several sheets of paper in front of him and began, "Jackie Porter Clayton, you are accused of an act of Treason Felony as any who imagine, invent, devise or intend to levy war against the sovereign to compel her to change her measures or counsels or to put any force or constraint upon or to intimidate or overawe both Houses or either House of Parliament. The penalty for the commitment of such a crime is punishable by life in prison."

The Clerk turned toward the prisoner's dock. "How do you plead?"

"Not guilty," Jackie said in a strong, positive projected voice.

The Lord Justice turned to the prosecutor for the Crown, "Sir, the accused has pleaded not guilty to the charge. What specific information do you have today to set before this court to justify and refute such a plea of innocence?"

Before the Crown's prosecutor, Sir Timothy Leggarder rose, Ian stood and interjected. "My Lord, might I have a moment? We believe that the charges are highly inflated and inflammatory. The Greystoke Trust management, including the defendant, was only recently made aware of such alleged illegal activities. As soon as management had an awareness of them, it moved to locate the cause. I am happy to report that the management was successful in finding the responsible individuals and have taken appropriate disciplinary action to see that such behavior is not done in the future."

Leggarder jumped in and said, "We have not brought these charges lightly."

Ian fired back. "I believe that my honorable colleague, Sir Timothy, has so highly polished the charges that they might look like diamonds, when in fact they are but gravel. Thus, I move that all charges against the defendant be dropped without prejudice and that the defendant be released immediately."

Before the judge had time to respond to Ian's request, Leggarder once again jumped to his feet, "My colleague has made a gross misrepresentation of matters; once more he has not heard the specifics of the charges. What the Crown has are specific and definitive records substantiating that the accused knowingly and willfully caused the transfer of monetary funds from his family's Trust to various groups and individuals classified by the international community as terrorist groups; such groups including but not limited to Castro's Cuba, the Nicaraguan Contras and even to several individual accounts in Russia. Most importantly, being of a clear and present danger to our Kingdom, funds flowing to the Irish Republican Army."

The specifics of the charges were beyond what Ian had ever anticipated. Jackie and Ian exchanged looks of bewilderment. The IRA was truly at war with Britain, bombing buildings and attacking and killing British soldiers. In 1983, it had launched a daring attack against 10 Downing Street. Fortunately, the attack was foiled by a special branch of MI6.

The Crown's prosecutor noticed the exchange of views between Jackie and Ian and charged forward. "The person who has been most supportive in not only bringing such action to our attention, but also fully cooperating in the gathering of such data, is willing to testify on behalf of the Crown."

Ian was dumbfounded. At the same time Jackie's composure, after the initial shock, seemed undisturbed.

Leggarder knew he had his opponent on his heels and pressed forward. "Because of the severity and sensitivity of the charges we request that the trial be held within ten calendar days from today, or sooner."

All eyes turned to Ian fully expecting a vigorous objection. Instead, Ian looked to Jackie for some guidance. Jackie gave an affirmative nod of his head. Ian turned back to the judge. "Such a request is most highly unusual. No trial to my knowledge, especially one of such high accusatory and consequential circumstances, has ever been convened in such an abbreviated time. Having said such, my client is more than willing to agree to such an extraordinary request."

Sir Bloweather shook his head in disbelief, then commenced with the remaining pomp and circumstance of the Court to secure the trial date and adjourn the procedures.

A HALF AN HOUR LATER Jackie was back in his cell. Ian had joined him and was pacing back and forth. "You're the client, but it's insane. There is so much work to do. Why did you agree to such a quick trial date?"

"One, because I know I'm innocent; two, we only need two items to resolve the matter; and three, I have great faith in your legal abilities."

Ian did not look convinced. Jackie went on, "If they found money trails, then we can too. After all they're our records. Put Otto, and only Otto, on finding those trails. No one, and I mean no one, else is to know what he is doing. Also, I want to see all the transfer points and the transaction sheets with signatures. Get me that and I'll give you what you need to put the Crown in its place."

Ian started shaking his head from side to side. "Jackie, you don't seem to understand that you're facing the rest of your life in jail if the case goes against you. That's a heavy burden."

Jackie stood up and grabbed Ian by both shoulders. "Look at me." Ian raised his head. "I know what I'm doing. For once in years my mind is clear. The ghost of Irene has been flushed from the system. I'm thinking clearly and if you will do what I say, The Trust will be saved, our honor restored. I'll be a free man again, and then I can torment you until we both live to ripe old ages. Is that clear?"

Ian reluctantly nodded his agreement. "If you say so," was his doubt-laced response.

Jackie turned Ian around, put a comforting arm around his shoulder and escorted him to the door. Two quick raps brought the guards. Ian mumbled a couple of words of departure then disappeared through the door.

As he passed through the door opening, Jackie said, "Get Otto on it right away, and let me know tomorrow what he's found. It should be easy. You'll see. Trust me."

Ian waived his hand good-bye, without looking back. If Jackie could have read Ian's mind at that moment he would not have been so optimistic.

Chapter 35: STANDOFF

A LITTLE LATER, A WHITE man with his hands tied in front and three African guards walked out of the dark passageway into the main cavern. One of the guards was considerably lighter than the other two and fidgeted in his too tight uniform. The white man slouched as if weakened, and kept his head down. A crude bandage wrapped his head, obscuring his face.

The four made their way quickly down the side of the main cavern back to the first passageway they had encountered. Their captive had sworn to them that he did not know where the women were. He had been certain they were in the room where they had found Korak. He had sworn again that there was nothing down the first passageway but troop quarters. He knew nothing of the passages on the other side of the main chamber as they were off limits to the troops. The officers' quarters were there and he did not know what else. They had left him, tied and gagged, in Korak's cell.

Korak and Nubiby ran down the first passageway leaving Jon and Zuberi at the entrance. It was longer and better lit than the one outside Korak's cell. They slowed to a walk as they heard footsteps coming the other way. Two guards looked them over as they passed. One hesitated as if he was going to ask them a question but the second interrupted him with a comment in a language Korak did not recognize. The first guard laughed, and they walked on towards the main chamber. Korak and Nubiby continued along the passage for some way diverting briefly to examine two side passages which dead-ended in piles of tumbled rocks.

They passed several more of Chertok's men in uniform. All spoke in some language unknown to them. Korak mumbled and nodded his head but kept going projecting a rushed and purposeful attitude. It worked. No one stopped them.

At the end of the passage, they came to an open door that led into a large dimly lit chamber containing rows and rows of three-tiered bunks. Most held mattresses rolled and tied – only the first two rows seemed occupied. There were several passages off this room but Korak figured the women would not be kept so close to the troops. If they weren't down this passage, they must be on the other side of the main cavern.

Korak and Nubiby ran back down the passageway, this time encountering no one. Jon and Zuberi were not where they had left them. They looked rapidly around thinking they had been captured when a loud "*psst*" drew them back to the original passage. The cluster of men watching the battle had not moved and the pop-pop-pop of gunfire could be heard in the distance.

Korak wanted Jon to wait there for them as the color of his skin was a liability. Korak's face was deeply tanned and could pass for a lighter-skinned African. Jon could not.

"There are white officers. We will be going towards their quarters. I am going."

"You will give us away."

"So, will you. Only Nubiby and Zuberi are unknown to them."

Korak nodded. He could not counter the argument. "You should go as an officer. Their uniforms are different. Wait here." He signaled Nubiby to follow him. Jon and Zuberi once more remained behind.

Within a few minutes Korak and Nubiby returned with an officer's uniform which Jon quickly donned. Korak said only "Someone tripped – had a bad fall."

The four left together for the main cavern, Jon leading with Korak just behind him and to the right, Nubiby and Zuberi behind Korak.

The plan was to stay in the shadow of the walls as they moved around the cavern to the other side, keeping the military gear in the cavern between them and the soldiers watching the battle.   It did not work out that way.

AS SOON AS THEY ENTERED THE MAIN CHAMBER, Jon spotted the Chief and three white men, one in the uniform of a Russian general, coming their way from the back of the cavern – the way Jon and Nubiby had come originally. Jon's group had already made the right turn from the passageway towards the back of the cave and to suddenly stop and switch directions would draw attention to them.

Jon hissed to Korak. "The Chief, that's the chief from Ashanti's village."

Korak did not answer. He had recognized two of the white men as Russians from the camp, the general and the one he knew had killed Dian Fossey. He did not know the other. The brim of his hat was down. Perhaps they would be lucky.

He saw the Chief speak to the Russian general who turned his head to look more closely at the oncoming group. He held the look too long, Korak thought. Then he said something to the African.

"We are made," Korak whispered. "We take them... Now!" They raised their guns in unison. At the same instant, the Russian commanded his group to do the same.

"Drop your weapons, gentlemen," the Russian said. "You have no chance here. You have nowhere to go, and no help. Please. Let's have no more bloodshed. And gunfire in the cave is so painful to the ears, as well as dangerous. Ricochets, you know."

"Don't do it, Grandfather. They'll just kill us."

"Agreed," Korak said. He turned toward the general "My grandson doesn't recommend dropping our weapons. I tend to agree. Perhaps we settle this here. Take our chances with the ricochets."

While Korak was talking, the four spread out from each other, making sure there would be four targets for their opponents to worry about.

The Russian general gave a loud command and suddenly the soldiers watching the battle turned, grabbed their rifles and ran to his aid. Jon, Korak, Nubiby and Zuberi were now surrounded by the soldiers, the Russian officers, and the Chief.

"Lower your weapons, gentlemen. You cannot win."

"Maybe not," Korak said "but we can take you out and a few of your men." Nubiby and Zuberi had turned to face the soldiers. Jon and Korak maintained the stalemate with the Russians and the Chief.

"I want him alive. He must be alive," the Chief said. "He has no value to me if he is dead."

"You're just going to kill him. What's the difference? Here or there." the second Russian said.

The Chief glowered at him. "You are not of Africa. Power is different here."

"Bunk. Power is power. Kill him and take his body back. They will get the message."

"No. I must be seen to kill him...by the village...by my people."

"That is the most insane...."

"Gentlemen," the general intervened. "We have other concerns here. We will preserve your sacrifice for you. They will surrender."

"We will?" Korak raised his eyebrows.

"You will. Or we will kill your wife. Meriem is her name, is it not?" The general gave a command and three of the soldiers facing Nubiby and Zuberi ran toward the right side of the chamber.

"Now gentlemen," said the general. "We wait."

Within minutes, three women, hands tied behind their backs, appeared in the passageway and were escorted across the cavern to stand beside the general. Ashanti scowled at Jon. Meriem beamed at Korak. Jane's eyes searched in all directions for a means of escape.

Both Jon and Korak braced themselves as they saw the women.

"Ashanti," Jon said. "How…?"

"They used me," Korak said. "I told her to run. She didn't listen."

"She never does."

The general grabbed the closest woman and held her with his left hand across her shoulders. His right hand held a knife at her throat.

"Well gentlemen. What say you? Do we spill the blood of this lovely woman today or will you drop your weapons?"

The woman shook her head. Jon and Korak looked at each other.

"It's only Jane."

"Just Jane. Not my she. Not my problem."

"Jungle Law?"

Korak nodded. "Mangani tradition."

"My grandmother though."

"*Great* grandmother," Korak emphasized.

"True. I do have another grandmother."

"Gentlemen, I grow tired of these games." His left arm tightened across Jane's upper chest and the knife in his right hand rose under her chin, nicking the skin and pushing her head up. A single drop of blood dropped to the rock floor.

"Tarzan will kill us both." Jon and Korak said in unison.

Outwardly Jon was nonchalant. Inwardly he was a maelstrom of grinding teeth, racing heart and seething blood. They were stalling, searching for a way out, anything, no matter how small. Within seconds, they would have to give up and he did not think they would survive. They really, really needed a distraction.

And then they got one.

Chapter 36: ON MOSCOW STREETS

WHILE THE FLIGHT WAS MUCH SHORTER than any commercial flight, it was several degrees less comfortable as the back seat of the fighter jet was designed for a much smaller person. They travelled at forty-five thousand feet and then made a sharp descent on landing at the military base outside of Moscow. As promised, there was a car waiting to whisk him off to the French Embassy where he was met by Monsieur Jean Baptise Kortad, the Director of Information, who, as with most embassies around the world, was in fact the head of intelligence for the embassy.

After exchanged introductions, Kortad walked Tarzan to his office. Tarzan sat in an oversized Empire-style chair while the DI took up his normal position behind his eighteenth-century partners' desk. "I have been in contact with your friend Monsieur D'Arnot and I will work with you in every way I can; however, I'm sure that you know that I do have restrictions beyond which I cannot reach without putting persons and nations into troublesome situations."

"All I need is transportation, a few directions and some rubles. I do not wish to inconvenience you."

"No, no, no. You are not, as you say, inconveniencing me, or the French government." Then Kortad pulled open a drawer to his desk and extracted a manila envelope. "You will also need these. You are now a French citizen by the name of Jean Pierre Claytonne, here on business, a participant in an international trade mission. Should anyone give you any problems, do not answer their questions; instead insist upon them contacting me. All will be taken care of. I am at your service."

Tarzan glanced through the material. Satisfied with the contents, he turned to Kortad and said, "Thank you, I should be going on my way."

"Oui, monsieur. I will have your driver bring your car around."

"That is not necessary. I can use taxis."

"Ah, but no! A person with your stature, remember you head an international trade delegation, would not travel by public transportation. You would have your own driver. It is most *necessaire!*"

Tarzan wanted to be on his own to do what was necessary without the restraint of others, but in this case, he acquiesced, knowing how the French always had to stick to their protocol, regardless of the circumstances, even if it meant defeat. Honor and decorum were at stake.

As he rose to leave, Kortad said, "One more thing. I almost forgot. I am ashamed of myself. Monsieur D'Arnot insisted that you should carry this with you." It was a miniature recording unit, one that could be easily concealed on one's body. "I know not what this is for, but then, it is not for me to ask... only serve." Tarzan took it with a wry smile. *My careful friend, Paul. "Je vous remercie, Monsieur Kortad."*

Kortad walked Jean Pierre Claytonne to the front of the embassy where a black four-door Peugeot was waiting. Kortad opened the front door of the car, exchanged words with the driver and then turned to Tarzan. "Your driver, Philippe Martin, will take you wherever you need to go."

He held the door open then closed it once Tarzan was seated. Through the open window he said, *"Bonne chance, mon ami."* And with that, the driver shifted gears and headed out of the embassy grounds into the streets of Moscow.

MADAME ROKOFF LIVED on the other side of Moscow from the French embassy. It was but a short distance, but with the amount of traffic, the trip took nearly an hour. Lines and lines of cars crept, stopped, then crawled some more. It was normal Moscow traffic. No one was in danger of getting a speeding ticket. Tarzan felt he could have walked the distance faster.

Several glances into the car's side-view mirrors gave Tarzan the feeling that they were being tracked by another car. A few more glances solidified his belief. He didn't know whether his pursuers were Russian, British or some other group. He would have to wait for events to unfold and see what developed.

As they approached Madame Rokoff's building, Tarzan told the driver not to stop but to continue. He wanted to see what the trailing car would do. He also wanted to see if there was any ground surveillance in the area. Everything appeared to be normal. People were walking on the street, a two-man work crew sweeping the gutters. There were even a couple of children playing on the steps of Rokoff's building. All seemed in order.

He instructed the driver to go down two blocks then circle back around. As they passed by again, everything seemed to be as previous. Then one point stood out, the work crew was sweeping the same spot. His keen eyes noted that their hands were soft, manicured, not calloused as someone doing such work for any amount of time.

He had seen enough. A trap was set…waiting for him.

As Tarzan's car slowed for a red stoplight he saw his opportunity. He hit the door handle and leaped from the car. Before the driver could even turn around in his seat, he was out of the car and into a dark alleyway. The driver slammed on the brakes, jumped out of the car and ran into the alley. "Monsieur Claytonne! Monsieur Claytonne!" The only answer he received was the yowling protestation of a stray cat whose meal of rotting garbage had been interrupted by his shouting. Monsieur Claytonne had disappeared…Vanished.

TARZAN LOOKED DOWN from his perch on a fourth-floor balcony. It had been an easy ascent, using the windowsills as hand and foot holds to scale the building. He saw the bewildered driver searching in vain for his passenger. Then the driver was joined by the two workmen!

All three searched, but found nothing. No one thought of looking up. They must not have briefed on who it was they were setting up. Frustrated by their lack of success, they began to discuss what to do next. The entire discussion was in English… British English. After several minutes, they concluded that there was nothing to do but report back to their respective bases.

Tarzan waited an additional five minutes before continuing his ascent to the roof of the apartment building. Before climbing onto the roof, Tarzan raised his head over the coping of the top of the building to inspect the surroundings. As he had suspected, there was an armed Russian soldier on the roof. It was obvious to Tarzan that the British and Russians were working together to catch him. He had cleared the first defense perimeter when he lost the driver and his accomplices. Now he had a second, an inner perimeter to traverse.

The soldier was focused on the doorway that led to the stairs descending into the building. His back was towards Tarzan. Tarzan silently raised his body up and over the edge of the building and with the stealth of a jungle cat moved across the roof. Before the unsuspecting soldier knew what was happening, a steel-talon hand clamped over his mouth and pinched his nose closed, cutting off his breathing completely. Iron fingers of another hand bit into his trapezoid muscle, paralyzing any motion that he might have contemplated. He collapsed to the floor, unconscious.

Tarzan bent down and disarmed the soldier of his AK-47S rifle. He slung it over his shoulder. *Who knew when it might come in handy?* He then checked the soldier's pulse. His intent was to immobilize, not to murder. He only killed when he had to, in defense of loved ones or self or to satisfy the need for nourishment. There was no other reason to take the life from another. A pulse was felt… the soldier was not dead.

Only a single outpost on the roof indicated to Tarzan that Madame Rokoff was either supremely confident or very sloppy. And the woman who began this war on his family was certainly smarter. He sensed this must be another layer to her trap.

Tarzan advanced to the door, grabbed the handle and slowly turned it. He heard the click of the lock as the bolt cleared its opening. He waited. Nothing. The door was simply unlocked. *Yes, another trap definitely awaited.* He opened the door to an empty stairwell. He began descending, pausing after each step, always listening for any sound of danger. Long years of experience had taught him that the traps set by man could have multiple bands of defense.

There was another door at the bottom of the stairwell. He unslung the automatic rifle, made sure the safety was off, and gently opened the door. He saw nothing. He heard nothing. All was quiet. He moved into the hallway and realized that he was on the eighth floor, Madame Rokoff's floor. Based upon the number that Ambassador Garner had provided, her apartment was near the other end of the building.

Twenty-three steps down the hall, the doors at either end of the hallway flew open releasing four heavily-armed soldiers — two from each door. They rapidly moved to take up positions within three feet on either side of Tarzan. The trap had been sprung. Tarzan had expected something just like this. Outnumbered and out positioned for the moment, he laid down his weapon and raised his hands above his head. Now, these men would escort him to his opponent's lair. He hid his smile.

Chapter 37: DAY IN COURT

IAN AND JACKIE were in the prisoner's holding cell of the Old Bailey doing their final review of the evidence and the counterpunches that Ian intended to employ. Otto would be their key witness in proving Jackie's innocence. He was primed and ready to testify. Jackie had reviewed the material Ian would put into evidence: signoff sheets, three-dimensional timelines, signatures, and a myriad of other documents aimed at discrediting the Crown's yet to be identified star witness.

By the time they had concluded playing the devil's advocate with all the data, it was time for them to get ready for court. Ian left to go to his chambers for his robes and wig, while Jackie was given the suit Louise had picked out for him. Like all his other suits, it was tailor-made. Now, because of his prison life and his self-imposed rigorous rehabilitation program, the shoulders were tight while the waist was baggy. In addition, the pant legs drooped in the absence of the brace.

As soon as the guards saw that Jackie was ready, they escorted him to the base of the staircase to the prisoner's dock. He was nervous, yet confident. They had done their work and this time he WOULD walk out a free man. The overhead light went on signaling that the court was ready for his appearance. The guard on his left nudged him forward. He needed no encouragement. He began the ascent to the courtroom and his eventual freedom.

ALL THE PARTICIPANTS were in place. The gallery, unlike for the Commitment Procedure, was open to the public. Even though the case wasn't written about in the press, word of its importance had been widely circulated. The gallery was packed to standing room only. People were poised to hear all the dirty details of the case, reminiscent of when Madame Defarge and her gaggle of cronies sat waiting for the decapitation of French royalty, or a crowd at the British Grand Prix race awaiting a major crash. There was much more interest in the anticipated titillating discoveries than in justice being served.

The Clerk called the court to order, Lord Justice Bloweather entered from his chambers, assumed his usual position and the trial began. Leggarder, the Crown's prosecutor, launched into a lengthy monologue on how Jackie had done this and done that, all with malfeasance in mind and the goal of supplying financial aid and support to enemies of the Crown, most specifically the Irish Republican Army.

He then produced stacks of paper that laid out a trail of transactions that over time had moved hundreds of thousands of pounds from The Greystoke Trust through a myriad of global financial institutions ending up in Ireland with the officers of the IRA, thus providing them with readily available funds to buy weaponry and influence. A total of thirty-eight different pieces of documentation were entered into evidence, documents allegedly carrying Jackie's signature of approval for the transfer of vast amount of funds.

The Lord Justice interrupted the proceedings several times to specifically ask Ian if he wanted to object. In each case, Ian declined. Finally, Leggarder said, "The Crown rests its case."

The Judge turned to the defense table. Ian rose and began. "The Crown's most eloquent spokesperson has piled page upon page, document upon document upon the court, yet how do we know the validity or worth of any of the words presented. They are sheets of paper without source identification. From whence did they materialize? Yes, they document the transference of funds through a chain of institutions, but where is the human factor that testifies to their validity and authenticity? Without such they are just paper...useless paper.

"Who was the person or persons that brought this pile...," leaning on the stack of papers in front of him for emphasis, "...of rubbish forth as evidence against my client? There has not been a single sworn testimony by any person or persons that these...," he picked up a handful, "...are anything but someone's writings of fictional events, easily and justifiably dismissible as any form of evidence. The Crown has not presented a continuous chain of evidence in regard to this material, only an implied link here and there. It's poppycock I say, pure poppycock! Malarkey, blarney, hogwash." The gallery gasped in unison at the use of such language. Ian continued.

"Let the honorable Crown Prosecutor bring forth his alleged 'star' witness...," pausing only momentarily for affect, "...or let all these malicious charges be thrown out the proverbial window as litter on legality."

Leggarder's jaw dropped open at such outrageousness. At the same time, the gallery leaned forward in greater anticipation of the verbal brawling to come. This is what they had come for!

Throughout the eruption, the Judge banged his gavel until order was restored. "Mr. Leggarder, the defense has made a good point, although quite flowery in doing so. You have put forth documents into evidence, yet you have not revealed the identity of the person or persons who brought you such evidence. Nor have you provided a chain of possession for such documentation."

Leggarder rose in response. "The documentation is on The Greystoke Trust paper, and the person who brought it to our attention is a highly positioned and respected person within The Greystoke Trust. Because of the high sensitivity of this matter, I had hoped the presentation of the documentation would be of such impact that the provider's identity need not be exposed. If the defense, however, so deems it, we are prepared at this very moment to produce the provider of the documents."

The Lord Justice turned to Ian. "I realize that the Crown has closed its case and that by the canons of law is not entitled to reopening it; however, since you have called the Crown out, in a most aggressive manner, I am inclined to grant the Crown's representative the opportunity to produce said witness, provided you are in agreement to do so, fully knowing that to reject the introduction of this witness is well within your right, and would most certainly result in an appeal of decision whichever way the decision of this court may go, based upon the inadequacy of service provided to it by the Crown's current representative. If that was to happen the Crown's representative could, and would most probably, fall into a state of disgrace for failing to most effectively represent the Crown."

"My Lord, I would not like to bring such disgrace on one of my colleagues of the court. Thus, I would not contest your permitting the Crown's representative in reopening his case against my client, provided that the defense has the right and privilege of direct cross examination of said purveyor of these platitudes of falsities and that such reopening be limited to the introduction of the called witness."

The Lord Justice turned to Leggarder. "Are you ready to produce your witness, now?"

"Yes, my Lord."

The Judge cleared his throat to say "proceed", when he was interrupted by the bailiff mumbling, "Ahhem." The judge looked toward the bailiff who was gesturing at his watch. The judge, in turn, looked at his watch, and then looked out at the courtroom. "It has been called to my attention that should such testimony begin now that it would be incomplete prior to the normal time of adjournment for lunch. Therefore, to keep the testimony intact, I hereby declare a temporary recess for lunch. Court will reconvene at 1:00 p.m." With that said the judge gaveled the court to recess. Everyone stood as the judge left the courtroom, then each in turn left to wander the halls of Old Bailey. Jackie was returned to the holding area for a brief meal and to bide his time until court reconvened.

Ian, appearing in somewhat of a lather, elbowed his way through the departing crowd to work his way to the entrance to the prisoner holding area. Jackie was sitting at a table and upon seeing Ian enter, pointed to the chair across from him for Ian to take a seat.

"I must be balmy to let you run your own defense, but so far, the Crown's played into your hands. Everything is riding on the Crown's key witness. If it isn't who we think it will be, then we will be in a sea of sewage!"

"Ian, you worry too much. There is no way for anyone else to walk through the door. You just wait and see. Now, if you don't mind, I'd like to eat my delicious bologna sandwich with my wedge of cheddar. I've grown so accustomed to prison food I think I'll have it placed on the menu of The Trust's dining room." Neither could keep a straight face and both broke out into laugher…a most unique sound considering the room in which it resonated.

At precisely 1:00 p.m. the Lord Justice emerged from his chambers and called the court to order. "Mr. Leggarder, please call your witness."

Leggarder acknowledged the Judge's order with a nod and then turned to the Clerk and nodded once more. The Clerk turned to open an outside door to let the key witness enter when a door at the opposite end of the courtroom flew open.

"My Lord, please pardon this intrusion. I have need to address this court on a matter of the highest urgency." The entire court focused on the intruder, a man of dignified diplomatic dress. Without hesitation, he moved toward the magistrate. The Court's Usher moved to stop him but the man simply brushed him aside and continued walking towards the magistrate. It was a performance of outrageous action draped in a cloak of dignity.

"I have information germane to this matter. If you will but read this note, I believe things will be made clear." The man extended the envelope he had been carrying to the judge.

The Lord Justice took it, opened it and after scanning its contents, announced, "This court is in immediate recess for an undetermined time. Clerk, please bring this gentleman, along with the Crown's and defendant's representatives, to my chambers immediately. Return the defendant below. Thank you."

The entire courtroom was wallpapered in silence. Ian looked at Jackie and shrugged his shoulders out of disbelief of what might be happening. Leggarder was in the same state of unknowing. It was a full twenty seconds before the silence of the room was broken by people in the gallery shaking off their disbelief and bursting into loud, speculative conversation as to what had just gone on, what might happen next. Representatives of the Press in the gallery stumbled over each other in a mad dash to phone in their reports. Such action was unheard of; a case like this had never been suspended in such a matter. None of the speculation proved to be even near the actual truth.

EIGHTY-NINE MINUTES after the judge had suspended proceedings, an extended-frame black Bentley limousine with heavily tinted windows pulled up to a side door of The Old Bailey. Its back door opened. Two people emerged from the court house and entered the car. The surrounding area had been cleared to assure privacy and anonymity. As soon as the occupants were seated, the limousine sped away, out into London traffic, headed for an unidentified destination. The public was left to speculate what had happened.

Chapter 38: BLOOD FEUD

TARZAN WAS SURROUNDED. The five foot, nine inch figure of a man of square jaw and body emerged from a door at the opposite end of the hallway. Heavy thick eyebrows dominated his forehead above his small, almost beady, eyes. He was in full military attire from his oversized hat to the spit-shined shoes. He walked past the soldiers as if they were not there and approached Tarzan.

"Ah, Lord Greystoke, it is an honor to meet you. I must say I'm a little disappointed. Based upon the stories of your adventures, I expected you to show up in a loincloth with a bow and a quiver of arrows across your shoulder."

Tarzan just stared at the man in front of him. "Different Jungles require different attire."

"Well said. I am Major Gregor Gregorvich. I am commander of this military sector. Please, lower your arms. You are among friends," breaking into a gap-toothed smile. "Your government is most interested in, how should I say it, catching up with you. But first, I think we should have a private discussion that might be more beneficial to both of us. Come with me." Again, the gap-toothed smile, this time combined with broad squinting of the eyes.

Tarzan said nothing, lowered his arms and followed the Major to a room from which the Major had initially emerged. They entered alone, the soldiers left to stand guard outside.

"Please, be seated", the Major said pointing to a well-worn sofa. "Your government said that you might try to see Madame Vokolesky. They implied that you might want to cause her some bodily harm. They asked us to retain you and return you to them should you show up." The Major paused for a reaction.

"Tarzan said, "You mean Madame Rokoff."

"Ah. Why do you call her that?"

"Because her grandson is the very image of her first husband, Nikolas Rokoff."

"You are correct. Nikolas Rokoff was her first husband. And, I believe you were responsible for his demise. Is that not so?"

"He was responsible for his own demise. He also tried to sell my son to a group of cannibals. He was a most despicable man who died in the jaws of Sheeta, the panther. I had no hand in it."

"We try to cooperate with all governments, especially Western ones. That is what I've been instructed to do. However, I have some objectives that might be better served by you remaining free. Would you be interested in hearing them?" Tarzan gave an affirmative nod.

"Good. You see I have had to put up with Madame Rokoff for many years. The State made me her keeper. If I had my way she would be long gone; but she has champions in very high positions that keep her in residence, people who remember her sacrifices for the Revolution and beyond." He paused again, cleared his throat and then proceeded.

"I know every detail of Madame Rokoff's life. You are the wild man she blames for her husband's death, even though he was truly a pig of a man and an opportunist of the highest degree. I have a fairly good idea what you want from her. You believe she is the root of the problems that your family has been experiencing. Is that not so?"

Tarzan nodded his agreement. The Major went on.

"I don't care what is between your families, but I do wish her gone. On more than one occasion she has interfered in my career, resulting in me being overlooked for promotions.

If she doesn't get exactly what she wants, when she wants it, she causes all sorts of trouble. Her age has passed, but somehow her influence has not diminished, if not grown.

"Let me put it this way, you have certain goals, as do I, and both are tied to Madame Rokoff. If you help me, then I might be in a position to help you. Or, as they say in your country 'we watch each other's back.'

"I have a plan that I think whereby our individual goals can be mutually achieved."

Tarzan knew exactly what the Major was implying. The Major wanted Tarzan to kill Madame Rokoff. He would not kill Madame Rokoff to help the Major achieve his objectives, but he would let events play out.

Tarzan finally spoke. "Excellent. Let us go see her now, the sooner the better."

"Before we go, I must warn you that she has several cats. Their urine odor combined with perspirations of an old woman can be quiet offensive to one's nostrils. That said, let us go."

MADAME ROKOFF WAS in her rocking chair in front of the large picture window that gave her a complete view of the park across the street. She was humming a childhood song, reminiscing over recent events. One cat was draped around her shoulders, another curled up and purring on top of the afghan covering her lap. The other seven cats were lounging in various areas of the apartment.

She was daydreaming. *It was all coming to pass, and* Pravda *was reporting it.* Pravda *loved stories of the decadent capitalistic West collapsing upon itself. Such stories proved the Communist way to be right! The Greystokes were symbols of Capitalism and she was destroying them. Their plantation was gone. Their wealth accumulated from bullion and gems stolen from Nikolas was being siphoned into her coffers. The entire family was falling into disgrace. Yes, it was all finally happening.*

A knock on the door and deadbolts being turned interrupted her musing. She said, "Who's there? What do you want?"

The door opened and the Major stepped forth. "Good afternoon Madame Rokoff. I've brought you a present." He stepped aside revealing Tarzan standing with his head hung down and his hands seemingly tied in front of him, when in fact the binding was the cord that ran from the microphone cupped in his hands to the recorder in his pants pocket.

The look on Madame Rokoff's face was ecstatic. A smile streamed across her withered face to the extent that her multiple layers of wrinkles virtually vanished. Tears came to her eyes. "Major, Oh Major. You could not have given me a better present."

She looked at Tarzan, her joy of ecstasy turning to disgust and vengeance, "You. You. You cheated my husband. You cheated me. You robbed us of his rightful finds. You took the gold and diamonds of Opar. They belonged to my husband. He found them, but you stripped him of all that was rightfully his. Now is your judgment day. Your family is being destroyed...and rightfully so...by mine!"

What he had heard and recorded went a long way in proving the innocence of his family, but not far enough. He decided to take a risk, to throw out a bluff, in hopes she would believe it.

"You are wrong, Madame Rokoff. My family has and will survive. I have come to tell you that your plotting and scheming has been for naught. Your lies are being stripped away. Your grandson who tried to destroy us rests in the dirt of Africa – along with the dried bones of his lying cheating grandfather."

The words burnt into the bitter-eaten soul of Madame Rokoff. A blood-curdling scream spewed out of her mouth. "You lie! You're a liar! My grandson lives. He must live! He's the last male heir. He will be victorious!"

The Major saw an opening and took it. "I am sorry Madame Rokoff, but Lord Greystoke speaks the truth. Your son is missing and presumed dead." A false mask of grief covered the Major's face.

The Major's affirmation of Tarzan's ruse snapped what little vestige of sanity that remained in Madame Rokoff. She leaped out of her chair, throwing the cat from her lap. Wielding a pair of long scissors that had been concealed in the folds of the afghan on her lap, she lunged across the room at Tarzan. He did not move. He simply raised his hands to intercept the downward sweeping arms of his attacker.

Madame Rokoff could not, try as she might, break the firm steady hold of Tarzan. Out of a mixture of frustration, bitterness and anger she screeched unintelligible sounds. She began to convulse, her whole body shaking. The scissors dropped from her grasp. Her skin color went from flush red to a grayish pallor. A gurgling sound came up from the depths of her body followed by an outrushing of blood from her throat. She went limp. The trauma had been too much. Her own vengefulness had brought on a massive heart attack. Tarzan lowered the frail body to the floor; the seven cats on the floor began circling around her as if trying to form a protective shield.

The Major beamed. "This is better than expected! You get your confession of conspiracy …and she dies of natural causes! What could be better?"

He turned to Tarzan. "Now we must address your situation. As much as I would like to let you go free my obligations to my country are more demanding. I'm afraid that I will have to escort you to the Lubyanka where a few of your countrymen await your arrival," at which point he drew his pistol, pressed it against Tarzan's chest and called for the soldiers waiting outside to enter.

Tarzan had expected nothing less and so he was not unprepared. He made a low hissing sound. Immediately two of the cats attacked the Major; one leapt up from the floor biting the Major's wrist, while the other bolted from the back of the sofa at the Major's face and hand. Four sets of claws dug deep into the Major's face. The Major gave out a hysterical scream, dropped his pistol and reached for his face in an attempt to extricate the tearing talons.

The door burst open and the first two of the four soldiers who had been waiting outside rushed in. Tarzan was ready, having moved to the opening side of the door. He grabbed the arm of the first onrushing soldier and spun him around and smashed him into the wall. He crumbled to the floor. Tarzan tripped the second one who went sprawling on the floor where the other seven cats immediately attacked him.

As the remaining two soldiers rushed in, Tarzan picked up the Major's revolver and turned to face them. They immediately realized that they were at a disadvantage. Tarzan motioned for them to lay down their weapons. He murmured something else and the cats immediately stopped their attack, striking a stance of attention.

The Major, his face covered in blood that partially blinded him, tried to take advantage of Tarzan's back being turned to him. He reached into his boot, pulled out an eight-inch stiletto, raised it over his head and charged.

Tarzan heard the footsteps but before he could react the largest of the cats, the one that had been draped around Madame Rokoff's neck, leapt into the air. It jumped to a nearby stuffed chair, then onto the mantelpiece, ultimately landing on the nape of the Major's neck. Claws dug in. White fangs flashed as they dug into the Major's jugular vein, ripping it wide open. The Major bled out in seconds.

The two soldiers were shocked. They had never seen such savagery. Tarzan didn't flinch. He had seen it many times over. He used the opportunity to knock out both soldiers at once by brutally smashing their heads together. He quickly stripped the soldiers down to their underwear. He then took lamp cording to securely bind each in such a way that if one tried to get untied the loop of cording around his companion's neck would tighten. As he was doing all this, the cats moved in and out between his legs, purring their pleasure of the moment.

When the soldiers were secured, Tarzan changed into the uniform of the soldier closest to him in build. The fit was tight, but acceptable as long as he did not have to fully flex his muscles. Lastly, he went to the kitchen and laid out ample food for the cats. He didn't know how long it would take before they were discovered and he didn't relish the idea of nine hungry cats banqueting on the remains in the living room over several days.

He went down the hall to the first room the Major had taken him. A strong nudge of the door was enough of a key to open it. He went directly to the telephone and while he spoke some Russian he hoped he got an operator that spoke English. His luck held, and within minutes he was talking to D'Arnot.

"My friend," it was D'Arnot speaking, "I think it best that we need to go the non-diplomatic route to extract you from there. How long can you stay where you are?"

"Not long. Why?"

"So, I know where I can reach you. I have to make a few calls to see what can be done."

"Don't bother. I'll call you back. I'm heading to the airport. I'll call you back in two hours. Talk to you then." He hung up noting that the whole conversation had taken just under two minutes, just under the time it took most calls to be traced. He didn't know whether the phone was bugged or the call traced, but jungle knowledge taught him to be thorough and wary.

All the time he and D'Arnot had been talking, Tarzan had been tapping out a much different message in Morse Code on the mouth piece: going to train station...will call back in an hour.

Moments later, a solitary soldier walked into the snow-covered air of Moscow and headed for the nearest metro station.

Chapter 39: FROM RUSSIA WITH HASTE

IT WAS LATE IN THE AFTERNOON. The rail station was full of commuters. The trip from Chistye Prudy station to Moskva Belorusskaia train station took thirty-seven minutes giving Tarzan twenty-three minutes before calling D'Arnot. He used the time to do some reconnaissance. Assuming the ramrod position of a well-trained soldier, he moved through the crowd virtually unnoticed. A Soviet soldier always had the right of way. People looked away. It was best not to know a face, as someone might someday come in the middle of the night to take you for a lengthy stay at one of many Siberian re-education camps.

The stroll around the station proved most interesting. There were at least three groups of two men each who seemed to be acting as nonchalant as possible and by doing so made themselves stand out: One pair Russian, a second French, and the third English. Each group's behavior gave off an aura of a wasted assignment. They would do what their superiors told them to do, but not expecting any results. Tarzan knew what their assignment was: Find him!

It was time to make his call. He found a pay phone and dialed the number to make a long-distance call. A long-distance operator picked up. While Tarzan knew some Russian he hoped his operator spoke English as many international operators did. His luck of the draw was only marginally successful. The operator spoke little English and comprehended even less. After repeating, and repeating again D'Arnot's number the operator placed the call and instructed Tarzan to deposit fifty-six rubles for three minutes. He did. The call went through.

"You are very prompt my friend, but then I would expect nothing less. I am afraid that my hands are tied. I've even tried using my DGSE *(Direction General of Security External, i.e., the French equivalent of the CIA)* connections and in turn their relations with the KGB. No luck. Seems the Russians are furious about the presents you left for them."

"Are you saying I'm on my own?"

"Yes, but not quite. I have contacted Meriem's brother, François Jacot, who you know is very active in trading with the Soviet Union. Cardifaire is a major supplier to ABK, the Soviet market group. In turn, his company is one of the largest importers of Russian goods to France. It's my understanding that he may have employment for you should you find yourself in such need."

"Where would I find such employment?"

"Go to the freight area. Look for the Cardifaire area and ask for Fred Schump. He is Cardifaire's man in Moscow. As I understand it there is a shipment of caviar and sturgeon leaving for Paris tonight. I wouldn't waste my time."

"Thank you, Paul. I'll look into it right away."

As Tarzan turned around and stepped out of the phone booth, he came face-to-face with another Soviet Soldier who said, "Why *do* you talk French on the telephone? Who are you?"

Tarzan responded, "Why were you listening?" Without giving the soldier time to respond, Tarzan kneed him in the groin and at the same time clamped his hand on the soldier's windpipe. Tarzan lifted him off the floor and in one motion pivoted and slammed the soldier's head on the back wall of the booth. The soldier was knocked out. Tarzan lowered him onto the phone booth's seat. He then took the receiver and cradled it under the soldier's chin as if he was in a conversation on the phone. Closing the booth's door, Tarzan slowly walked away. No one seemed to have noticed the entire incident.

IT TOOK NEARLY twenty minutes of meandering through the station to find the freight area. It wasn't that the freight area was hidden or hard to find, it was more to be sure he wasn't being followed. The whole area was a scurry of activity as boxcars of fruits, vegetables, cheeses and wine were being unloaded and as rapidly refilled with caviar, sturgeon, vodka and other Russian dining delicacies. Tarzan stopped a stevedore, asked for Fred Schump, and was directed towards a stocky heavily muscular individual several boxcars down.

Tarzan approached the man and said in French, "Mr. Schump? I was told that you had a job opening that I might fill."

Schump hesitated then responded. "Yeah? Why would I have a job for you? I don't need any extra security. Who told you that?"

"Francois Jacot."

"He's always recommending someone to do something." Schump then scanned Tarzan from head-to-toe. "You might work out. You look like you're strong enough to last a night or two. Come with me. Before you start you've got to fill out some paperwork."

Schump turned and started walking toward a door over which a light bulb dangled. No fixture, just bare bulb wiring. Once inside the small room, Schump said, "Okay. Don't take any offense to the performance out there. You never know who might be listening. I was expecting you. You can't work in that outfit. Look through that pile over there. You should find something to fit. And get a heavy coat. You're going to need it. Leave the uniform. I'll get rid of it."

Tarzan did as he was told. Schump continued to talk. "Here's the plan. You're going to be the inside loader on tonight's train. Thing is when it's all loaded you stay inside. I'll personally close and lock the door. There shouldn't be any problem with the inspectors. They all get paid off on a regular basis."

"The train's destination is Paris. In total thirty-eight hours. It makes multiple stops, seventeen to be exact, but you won't be able to get out. That's why you need the warm coat, plus that bag of food over there," pointing to a package on the desk. "Don't want you eating into the company's profits — as if no one else does." Schump laughed at his own joke.

As soon as Tarzan changed, the two men set to work loading the boxcars. It would have been physically challenging for most men, but Tarzan relished the chance to be physically active as there was too little time in the modern world to do so.

He and Schump were halfway through loading the last palette of vodka when four men, two in military uniforms, and two in civilian attire, appeared. Tarzan knew immediately their presence meant trouble because one of the soldiers was the same one he had knocked out and stuffed in the phone booth, and the two civilians were the English team from the station.

"That's him! That's the one!" The Russian shouted in broken English while pointing at Tarzan. The other soldier raised his AK-47 into the ready position. The two English agents stepped forward in front of the soldiers. The larger of the two said, "That won't be necessary. I'm sure Lord Greystoke will come along peacefully."

It was at this point that Tarzan took the case of vodka he had been holding, raised it over his head and hurled it at the four men. Simultaneously, he pushed Schump out of the way. "This is my fight. Stay clear."

The men never thought Lord Greystoke would attack and not submit to the Crown. Before they could recover, he hit the lead man in the solar plexus with a forward leg kick, completely knocking the wind out of him. He fell back into the other three. They crumbled into a mass of entangled arms and legs fighting each other to untangle and regain their balance.

Tarzan dove into the pile of flaying arms and legs. He drove a left cross into the man on the outmost part of the pile

and let the punch follow through, connecting his elbow squarely to the man's chin who was next to him. Both crumpled like
a bag of bones.

The only remaining adversary was the armed Russian
soldier who was raising his weapon to fire. Tarzan grabbed the
barrel of the AK-47 and ripped it from the soldier's grasp. The
Russian stared in disbelief, and while he was doing so, he felt
himself being lifted into the air and being hurled at the nearby
concrete wall. His head collided with the wall, making a noise
like a watermelon breaking open.

Tarzan stood among the human rubble that he had
created. He turned to look for Schump and that's when something heavy hit him squarely in the back of his neck. Everything
went black.

"I must apologize for that, but you of all people should
understand survival of the fittest. I have to continue to live
here," said Schump. Tarzan had been struck down by the only
force that ever momentarily defeated him…man's ability at
deception and conspiracy for one's own betterment.

Meanwhile, the men were regaining consciousness.
They saw Schump standing over the motionless Lord Greystoke.
The lead English agent said, "Respectable job. We'll take it from
here."

He slowly rose, shaking his head in an attempt to clear
his thinking and walked to where Tarzan lay. As he did so,
Tarzan began to move. Seeing that, he hollered at his co-
conspirator, "Get up! Get up! Hold him down before he can
do any more damage."

As the second man threw himself on Tarzan, the leader
withdrew a case from his coat pocket, and opened it, revealing
a syringe and a vial, and loaded the syringe.

"Hurry up, he's starting to come around. He's starting
to move! I don't think I can hold him!"

The leader quickly knelt, grabbed Tarzan's forearm, and stabbed Tarzan with the syringe. A warm feeling coursed through Tarzan's body. Then, he fell back into blackness.

"There. He should sleep for a good four hours. Let's get him out of here."

TARZAN'S SUPERIOR BODY assimilated the drug in a little over two hours. He slowly woke, feeling his arms and legs restrained and lying on a makeshift bed, possibly a cot of some kind. He slowly opened his eyes. The room was heavily shadowed and it took a couple of minutes to bring things in focus. The first thing he saw was a familiar portrait. He instantly knew that he was in the British embassy, because where else would one see such a large portrait of Queen Elizabeth the Second.

"His eyes just flickered. He's starting to wake up. Go get the ambassador," said a voice beyond his vision. A door opened then closed. Silence returned. Tarzan did not move. He quietly waited to see the intent of his captives.

Eight minutes later the door opened again and then closed. Footsteps crossed the room to the cot on which Tarzan lay. A slight opening of one eye let Tarzan see a tall, slender man in his sixties. He knew the face, the face of Lord Ellington, Britain's ambassador to the Soviet Union. He did not acknowledge the identification; best to wait to see what develops.

The ambassador's first words were, "For God's sake. Remove those shackles. He's an English lord, not a criminal. We're more civilized than that." He then turned to Tarzan. "Lord Greystoke, John, can you hear me?" Tarzan nodded. "Good. First I must apologize for the treatment that you have undergone. It was quite unnecessary. Underlings do so many times misconstrue their instructions."

Tarzan took the opportunity and said, "So why am I here? Why have you been hunting me down?"

"Excellent question. The answer is we need your help. Claytons seem to be in trouble all over the place. First your son's involvement with Fossey, then your grandson being accused of high treason and your African compound attacked.

"And then when we tried to meet with you, you evaded us and sought help from the French. It made the Home Office quite nervous. MI6 thought you might be trying to run. When you came to Russia, it seemed to validate the concern. We couldn't have you running around free, until we discovered just what was going on."

Tarzan didn't speak, but his posture and face showed that he was not buying the entire package that the ambassador was trying to sell him. The ambassador went on.

"When you were searched for any weapons, we found your tape-recorded visit with Madame Rokoff. That clarified one issue; you weren't running, you were pursuing.

"Of course, you must understand that because of your actions the Russkies very much want to talk to you. You did, after all, leave quite a mess behind; Madame Rokoff dead, as well as Major Gregorvich. They very much want to hear your story. Don't worry. We'll handle that end. There are more important matters."

"I agree."

"Fortunately, while we've been trying to catch up with you, events have been resolving themselves. Let me give you a quick synopsis of the latest lay of the land.

"Concerning your son, the good news is the Rwandans are focusing more on the American student, Wayne McGuire, and on Emmanuel Rwelekona, a tracker that Fossey had fired because she suspected him of working with the poachers. The bad news is your son's current location is still unknown. His wife is also missing."

"Where he is shouldn't be a concern. He can take care of himself. He's probably in the jungle with friends."

"While I can't go into details and while I don't have confirmation I do believe that some kind of solution is in the works for your grandson and your Trust. I'm being told that there's been a royal 'screw-up' between MI5, MI6 and the Home Office. Seems no one cared to inform the others what they were doing."

Tarzan started to ask for more details, but the ambassador said, "I wish I could tell you more, but I can't...at least on that matter. I can however tell you more about the attack on your home.

"The latest intelligence reports we have is that there's a large contingency of Zairian Special Forces who have launched an attempt to overthrow the government. There are Russian bear paw tracks all over the place. Our sources believe the Russians are more interested in creating a conflict so they can gain complete control of the mineral rights in the area. If true, it puts our influence there at jeopardy... too much at risk economically. Something we can't tolerate. We believe the attacks on your home and other surrounding plantations are a direct attempt to eliminate your influential opposition to the mining of such minerals, metals and other resources."

"That makes sense. We've been approached before and have rejected all such offers. The land belongs to the native Africans. They should be the ones to determine what is best for them and their communities."

"Right," said the ambassador. "That's why your country needs you to go back to Africa and use whatever means available to investigate these claims and if necessary put an end to the Bear's influence. Once you determine what is needed, you will have the full resources of your country to carry out whatever is necessary."

Tarzan grew suspicious. "You, in essence, want me to do your political spying?"

"Well, yes, you could say that; however, there is something else you need to know...something on a more personal level." The ambassador paused, cleared his throat and continued. "The escort that was taking your wife back to your compound was ambushed. Her escorts were killed but there is every sign that she was taken captive...by the same group leading the coup."

The scar on his forehead, given to him many years before during a fight for tribal supremacy with Tublat the ape, turned crimson. Tarzan was enraged. His gray eyes narrowed in fury. His entire body leaned forward, and his hands turned into fists. *If Jane was in danger, he would do whatever was asked.* "How soon can I leave?"

"I anticipated that, old boy. There's a car downstairs to take you to a plane that is fueled and waiting for you at Sheremetyevo-Two. It's flying under diplomatic immunity so you won't have any trouble from the Russkies. Pop on those clothes over there," pointing at a pile on the desk across the room, "and we'll have you on your way."

Then Lord Ellington, having completed his mission, bid Tarzan farewell and left the room.

Within ninety minutes, Tarzan was pacing like a caged lion in a British BAE 146 CC2 winging his way to Africa and the confrontation that awaited him.

Chapter 40: DIVERSIONARY ACTION

WHEN JON, NUBIBY AND ZUBERI DISAP-PEARED down the hole in the earth, Kerkuk addressed his fellow apes, imploring them to join him in aiding these humans at the front of the cave. The apes refused. The game with the two gomangani had been fun. But now it was time to forage and return to their shes. They began to disperse.

Kerkuk challenged them. This was Tarzan, part of their tribe. Yes, their ape minds reasoned. Tarzan was part of their tribe. But Tarzan was not here. Tarzan was not in trouble. Hence, they would not act.

Kerkuk, in the manner of his kind, reasoned this way himself and could not have explained why he was intent on saving Korak.

They ignored him, moving off into the jungle. He roared his frustration at them. "I will go alone. I will do it. I will bash the skulls of the gomangani. The same gomangani who plague you, kill your tribe, leave your shes unprotected and alone. I will do it. Go. Eat your fruit. Find your shes. I, Kerkuk, will do it for you." He was enraged, pounding his chest and ripping branches from the nearest tree and throwing them after the departing apes.

They got the message. The group returned and stood before him. They wanted very much to crush the skulls of the gomangani who had plagued them for so long.

THE SCENE IN THE CAVERN was tense. Jon, Korak, Nubiby and Zuberi had turned right from a passageway headed towards the back of the cavern, avoiding the men watching the battle from the immense cavern mouth. They intended to skirt the walls to the other side where they hoped to find Meriem and Jane in a passageway there. Almost immediately, they had encountered four white men, including the Chief and a Russian general. Jon and Korak now faced them, rifles raised. Nubiby and Zuberi had turned 180 degrees towards the cavern mouth when the general's men, at his shouted command, had run to block any escape and were now pointing rifles at Nubiby and his son, who were pointing theirs back. Facing Jon and Korak, the Russian general held Jane with a knife to her throat. Meriem and Ashanti were a few feet away, each held tightly by one of the general's men.

INTO THIS TAUT SCENE, Kerkuk led the apes. They climbed down the cliff face above the cavern through the trees and hanging vines, and dropped onto the rock floor at the mouth of the cave, roaring and hooting their arrival. The combined roars of seven bull apes was as stunning and unexpected as it was deafening, echoing off the walls of the cavern and drowning out the sounds of the battle raging down the valley.

The soldiers facing Nubiby and Zuberi had their backs to the cavern opening and did not see the apes arrive. Startled by the roars, they turned reflexively. Nubiby and Zuberi took that opportunity to fire, killing three immediately and scattering the others into the passageways.

At the same time, the guards holding Meriem and Ashanti turned sharply toward the commotion. It was enough. Meriem and Ashanti pivoted and brought their right feet solidly into the groins of their respective guards, sending them to the floor writhing in agony.

As every action has an equal and opposite reaction, Meriem and Ashanti, whose hands were tied behind them, suddenly found themselves off-balance and falling backwards.

Jane felt the General's attention diverted for just an instant and collapsed into a heap on the floor. The general grabbed for her as she fell but he was too late. Jon and Korak fired staccato shots in unison. The General's body jerked and twitched like a hooked fish, then toppled backward to the stone, his chest a sieve of oozing blood.

Meriem and Ashanti collided with Chertok and the Chief, all four collapsing in a heap on the cavern floor. Chertok scrambled for a hold on Meriem and dragged her to her feet, stopping Jon and Korak in their headlong rush towards them. The Chief grabbed Ashanti's tied hands and dragged her towards one of the back passageways. This was going badly for him and the witch girl was better than nothing. But Ashanti wasn't going quietly. She kicked and twisted violently, jerking the Chief one way and then the other like a shark being landed in a small fishing boat and taking its vengeance before it died.

The Chief could not hold her. He released her and attempted to bring the butt of his gun down on the top of her head, but she rolled to the side and the butt connected with the granite floor sending daggers of pain up to the Chief's shoulder, rendering his arm useless. He looked wildly around at the scene, then disappeared down a passage.

Ashanti shimmied up the back wall to regain her feet. To her left, Chertok struggled to hold Meriem who twisted and turned like a snake trying to break free of his grasp. Jon and Korak inched towards them, guns pointed, waiting for the first clear shot.

Chertok spoke in Meriem's ear. "Stop or I will fire now." She stopped, realizing that Korak or Jon might kill him but he could still fire first and kill one of her family or Ashanti. Had he fired then, the dynasty of Tarzan would have ended there in that cave. But in true Chertok family fashion, he gloated, enjoying his moment of triumph and the imminent deaths of the two Claytons at his hands.

"Who would like to die first?"

He was met with silence. Chertok, intent on his prizes, had blocked out the hooting and chest pounding of the apes in the front of the cavern. The soldiers at the front were dead or running. Nubiby and Zuberi were in Chertok's line of fire and unable to help. Behind him, one lone ape advanced slowly along the cavern wall to the back of the cave, eyes focused only on him.

"If you will not choose, I shall choose for you. I think it is hardest on the old to see the young die first. So, young Clayton, you are first." Chertok laughed and fired. Ashanti had pushed off from the cave wall running straight for Jon as Chertok spoke the last sentence. As she collided with Jon, she felt small stings cross her back like small children pelting her with pebbles. Then she felt nothing.

Jon's attention had been on Chertok and Kerkuk who he expected to roar a diversion at any second. He did not see Ashanti's dash and collapsed onto his back under her weight.

"Ashanti." She was lying across his chest. His arms went around her. He felt a sticky wetness on her back and, panicked, pushied her up and over sharply onto her back, knowing but refusing to know she was gone.

"Ashanti," Jon looked into her eyes and watched their spark vanish. No fire. No humor, no vexation, no protest, nothing. He closed them and cradled her, tears dropping onto the whorls and curls of her beautiful face.

Jon felt Meriem drop down to the floor beside him. He turned to her and she was jolted by the despair in his eyes. Meriem took his arm and rested against him.

"She loved you, Jon."

As Ashanti and Jon collapsed to the floor, Korak had run to intercept Chertok from the side hoping to get a clean shot. Chertok held Meriem in front of him, his left arm threaded through hers, still tied behind her. When he fired at Jon, Meriem screamed and threw her body backwards into Chertok desperate to knock them both to the ground and give Korak, now rushing towards them, a chance to intervene. As they fell backwards in tandem, Chertok fought to keep his balance and took the only chance he had left. He fired at Korak who saw his intent and dove to the floor. There was no need. Chertok, still struggling to stay standing, could not hold his aim. His arm flailed like leaves in a storm and the shots went wild.

Just as it seemed Chertok and Meriem were bound to fall, a long hairy arm snaked around Chertok's waist and jerked him backward and to the side, free of Meriem. At the same time a second hairy arm smashed down on his gun hand and then enveloped him from the other side, pinning that arm. The gun clattered to the floor and Kerkuk dragged his prize off towards the front of the cave. Chertok screamed and writhed in the ape's grasp, his feet scrabbling over the stone but finding no purchase.

Korak watched from the cavern floor and left justice to the ape. Jane came to stand beside him and he rose to his feet, drawing his knife to free her. Jane and Korak stood together and watched the ape drag Chertok to his fate.

Chertok could not break the relentless squeeze of the ape. He went limp, feigning unconsciousness, hoping for something to distract the ape and loosen his grip. The ape mind is notoriously distractible and Kerkuk was no different in that regard. He curled his left arm around the waist of the limp Chertok, dangling him above the ground and freeing his right as the six other bulls surrounded him. Kerkuk growled and gestured, warning them that this was his kill and his alone. Chertok saw his chance and gave his body one last powerful twist and broke free. He fell to the stone and scampered off on hands and knees, thinking he was free and that Kerkuk would be distracted with the other apes. But once again, Chertok underestimated his enemy. Kerkuk would find it difficult to explain his loyalty to Korak or his rage at Chertok in ape terms.

He knew only that nothing would keep him from this tarmangani–not food, not other apes, not even a she.

Kerkuk lunged towards Chertok, rolling him onto his back, the momentum carrying the ape over him. They rolled, first one on top, then the other, Kerkuk squeezing ever more tightly, until they reached the lip of the cave and disappeared into the dense foliage below.

272

Chapter 41: COMPOUND POW-WOW

I T WAS EARLY MORNING WHEN TARZAN got his first glimpse of eastern Africa. It would take another hour and one half before the wheels touched down at Jomo Kenyatta International Airport Nairobi, Kenya. As soon as the plane came to a halt, Tarzan was up and out the door. A black limousine was parked just forty feet away. As soon as the door to the plane opened so did the rear door of the limousine. Its occupant immediately headed toward the plane. Ambassador Garner started talking even before the two were face to face.

"You're a great sight for sore eyes. I don't know how you do it, but you're one incredible surprise after another."

Before he could say more, Tarzan cut him off, "Cut the diplomacy. Let's cut to the chase. How many of the arrangements that I requested have been made?"

"All of them. Besides the chopper you requested, I've also arranged to have two other Chinook HC2 to accompany you. Each is heavily armed with machine guns and air-to-ground missiles. Per your request all markings have been covered over so no one will know who you are. There are thirty British Special Forces onboard each. If you need more support, all you have to do is call for it."

"What about the Zairians? Do we have air clearance with them?"

"Yes. Président Joseph Pelo Sakumbi has pledged his full co-operation. I believe he's scared to death that the rebels are renegades from his own army. He doesn't want to send in any of his regular army for fear they'll join forces in opposing him. He also wants to have someone to blame if things do go wrong."

"Understood. What about the whereabouts of my wife and family? Any word on that?"

"No specifics. The intelligence coming from the interior is disjointed and contradictory. Radio communications is intermittent at best. That's why we need you on the ground, to find out what is truly happening. Where do you plan to go first?"

"I'm going to our compound first. I need to see the damage first-hand. My people will have a better knowledge of what is happening. Where are the choppers?"

"Across the field."

"And the items I requested?"

"All are onboard your chopper. But how you plan to fight armed rebels with a knife, bow and arrows and a rope is beyond me."

"They're comfort apparel. Now, let's go."

Twenty minutes later the three Chinooks were airborne and headed to the Greystoke compound."

AS THE HELICOPTERS NEARED their destination, Tarzan contemplated the best way to their approach. Not knowing whether a communications center had been reestablished after the attack on the compound, Tarzan chose to be cautious in approaching the compound. He spoke to the pilot. "Take a swing around and then hover over that area by the large rock pile. That used to be my home. Have the other two choppers spread out and hover at a higher elevation." The pilot nodded his understanding.

As they circled and came into a hover position, Tarzan's keen eyes scanned the land to see what might be happening. He saw no one, but a single, old, very old native standing in the middle of the compound with his hands clasped behind his back. Tarzan recognized the man immediately. It was old

Mubuto. While no one else was in sight, he spotted movement among the piles of debris. Men were positioning themselves to have a direct line of fire on the chopper.

After hovering for two minutes, Tarzan gave the pilot his next instruction. "Now, slowly lower down to a very soft, very slow landing." As the pilot was doing so, Tarzan kept a sharp eye on the ground, being leery of a potential attack from any direction.

The chopper came to rest, its blades churning up a miniature windstorm. Mubuto remained stationary, as a stoic figure standing quietly in the face of impending danger.

From inside Tarzan shouted to its occupants, "Open the door, but stay out of sight. Armed soldiers are the last thing they want to see. The wrong impression now would do no good for anyone."

The door opened and Tarzan stepped out wearing nothing but his loincloth, his bow and arrow quiver over one shoulder, his rope over the other, and his new knife on his hip. "Habari rafiki yangu. (*Hello, my friend*) It is good to see you again."

Mubuto's face burst forth a broad smile. "It is good to see you again!" He then turned and shouted in Swahili, "It is Tarzan! Come! It is Tarzan!"

What was once empty space was suddenly filled with joyfully shouting natives. "He's back! Tarzan is back!"

As the celebration continued a path was cleared from the outer edge of the crowd toward Tarzan. The figure of a white man moved towards the focal point of the group. Tarzan had his back to him and because of the loud shouting did not become aware of the person until they were only a few feet apart. Tarzan turned toward the presence, his jungle instincts responding.

Both men looked at each other and then rapidly closed the remaining small space between them. Each hugged the other! "Jackie! Is that you...walking?"

"Yes, Granddad!"

"How?"

"The paralysis was more in my head...tied to the accident."

"I thought you were in London. Who's running the Trust?

"Ian and Otto."

"Not Louise?"

"No. Hopefully she's sitting in the same cell I occupied."

"What?"

"Remember when Willoby at MI6 recommended her so many years ago? Louise, it turns out, was a Russian agent that MI6 turned and Willoby was her control.

"When I heard the charges and that there were signed documents as evidence I knew that if I hadn't signed them, then there was only one other person who could have...Louise. She'd mastered my signature long ago for mundane types of correspondence. Realizing that, I told Ian to dig up everything he could, using whatever resources necessary, to find out as much about her as possible. I wanted facts, not the contravenes that Willoby had foisted her upon us.

"Ian came back with a ton of information. Noiseworthy supplied the key...he used his State connections to learn that Louise was the great niece of one Madame Deniska Vokolesky who raised her after her parents were killed in a purge. The Vokolesky name didn't mean anything until Ian added 'wife of Nikolas Rokoff.' Ian didn't recognize the significance of the Rokoff name, but I certainly did."

"I've been recently reminded of those names too," said Tarzan.

"How was your trip to Russia?"

"The old woman and her connection to the Russian military is dead."

"That's a relief. Well, it seems Willoby planted Louise with us to feed the Russians bogus economic and financial information knowing they would accept as fact because it was coming from the Trust.

"He suspected that she was stealing from us on the side, but considered the information she was providing on the Russians well worth the exchange...especially since the cost was not coming out of his budget but our pockets. He and his cronies felt their operation was so top secret that we couldn't even know about it. They were going to let me swing in the wind, believing that I would eventually be acquitted.

"Only during a casual conversation with someone at Whitehall about the trial did Willoby find out that Louise was the Crown's star witness. I'm told that he turned a bleached shade of white knowing her testimony would throw everything into the public's eye. That's why he interrupted the trial proceedings. He couldn't risk MI6 being exposed."

Tarzan shook his head from side to side in disgust. "As soon as we're back in London I will have a talk with Willoby." The look on Tarzan's face made it clear that Willoby would not be participating in a congenial conversation. "Right now we have more pressing issues."

Tarzan turned and shouted at his pilot. "Bring in the others." To the crowd he said, "We've work to do. Help unload the choppers. Jackie, Mubuto and I have matters to discuss.

The three moved to the shade of one of the makeshift buildings that had been constructed out of the rubble of the compound. Jackie quickly explained more fully his new-found ability to walk and that he had only arrived late the previous evening.

Tarzan turned his attention to Mubuto. "What do your men tell you of what is happening? Where is the rest of my family? What of the attackers? Where are they now?"

Mubuto just shook his head. "Monsieur Clayton, you have always been impatient, and for these matters I understand your urgency. Remember, however, many more of my people and family died than yours. I will tell you what I know and of what I hear.

"The drums say that the Lady Jane and Meriem are being held captive to lure you to their rescue. Korak, young Jon, fifty Waziri and a handful of guerillas are planning to attempt a rescue; but my eyes say that they will fail without your help. They are all in imminent danger. You and your men must hurry."

"Yes, but where do the drums say to go?"

As if on cue, the jungle began to resonate with the sound of drums, the telegraph of the natives. All listened intently. Tarzan's scar flashed red. Jackie unconsciously began squeezing his hands into fists. Mubuto's face scowled. The only good part of the news was it told the location of the insurgents' camp. It was in the high plains; an area peppered with caves.

The rest of the news was bad. Fighting was going on, but it was not going well. The drums went silent. Tarzan, Jackie and Mubuto looked in silence at each other. Tarzan finally spoke.

"Mubuto send word that we are on the way. Jackie, you ride in the second chopper. I'll be in the lead one. I'll direct the pilots as I know the way via the landscape. Let's go."

Tarzan was a man of few words and of more action. He followed the belief written by a famous author that had once written, "If man only spoke when he had something worthwhile to say and said that as quickly as possible, ninety-eight per cent of the human race might as well be dumb, thereby establishing a heavenly harmony from pate to tonsil."

Tarzan, Mubuto and Jackie moved as one toward the choppers, shouting farewells. As the three helicopters lifted off in one cloud of dust and verged toward the northwest, Mubuto mumbled, "May the great Tarmangani save Little Numa from the death coils of Histah. Let it be so."

The three metallic birds of prey faded into the distance, heading for an unknown dest

Chapter 42: CALL TO ACTION

THE PLAINS WERE TEEMING WITH WILD-LIFE: one and one half million wildebeest, three hundred thousand zebras along with a multiple variety of antelopes. They were the survivors of the eighteen-hundred-mile trek from the southern plains, following the path of their ancestors to give birth to their offspring.

They were not alone. They were joined by prides of lions, leopards, cheetahs as well as packs of hyenas and wild dogs who continually stalked the herds to feast upon the weaklings and the new born. It was life in its most natural and violent.

As they grazed three images broke the horizon. The herds paid little attention. The images looked like dragonflies. Then they grew in the size of birds of prey, gyrfalcons. The noise of engines trailed behind. Yet the herds continued to be indifferent. They had seen and heard such sounds before, bringing tourists to see from the air the gathered array and spectacle of species on the plains.

AS THE THREE HELICOPTERS neared the battle zone, Tarzan and Jackie realized that there was not one battle line, but three different areas of conflicts.

"Take us down closer. We need a better look." Tarzan told the pilot of his helicopter. "Tell the other two to hold their positions."

The chopper dropped to eight hundred feet. The three groups under attack became clear. One group appeared to be in the midst of the insurgents' camp. Clearly, they had been able to gain entrance to the camp before being discovered. There was every appearance that the battle was going hard against that group as the area of fighting had a visibly shrinking circumference.

The other two groups appeared to have attacked the camp using a two-prong strategy. The group to the left was dressed as guerillas; while the group to the right was clearly natives who Tarzan immediately recognized as the Waziri.

Both groups were severely outmanned. Tarzan's initial estimate was eight to one. Each group's only successful retreat laid in reaching the sharply rising cliffs behind them; however, heavy fire from two artillery installations cut off any chance they had of reaching the cliffs. Both groups were trapped. They were being slowly squeezed into annihilation. The noise, intensity and smoke of the battles blocked out any awareness on the ground of the helicopters hovering overhead.

The only element that had kept the Zairian rebels from sweeping to a rapid victory was the terrain's funnel shape that swept from wide open plains to narrow canyons. The effect limited the battle line to where only a reduced number of its troops could attack at a time.

Tarzan gave a thumbs-up to the pilot to return to their original level. As they ascended, he gave instructions to the other two choppers. "Two, see if you can't take out the battery on the left. Three, do the same to the one on the right." Both choppers changed course and dove out of formation headed for their appointed targets. Tarzan called Chopper Two," Put on Jackie."

"I'm here."

"Were you able to get through to Garner? Where are the promised reinforcements?"

"He just radioed back. The RAF has been delayed by equipment failure and waiting for munitions to load. They can't get off the ground for another hour."

"That's too long!"

"I know, and so does Garner. As soon as he found out about the delays he checked with the French. They have two hundred airborne personnel on maneuvers about one hundred fifty miles off our position. They're diverting. They should be here anytime."

Tarzan scanned the skies. "They may be on the way, but I don't see them."

At that moment, a loud boom jolted the sky. The artillery crew below had spotted Chopper Three as it dove on its position. They scrambled to fire their short-range man-portable air-defense system (MANPADS) missile launcher at the approaching adversary. Chopper Three's crew simultaneously launched its missile. Both intended targets were hit. The artillery battery and Chopper Three disappeared from the battle and the face of the earth.

Chopper Two's crew was more successful. It delivered its payload, and then rapidly climbed back into the skies. Another ball of flames announced that the second battery had been eradicated. The dense smoke from the explosions blurred the visibility of the choppers' occupants.

As the smoke cleared, Tarzan re-evaluated the situation on the ground. Things were still dire. Movement at the end of the valley caught his eye. He picked up the high-powered binoculars that lay between him and the pilot to get a closer look. What he saw brought simultaneous joy and consternation. There were Jane, Korak, Meriem and Jon. Yet, their path was leading them directly into the conflict.

Tarzan rapidly formulated a plan. He set down the binoculars and turned to the pilot, "Does that work?" pointing at a toggle switch on the Chopper's instrument panel that was marked speaker.

"Yes," was the instant reply.

"Go back to the herds." Tarzan radioed Jackie to follow.

The pilots had no idea what Tarzan was contemplating, but they had been told to do whatever Lord Greystoke instructed, so each turned their aircraft away from the battle and back to the plains. It was a three-minute flight that felt more like three hours. As they approached the grazing herds, Tarzan instructed the pilots to fly beyond them, then circle back descending to as low altitude as possible. As the turn commenced, Tarzan flicked the toggle-switch. The next thing that happened nearly scared his pilot half to death. The loudspeakers mounted on the outside of the Chinook gave forth a cry that few, if any, human beings had ever heard. *"AHHHYEE AHEE AAAH!"* Tarzan had issued his call for help. He was asking the herds to follow him.

Zebras, wildebeests, elephants and antelopes, along with the lions and leopards raised their heads in unison to the summons coming from the sky. Once again, the speakers shouted, *"AHHHYEE AHEE AAAH!"* The Lord of the Jungle called a second time. This time his denizens responded. Predator, prey and scavenger alike all became a rolling mass of devastation charging toward the battle scene. The wildebeests formed the front line. The zebra and antelopes followed next. The elephant comprised the back wall. Lions, cheetahs, leopards, along with the wild dogs and hyenas, ran along either side of the main body.

NO ONE ON THE BATTLEFIELD anticipated what deadly destruction was thundering towards them. Soldiers close to the front lines were so anxious to engage in the action that they totally ignored what was going on behind them. Their enemy was in front of them; their own troops behind. They could concentrate on the battle in front. It was a mistake that would cost them dearly.

The rear-most troops were the first to sense danger raging towards them. They looked back and saw a brownish gray dust cloud…a dust cloud growing in density, height and width until it nearly blocked out the sun...a dust cloud coming to consume them.

Then, the earth trembled, first gently, then more intently with each passing second. Their initial thought being an earthquake was happening; but that didn't explain the billowing dust storm. Their equipment began vibrating, then violently shaking. They wanted to break and run, but couldn't. They could barely stand. It was only then that the strength and scope of the impending disaster became apparent. They only barely had seconds from the time they first heard the *gnu* snorting of the wildebeest until the lowered heads and fixed horns raked into them.

The wall of raging wildlife rammed the back lines of the rebel army. Horns ripped and tore. Bodies fell under the onslaught to be trampled by unrelenting onrushing hoofs. Cloth and flesh sliced, then shredded, then grist into meal, finally to be soaked up by the dust-laden African earth. Formations of soldiers were pinned upon each other. Weapons were useless.

At the front lines, the soldiers broke rank and ran for survival. Suddenly the battle meant nothing, survival everything. Few succeeded. The majority perished as their path to survival was blocked by the back ranks being crushed into them and the narrowing of the terrain in front of them.

One moment Terrik and his men were fighting for their lives; the next their attackers were running in every direction. Terrik used the unexpected opportunity to hastily move his badly ravaged troops back into the foothills.

The Waziri acted even faster. They understood the thunderous trampling sound that reached their ears. They also had seen the Chinooks, and a known figure, dressed only in a loincloth, hanging out the side of one of the copters. Tarzan was there! It fortified them. He was coming to fight with them, as he had done so many times before with their forefathers. They rapidly withdrew, moving in unison towards the protection of the nearby boulders and trees.

Tarzan watched from above as the events unfolded. The stampede was doing what no man-made weapon of destruction could do. It was annihilating the enemy, literally trampling it into the ground. It was then that Tarzan saw a new danger. Jon, Korak, Jane and Meriem had seen too late that their descent from the cliffs had placed them in the path of the onrushing herds.

Tarzan raised forth another, different cry, "*EYAAA HOOOTAY,*" attempting to divert the thundering mass. The back tiers of the thundering mass heard the order and responded. They slowed, coming to a standstill as if waiting more instruction. The front lines were deaf to it. The wildebeest, zebras and antelopes continued their mad dash trampling everything in their path.

Tarzan helplessly looked on as his loved ones were about to be trampled into dust. He tried again, "*EYAAA HOOOTAY*". Jackie, seeing and hearing what his grandfather was attempting to do, joined in. More stopped, yet more continued.

Korak was the first to see that they had exchanged one set of dire circumstances for another even more dangerous. They were in the direct path of charging animals. Escape to either side was blocked by the fleeing soldiers. Re-ascending the cliffs was out of the question. There was only one thing to do, something he had never done before. He raised his arms, cupped his hands over his mouth, inhaled as deeply as he could and gave forth a blood curdling sound that overrode the surrounding hysteria, "*EYAAA HOOOTAY.*"

The herds kept coming...three hundred feet...then two hundred. The charging mass continued. Jon saw his grandfather prepare to call out again. He stepped up to Korak's side and joined his voice with that of his grandfather's, "*EYAAA HOOOTAY,*" at the same moment that Jackie and Tarzan repeated their cries. The unison of the four voices reached the herd. The moving mass slowed, coming to a stop within fifteen feet of the little group. The herd looked around as if waiting further instruction. When none came they simply turned and headed back to their original grazing area to continue life before it was interrupted. There was nothing left of the enemy army. There were a few, very few, who had reached the protective shelter of the jungle. The rest had all been pulverized into oblivion and rested in the African soil as bits and pieces.

The two helicopters set down thirty feet in front of the small gathering. Before the runners of the choppers had touched the ground, a figure bolted from the interior of each chopper and rushed to the group. Jackie hugged Jon, while Tarzan walked over to Jane, smiled, and said, "You get into more trouble when I'm not around." She reached up and hit him on the shoulder and then both folded into a long embrace.

A small head peaked out from the door of one of the helicopters and looked all around as to be sure everything was all right. Tarzan was the first to see the inquiring face. "Mubuto, come. It is safe."

He stepped out and as he moved toward the group he said, "I do not think I want to be carried in a helicopter again. It is too noisy…most frightening."

He walked past Tarzan and Jane, and everyone else, coming to a stop directly in front of Jon. He put his boney hands on Jon's broad shoulders and looked him directly in the eyes. "When you were a little boy, you were afraid of all the animals of the jungle. The pitiful growl of an aging Numa made you cry. But today, today you stood with your grandfather… in face of certain death…without a concern for yourself…to defend your family. Today you showed that you have become a man of the jungle. And as a man you have earned a new name."

Mubuto shifted his hands to Jon's forehead. "From today forth you shall be Tarnuma, the white lion, for you have shown the bravery of Numa." Everyone burst into cheers with the Waziri chanting, "Tarnuma!, Tarnuma! Tarnuma!

The celebration was short lived. The roar of aircraft overhead broke the silence of the land. The sky became filled with hundreds of white clouds that turned into parachutes carrying battle-ready soldiers. Were they reinforcements for the insurgents, or something else? The small group waited to see what hand of cards Fate was dealing them next.

Chapter 43: ORDER RESTORED

THE DRONE OF THE AIRCRAFT overhead deafened all those on the ground. The first bodies hit the ground, rolled and came to a standing position. Others immediately followed. They looked around. Then they looked at each other. They had been sent to fight, but other than a small gathering of mostly unarmed people – several Africans, six white men and three women – no one else was around. Where was the enemy?

One person emerged from the group and walked to the small group. Broad shoulders rested on his six-foot frame. He had penetrating dark-brown eyes and was clean-shaven except for extended side burns. He addressed Tarzan in French. "Lord Greystoke, I presume. My great grandfather sends his greetings."

Tarzan responded. "Then you must be Pierre, Pierre D'Arnot. The last time I saw you, your grandfather was carrying you around on his shoulders."

"*Oui*, it has been a while, but we all grow up. I thought we were needed, but from the look of things I cannot calculate why."

With a grin, Tarzan responded, "We waited but the play had to go on. Sorry you missed the excitement."

The conversations carried on while plans for departing were implemented. The French would stay behind and secure the area until local troops arrived. Farewells were sounded. Jackie and Jon were the first ones to fly out. They took Ashanti's body with them so she might have a proper burial in the

Clayton compound cemetery. Terrik and his men, as well as the surviving PRP's, melted into the jungle. They had no interest in mixing with troops...any troops of any country.

The Waziri refused to fly. They needed to bring their dead home, and to celebrate their passing. The villagers along the way would know the sacrifice the Waziri had made to avenge the death of their own. Tarzan would return with them. Jane objected. She wanted him to stay with her. She even reminded him about his comment about her always getting into trouble whenever they were separated. He countered her plea by saying that she would be fine, being in the protective custody of their son. Besides, he said, "I've had my fill of flying."

Jane understood. What Tarzan was saying without saying it was his duty to accompany the Waziri and their dead. In addition, he needed to cleanse his mind and body of the overdose from the civilized world to which he was always leery. The jungle was his home with its undeniable honesty of living.

Korak, Jane, Meriem and a reluctant Mubuto boarded the remaining helicopter—destination, their home, the rubble of the Clayton compound. Tarzan and the Waziri watched the helicopter ascend into the sky and then veer southward. As it disappeared they turned in unison to start their march in the same direction.

THEY HAD JUST ENTERED the jungle's perimeter when the underbrush started to shake. All turned to the noise and drew their weapons. Was it Numa...or Sheeta...or perhaps Buto the rhinoceros? Tarzan's keen sense of smell told him differently and signaled the Waziri to lower their weapons. Out of the bush rose a gigantic form with hair-covered arms outstretched and fangs flaring. Matted hair from dried blood covered most of its head and shoulders, only adding to the ferocity of the beast. It set its gaze on one person. Then the huge animal dropped to all fours and raced to Tarzan's side. It was Kerkuk, who all had thought had died when he and Chertok had rolled off the edge of the cave into the jungle abyss below.

Tarzan and Kerkuk immediately became engaged in excited conversation. Tarzan had heard about Kerkuk's fall and how the ape had come to the aid of his son. Tarzan wanted to know how Kerkuk survived.

Kerkuk, through a series of grunts and growls, which only Tarzan understood, explained all. As he was falling he had been able to free an arm and reach out for a branch. The first branch broke under the weight of the two bodies, but the second one held. Chertok, still in Kerkuk's grip, didn't know that he was safe. He feared his captor more than the fall. He continued to struggle and somehow broke Kerkuk's grip, falling head-long into the dense foliage and toward the sharp boulders below.

Tarzan asked several times, but Kerkuk refused to say if Chertok was still alive. Tarzan wanted verification that Rokoff's grandson was dead, and thus the threat to his family, ended. Kerkuk would only say, "Bad man gone. No come back."

"Why bad man?"

"He kill Korak's friend."

"What friend?"

"Nice lady."

"How do you know he killed her?"

"I watch through hole in cabin floor; from place where new friend, Tiny, show me he and others go to watch the hairless tarkalan (*white woman*). Very funny."

"Kerkuk, pay attention! Tell me all, from the beginning."

Kerkuk looked down, feeling the reprimand. He continued "I wait for Korak, out of sight under cabin. He long time in nice lady's house. Then I hear loud noises. Big fight. Things breaking. I see through hole. Korak getting off floor from pile of wood. Bad man hit nice lady with big knife. I see bad man turn to hit Korak with big knife. Korak jump back. Slip. Fall. Hit head on edge of bed. I go help Korak. Push floor up. Bad man ready to hit Korak with big knife. He look at me. I roar.

Show teeth. Make bad man afraid. He drop big knife. Run away. I never forget face."

"What did you do?"

"I want to chase bad man. First have to see Korak safe. Know nice lady dead. Big hole in head. Much blood. I go Korak. He asleep. Will not wake up. Bad man gone. Take Korak out. Back through hole in cabin. I carry him. We run away. Hide in jungle. When he wake, Korak no remember things. I take him home."

Kerkuk's story matched what Tarzan had surmised when he had inspected the cabin. "You did well. I am very proud of you." Kerkuk encircled his arms around Tarzan and hugged him.

Kerkuk's wounds turned out to be superficial. Tarzan's sense of smell told him that a substantial portion of the blood on Kerkuk actually came from Chertok. Once the wounds were treated the trek back to home continued. All returned safely, except for Kerkuk who on the third day of the journey wandered off in pursuit of food. No one was worried. They knew his was not the longest attention span on the planet and they all also knew that he was more than capable of taking care of himself.

Chapter 44: OFFICIAL DENIALS

E VEN BEFORE TARZAN AND THE Waziri reached
the Clayton compound, word was spreading like wild-
fire of what had taken place on the Plains of Kisangani.
Within twenty-four hours the Zairian Press Office issued the
following press release:

FOR IMMEDIATE RELEASE

*Zairian Troops put down massive attempted
rebellion*
*Kinshasa, Zaire: Troops loyal to President
Sakumbi and the Zairian people encircled and engaged a rebel force of nearly 800 guerillas that would
depose President Sakumbi and enslave the Zairian
people. The battle took place at the edge of the jungle and the adjacent plains in the Kisanagi region.*
*Zairian aircraft led the battle from the air
by destroying the artillery of the rebel troops. Using
a coalition of local resources and militias the rebel
army was virtually wiped out, while there were
no casualties with only minor injuries sustained by
the Zairian friendly forces.*
*According to people on the ground, the Zairian
forces received some logistical intelligence from Lord
Greystoke and his family who were vacationing nearby.*

The local natives referred to Lord Greystoke as "Tarzan" because of his detailed knowledge of the jungle and area.

The government has declared the area off-limits to all civilians including correspondents, commercial camera crews, outside parties, photographers and others for security reasons. Only authorized military and governmental personnel shall have access to the quarantined area.

-30-

Anyone seeking more information should contact

The Zairian Press Office, 1223 Mybigfoot Way Kinshasa, Zaire

The press release was spread throughout the international news media in hopes of obtaining support for Zaire and President Sakumbi. Being somewhat skeptical of government produced news releases the networks and syndicates sent out their own people to find the facts and write the true story. Here are a few of the results:

The front-page headline in the *Guardian* was, "Lord Greystoke Calls On Friends to Destroy Band of Zairian Insurgents". The text went on to give probably the most accurate account, utilizing every possible moment to glorify the feats of a "native son".

In Paris, *Le Monde* took a different approach. "French Special Forces Rescue English Lord and Family from Certain Death," was the headline, while the body of the story glorified French Special Forces' participation, describing in great detail how they had parachuted in just in time to dispatch the Zairian rebels and rescue Englishman John Clayton and family.

Pravda in Moscow gave a different twist to the event. "Diplomat Heroically Dies Providing Aid to Zaire." Its article declared that an esteemed member of the GKES (State Committee for Foreign Economic Relations) Vladimir Chertok, had been murdered by Zairian rebels. It said Chertok had been on loan to the Zairian government in its search for possible mining

Battle of Kisanagi. The government is planning awarding him The Hero of the Soviet Union medal, the highest distinction our Nation can give to an individual for making the ultimate sacrifice for service to the U.S.S.R.

In the United States, broadcast media gave the event a brief mention as just another story of unrest in Africa. In the print media, only the *New York Post* picked up on the Tarzan angle with the headline "Tarzan Calls! Beasts Answer!"

The Italian press ignored the story as Italy was once again in the midst of changing governments.

As the various papers reached the Claytons, there was more than one laugh by the people who knew the real story.

Chapter 45: PRESERVATION RESERVATION

J OHN AND JANE CLAYTON WERE WAITING in the Jefferson Suite of the Mayflower Hotel in Washington, DC for a call that the limousine had arrived to take them to Worldwide Wildlife Federation Building for the formal announcement of a most aggressive and innovative plan to help save the African environment for apes and gorillas.

It had been seven months since the "Pulverization on the Plains" as the *Washington Star* had described it. A lot had had happened in between. Korak, Jane and Meriem had brought the compound back from virtual ruin to a highly viable farming institution. The latest in irrigation equipment and technology were proving to significantly increase crop production over pre-attack times. Glistening new buildings along with homes for the native Africans dotted the landscape.

The graveyard dedicated to the Waziri dead from that fateful day and the battle that followed lay to the North of the new buildings. Hundreds of Waziri had come to dig the graves and cleanse their dead. After these seven month, the morning time for the wives was over, and small shrines began to appear.

During the same time, Jackie had rebuilt the tarnished image of the Greystoke Trust. Once again it was a most highly respected global financial institution that was generating more cash flow than ever before.

While the others were busy with their pursuits, Tarzan, having seen the impending danger to his apes and gorillas had applied his statesman's skills to get unheard of commitments from multiple countries to help build environmentally safe zones for the gorillas and apes, while at the same time creating large revenues for their respective treasuries. It was the culmination of this effort that was being announced at the World Wildlife Federation.

"I don't know why people have to wear such things." Tarzan said, referring to the black bow tie he was unsuccessfully trying to get tied and correctly positioned.

Since there was no one else in the room to answer Jane responded, "It's the proper attire for the importance of the evening". Then with a small giggle, "It more likely was done to torment you." She got up from the edge of the king-sized bed, walked over to her husband, stood on her tiptoes and gave him a peck on the cheek. "Besides you look very dashing!"

He pulled her to him, leaned over to kiss her when the phone rang. Both sighed, and then Tarzan picked up the phone. It was Jackie. He and the others were in the lobby and the limousine was just pulling in. Tarzan said they'd be down in a minute.

Tarzan didn't understand why they had to be driven the short five blocks. It would have been much easier to walk. But then he looked at Jane's four-inch high heels that accompanied her green sequined ankle-length dress and decided the limousine might be the better way to go.

UPON THEIR ARRIVAL into the banquet hall the entire audience of attendees rose in unison and applauded the Clayton clan. It was not your standard Washington DC gathering. In fact, most people were from abroad. The Prime Minister of Great Britain, the President of France, the Chancellor of Germany, along with leaders of Zaire, Uganda, Rwanda, and Sierra Leone were in attendance. There was even a contingency from the Soviet Union, unintentionally seated at the very back of the hall.

The Clayton family took their positions at the head table. After the dinner and dessert were served, the President of the WWF stood, tapped on his water glass to get everyone's attention and proceeded to introduce Lord Greystoke who in turn introduced the members of the family sitting with him. Jane, upon her introduction, gave him a smile that said, "Go get them, Tiger!"

"Thank you all for coming tonight. Your attendance is an indication of just how important this program is not only to Africans but to rest of the world. If the rain forests where the apes and gorillas of Africa live are devastated, the rest of the world's environments are also endangered. That is why this program is so significant and I applaud you for recognizing it by your attendance tonight." Like most diplomats and politicians, they enthusiastically applauded themselves.

Tarzan immediately launched into the heart of the program: There would be Safe Zones designated where no surface mining or forest defoliation would be permitted. The Safe Zones would be patrolled and maintained by the individual countries. Underground mining would be permitted so countries would not lose out on potential revenues. The mining would be by lease and in compliance with terms and safety regulations of the country. Oversight would be done by Greystoke Trust personnel. The underground tunnels created by the mining would be eventually developed into passageways where tourists could travel to various viewing posts to watch the Safe Zone occupants in their natural behavior. The tunnels and view posts would also protect the inhabitants from tourist-carried diseases that might prove fatal to the apes and gorillas.

He concluded by saying, "To show our commitment to this project, we, through The Greystoke Trust, are committing one billion dollars a year for a minimum of the next ten years to make this a reality.

"Jon Clayton, my great grandson, will be in charge of the project working in conjunction with The Trust and you and your assigned delegates. Jon has discovered a real love for Africa and its wildlife inhabitants. Finally, I challenge each of you and your countries to make the same commitment." The building rang with applause of approval.

The speech over, it was time to mingle. Side conversations became abundant. Many political problems were privately discussed and even a few temporarily resolved.

It was only when virtually everyone else had left and the Claytons gathered to take the limousine back to the Mayflower that Jon's absence was discovered. Finally, after a cursory search, his dad declared, "He's gone. I hope he's off having fun with a blonde or a brunette.

Most of the attendees would have been shocked to know where Jon had gone.

Chapter 46: *NEW HORIZONS*

GILBERT SMYTHERS HAD BEEN the night watchman at the Smithsonian's National Zoo longer than anyone could remember. He loved his job. He loved the animals. During the day, he kept to himself. When it came to people, he was a loner. None of the people in his apartment building knew that the quiet gentleman that lived in apartment 25C was in fact their landlord. At night, he became gregarious carrying on a constant stream of conversation with all the animals as he passed by their enclosures, checking to be sure each one was okay.

Nighttime was his time. He had walked all the trails in the so many times he could literally walk them blindfolded. After forty-three-years on the job, a quick glance at any given building told him whether everything was okay. That's why he pulled up short as he approached the Large Primates building. There was a faint glow of light coming through the translucent pane of glass in the entry door, something that shouldn't be. He walked up to the door and saw that the door was slightly ajar. Something was definitely wrong.

He put his ear to the crack in the doorway, but heard nothing. Everyone seemed to be asleep. He withdrew his pistol from his holster, reached into his pocket for his two bullets which he then chambered. He took a deep breath and slowly, very slowly he pushed open the door.

Stepping inside the first thing he saw in the dim gray light was what appeared to be a man hanging from one of the upper branches of the glassed-in gorilla display. He grabbed his flashlight and directed a beam of light at the dangling object. He breathed a sigh of relief and surprise. It wasn't a man but the pants and jacket of a tuxedo, swaying gently in the breeze of the enclosure's circulating fan.

He slowly swung the light beam around rest of the enclosure, moving from the exercise tree to the far-right hand side of the glass enclosure. He physically jumped back at what he saw. There were the normal three occupants of the cage: Gregor the silverback accompanied by Henretta and Dolly two female mountain gorillas. That is not what shocked him. It was the nearly naked body of a young man snuggled up among the others.

Smythers wasn't sure whether the youth was alive or dead. The answer came almost immediately as the top arm of the person was raised to block the light of flashlight with the palm of his hand. Next, he simply gave a *"thumbs up"* sign and laid back down.

The night watchman knew the face of the young man and immediately understood. He had met the young man before when he had visited the zoo with his great grandparents. Smythers turned off his flashlight, mouthed the words "good night" then left, making sure he closed the door behind him. He was already looking forward to the next night when he could talk with Gregor, Henrietta and Dolly about their special guest visitor.

Jon Clayton slept among newly made friends and had one of the best sleeps of his life. He had faced his fears and conquered them. Along the way, he had found his life's calling: the preservation of the future for not only wildlife but also for mankind. Like so many others, his life's journey brought him to his calling - contrary to all the plans that he had made.

AUTHORS' NOTES

Who killed Dian Fossey? According to "official records," Wayne Richard McGuire, Fossey's last research assistant, killed Fossey. He was tried in absentia and many people believe that the trial was a cover up to protect government officials who wanted to be rid of Fossey because of her strong stance against poaching and tourism. (Her opposition to "gorilla tours" was based upon the fact that the gorillas were highly susceptible to infection from germs carried by such visitors.)

What we have put forth in this story is the possibility that her death was more about mineral rights than animal rights. Our theory is that an agent of a foreign government was the killing instrument used to clear the path for developing and exploiting the natural resources and minerals of the area.

In the mid-to-late 1900's many countries were trying to bring Africa into their sphere of influence, including Russia, China, Britain, France, the United States and even Cuba. Russia was especially active in trying to secure the mineral rights to vast tracks of land. While the Republic of South Africa was the primary target, all areas of Africa were explored to find significant amounts of precious metals, gems and minerals.

The latter part of the 1900's was the age when African countries sought their independence. Many of the struggles were carried out by groups of men and boys, living in the jungle, such as the PRP who were armed by countries trying to gain influence.

The Zaire of 1985 is now called the Democratic Republic of the Congo.

If Tarzan's physical fitness seems inconsistent with his physical age, please read *Tarzan's Quest* wherein he discovers a life longevity drug created by Kavandavanda, king, witch-doctor, and god of the Kavuru.

The GKES mentioned in Chapter 2: "Same Time, Different Place," is Russia's State Committee for Foreign Economic

Relations to aid developing foreign countries and to spread the Communist ideology.

More on Dian Fossey

The renowned paleontologist Louis Leakey referred to Dian Fossey as one of "The Trimates": three women who went on to do so much in the field of primate research. The other two were Jane Goodall who worked with chimpanzees in Africa, and Birute Galdikas who studied Orangutans in Borneo. Fossey concentrated her works in studying the mountain gorillas on the slopes of Visoke volcano in the *Parc National Des Volcans* of Rwanda.

She was born January 16, 1932 in San Francisco, CA and died sometime during the night of December 27, 1985. Her body was discovered by a compound employee the morning of December 28, 1985. Her burial was on New Year's Eve Day, Tuesday December 31, 1985. She was buried in a plain, plywood coffin and laid to rest in the cemetery of the Karisoke Research Center; the same cemetery where many of the gorillas that had been slain by poachers had also been interred.

Only a handful of mourners attended the funeral, among them one of her best friends, Diana McMeekin who at the time said, "Even though everyone of the gorillas has witnessed some atrocity perpetuated on their own kind by human beings, all are still willing to give humans the benefit of the doubt."

The Reverend Elton Wallace performed the services. His benediction was, "And if you think the distance that Christ came to take the likeness of man is not so great as that from man to gorilla, then you don't know men or gorillas, or God."

Fossey's grave marker reads:

NYIRMACHABELLI

Dian Fossey

1932 -1985

No one loved gorillas more.

Rest in Peace, dear friend.

Eternally protected

in this sacred ground.
For you are at home
where you belong.

NYIRMACHABELLI was Fossey's African nickname
meaning,
"The woman who lives alone on the mountain."

Ongoing Work to Preserve African Primates
If you would like to contribute to help in the preservation
of African Primates, please contact one of these organizations:
The original Digit Fund is now part of The Dian Fossey
Gorilla Fund International. Information on it can be found on
the web at https://gorillafund.org
Mountain Gorilla Project, African Wildlife Foundation is
headquartered in Nairobi, Kenya and has offices around the
world. Information can be found on the web at
africanwildlife.org
The Gorilla Organization is headquartered in London, UK
and may be contacted through its website info@gorillas.org
World Wildlife Fund information is available at
www.worldwildlife.org

TO READ MORE about Dian Fossey and her life, we
recommend the following two books, which we heavily drew
upon for our research.

Woman In The Mists by Farley Mowat. Published by Warner
Brothers Books.
Copyright 1987

The Dark Romance of Dian Fossey by Harold T.P. Hayes.
Published by Simon & Schuster on Tombstone. Copyright,
1990.

ADDITIONAL BOOKS that were of value in our research for the book.

Spellbound: Inside Africa's Witch Camps by Karen Palmer. Published by Free Press, Simon and Schuster, 2010.

Encounters with Witchcraft: Field Notes from Africa by Norman N. Miller, Published by Suny Press, 2012.

The Africans (Africa in the 1980's). By David Lamb. Published by Vintage Books Edition, 1987.

The Forest People (On the forest and pygmies). By Colin M. Turnbull. Published by Touchstone, 1968.

Congo by Michael Crichton. Published by Alfred A. Knopf New York, 1980.

NEEDLESS TO SAY we also recommend reading the entire series of Tarzan books written by Edgar Rice Burroughs. Not only are they good adventure reading but upon closer inspection you will find many gems of wisdom and humor. Here are just a few.

from *Tarzan and the Leopard Men*
"There was a great deal of oratory, most of which was apropos; but this is ever the way of men in conferences. Black or white, they like to hear their own voices."

"Life to the jungle-bred is a commodity of little value. It is given and taken casually as a matter of course. One loves or kills as naturally as one sleeps or dreams."

From *Tarzan's Quest*

"The jungle-bred veil their emotions and they move noiselessly always for thus do they extend the span of their precarious lives."

"Gato Mgungi *(African Shaman)* had never had any of the advantages of civilization (He had never been to Hollywood); but he knew what to do under the circumstances, for the psychology of celebrators is doubtless the same in Africa as elsewhere. When there is nothing more to eat or drink, it must be time to go home."

"She breathed the odors of the steaming jungle with a keen delight. The restrictions of ordered society, the veneer of civilization, fell away leaving her free, and she sensed this new freedom with a joy that she had not felt since she had left the jungle to return to London."

"Most everyone lives too long anyway for the good of the world. Suppose Congress got hold of 'em?" (em are the longevity pills of Kavandavanda in *Tarzan's Quest*.)

from *Tarzan at the Earth's Core*

"The temperature of Pellucidar is such that clothing is rather a burden than a necessity, but so accustomed is civilized man to the strange apparel with which he has encumbered himself for generations that, bereft of it, his efficiency, self-reliance and resourcefulness are reduced to a plane approximating the vanishing point."

THESE ARE BUT A FEW of the many thought-provoking ideas that Burroughs reveals while telling the adventurous tales of Tarzan, Lord of the Jungle. You'll have to read the series to find the rest.

The Tarzan Series:

Tarzan of the Apes
The Return of Tarzan
The Beasts of Tarzan
The Son of Tarzan
Tarzan and the Jewels of Opar
Jungle Tales of Tarzan
Tarzan the Untamed
Tarzan the Terrible
Tarzan and the Golden Lion
Tarzan and the Ant Men
Tarzan, Lord of the Jungle
Tarzan and the Lost Empire
Tarzan at the Earth's Core
Tarzan the Invincible
Tarzan Triumphant
Tarzan and the City of Gold
Tarzan and the Lion Man
Tarzan and the Leopard Men
Tarzan's Quest
Tarzan and the Forbidden City
Tarzan the Magnificent
Tarzan and the Foreign Legion
Tarzan and the Madman
Tarzan and the Castaways
The Tarzan Twins
Tarzan and the Tarzan Twins with Jad-bal-ja

THE WILD ADVENTURES OF

EDGAR RICE BURROUGHS® SERIES

1 Tarzan: Return to Pal-ul-don

2 Tarzan on the Precipice

3 Tarzan Trilogy

4 Tarzan: The Greystoke Legacy Under Siege

About Edgar Rice Burroughs, Inc.

 Founded in 1923 by Edgar Rice Burroughs, as one of the first authors to incorporate himself, Edgar Rice Burroughs, Inc. holds numerous trademarks and the rights to all literary works of the author still protected by copyright, including stories of Tarzan of the Apes and John Carter of Mars. The company has overseen every adaptation of his literary works in film, television, radio, publishing, theatrical stage productions, licensing and merchandising. The company is still a very active enterprise and manages and licenses the vast archive of Mr. Burroughs' literary works, fictional characters and corresponding artworks that have grown for over a century. The company continues to be owned by the Burroughs family and remains headquartered in Tarzana, California, the town named after the Tarzana Ranch Mr. Burroughs purchased there in 1918 which led to the town's future development.

www.edgarriceburroughs.com
www.tarzan.com

TARZAN

TARZAN
Return to
Pal-ul-don

The first authorized Tarzan
novel from the sure hand of the
pulpmeister, Will Murray, who
does a fantastic job of capturing
the true spirit of Tarzan – not
a grunting, monosyllabic,
cartoonish strongman, but an
evolved, brilliant man of honor
– equally at home as Lord
Greystoke and as the savage:
Tarzan the Terrible.
–Paul Bishop

Available at
www.ERBurroughs.com/Store

Edgar Rice Burroughs®

Visit
www.
ERBurroughs
com

Statues
and
Artwork

ERB Comic
Strip Tees

Books

Collectable
Dust Jackets

Online Comic Strip Subscription
featuring 17 different storylines

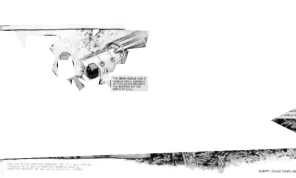

Tarzan Clothing
and much more!